BEST NEW FANTASY

DEC 22 2006

BRANCH

HAYNER PUBLIC LIBRARY DISTRICT
ALTON, ILLINOIS

OVERDUES .10 PER DAY MAXIMUM FINE
COST OF BOOKS. LOST OR DAMAGED
BOOKS ADDITIONAL $5.00 SERVICE CHARGE.

ANTHOLOGIES EDITED BY SEAN WALLACE

Horror: The Best of the Year, 2006 Edition
Horror: The Best of the Year, 2007 Edition
Japanese Dreams
Jabberwocky 1
Jabberwocky 2
Jabberwocky 3

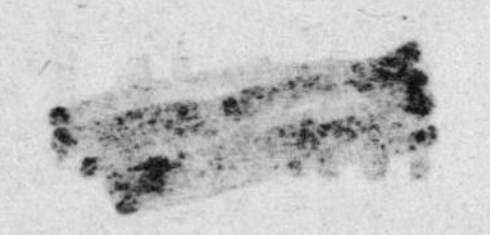

BEST NEW FANTASY

EDITED BY SEAN WALLACE

PRIME BOOKS

HAYNER PUBLIC LIBRARY DISTRICT
ALTON, ILLINOIS

BEST NEW FANTASY

Copyright © 2006 by Sean Wallace.
Cover art copyright © 2006 by Eikasia.
Cover design copyright © 2006 by Stephen H. Segal.

Prime Books
www.prime-books.com

Printed in the United States of America

ISBN-10: 0-8095-5678-2
ISBN-13: 978-0-8095-5678-6

S.F.
F
BES
617474863

CONTENTS

This year the first volume of **Best New Fantasy** marks the start of a new anthology series, showcasing an interesting mix of short fiction by some of the field's "newest" authors. However, the definition of "new" doesn't necessarily mean within the last five years—the standard for this anthology—but includes authors that have just started to hit their stride, for whatever reason, with novels, short stories, and more. (In other words if their name is constantly on people's lips, then they're probably fair game for **Best New Fantasy**). But, as with any anthology of this nature, what is best, and what is new, is in the eye of the beholder, and the hope is that you find a sense of wonder in all of these sixteen stories, as much as they have, for your editor.

Theodora Goss' short story collection, ***In the Forest of Forgetting,*** *was published by Prime Books in 2006. In 2004, she won a Rhysling Award for speculative poetry. Her short stories and poems have been published in* ***Alchemy, Realms of Fantasy, Polyphony, Strange Horizons, Mythic Delirium, Flytrap****, and* ***Lady Churchill's Rosebud Wristlet****, and have been reprinted in* ***Year's Best Fantasy, The Year's Best Fantasy and Horror****, and* ***The Year's Best Science Fiction and Fantasy for Teens.*** *Her short story "The Wings of Meister Wilhelm" was nominated for a World Fantasy Award. Visit her website at* ***www.theodoragoss.com*** *and find out more about her short story collection at* ***www.forestofforgetting.com.***

About "Pip and the Fairies," she says, "When my daughter was born, her real name, Ophelia, seemed too formal, too imposing, for such a small person, so we called her Pip. At one point, I started wondering what it would be like to write a story about her—and then, what she would think of that story when she was an adult."

Pip and the Fairies

Theodora Goss

"Why, you're Pip!"

She has gotten used to this, since the documentary. She could have refused to be interviewed, she supposes. But it would have seemed—ungrateful, ungracious, particularly after the funeral.

"Susan Lawson," read the obituary, "beloved author of *Pip and the Fairies, Pip Meets the Thorn King, Pip Makes Three Wishes*, and other Pip books, of ovarian cancer. Ms. Lawson, who was sixty-four, is survived by a daughter, Philippa. In lieu of flowers, donations should be sent to the Susan Lawson Cancer Research Fund." Anne had written that.

"Would you like me to sign something?" she asks.

White hair, reading glasses on a chain around her neck—too old to be a mother. Perhaps a librarian? Let her be a librarian, thinks Philippa. Once, a collector asked her to sign the entire series, from *Pip and the Fairies* to *Pip Says Goodbye.*

"That would be so kind of you. For my granddaughter Emily." A grandmother, holding out *Pip Learns to Fish* and *Under the Hawthorns.* She signs them both "To Emily, may she find her own fairyland. From Philippa Lawson (Pip)."

This is the sort of thing people like: the implication that, despite their minivans and microwaves, if they found the door in the wall, they too could enter fairyland.

"So," the interviewer asked her, smiling indulgently, the way parents smile at their children's beliefs in Santa Claus, "did you really meet the Thorn King? Do you think you could get me an interview?"

And she answered as he, and the parents who had purchased the boxed set, were expecting. "I'm afraid the Thorn King is a very private person. But I'll mention that you were interested." Being Pip, after all these years.

Maintaining the persona.

Her mother never actually called her Pip. It was Pipsqueak, as in, "Go play outside, Pipsqueak. Can't you see Mommy's trying to finish this chapter? Mommy's publisher wants to see something by Friday, and we're a month behind on the rent." When they finally moved away from Payton, they were almost a year behind. Her mother sent Mrs. Payne a check from California, from royalties she had received for the after-school special.

Philippa buys a scone and a cup of coffee. There was no café when she used to come to this bookstore, while her mother shopped at the food co-op down the street, which is now a yoga studio. Mrs. Archer used to let her sit in a corner and read the books. Then she realizes there is no cup holder in the rental car. She drinks the coffee quickly. She's tired, after the long flight from Los Angeles, the long drive from Boston. But not much farther now. Payton has stayed essentially the same, she thinks, despite the yoga studio. She imagines a planning board, a historical society, the long and difficult process of obtaining permits, like in all these New England towns.

As she passes the fire station, the rain begins, not heavy, and intermittent. She turns on the windshield wipers.

There is Sutton's dairy, where her mother bought milk with cream floating on top, before anyone else cared about pesticides in the food chain. She is driving through the country, through farms that have managed to hold on despite the rocky soil. In the distance she sees cows, and once a herd of alpacas. There are patches too rocky for farms, where the road runs between cliffs covered with ivy, and birches, their leaves glistening with rain, spring up from the shallow soil.

Then forest. The rain is heavier, pattering on the leaves overhead. She drives with one hand, holding the scone in the other (her pants are getting covered with crumbs), beneath the oaks and evergreens, thinking about the funeral.

It was not large: her mother's co-workers from the Children's Network, and Anne. It was only after the documentary that people began driving to the cemetery in the hills, leaving hyacinths by the grave. Her fault, she supposes.

The interviewer leaned forward, as though expecting an intimate detail. "How did she come up with Hyacinth? Was the character based on anyone she knew?"

"Oh, hyacinths were my mother's favorite flower."

And letters, even contributions to the Susan Lawson Cancer Research Fund. Everyone, it seems, had read *Pip and the Fairies*. Then the books had gone out of print and been forgotten. But after the funeral and the documentary, everyone suddenly remembered, the way they remembered their childhoods. Suddenly, Susan Lawson was indeed "beloved."

Philippa asked Anne to drive up once a week, to clear away the letters and flowers, to take care of the checks. And she signed over the house. Anne was too old to be a secretary for anyone neater than Susan Lawson had been. In one corner of the living room, Philippa found a pile of hospital bills, covered with dust. She remembers Anne at the funeral, so pale and pinched. It is good, she supposes, that her mother found someone at last. With the house and her social security, Anne will be all right.

Three miles to Payne House. Almost there, then. It had been raining too, on that first day.

"Look," her mother said, pointing as the Beetle swerved erratically. If she looked down, she could see the road though the holes in the floor, where the metal had rusted away. Is that why she has rented one of the new Beetles? Either nostalgia, or an effort to, somehow, rewrite the past. "There's Payne House. It burned down in the 1930s. The Paynes used to own the mills at the edge of town," now converted into condominiums, Mrs. Archer's successor, a woman with graying hair and a pierced nostril, told her, "and one night the millworkers set the stables on fire. They said the Paynes took better care of their horses than of their workers."

"What happened to the horses?" She can see the house from the road, its outer walls burned above the first story, trees growing in some of the rooms. She can see it through both sets of eyes, the young Philippa's and the old one's. Not really old of course, but—how should she describe it?—tired. She blames the documentary. Remembering all this, the road running through the soaked remains of what was once a garden, its hedges overgrown and a rosebush growing through the front door. She can see it through young eyes, only a few weeks after her father's funeral, the coffin draped with an American flag and the minister saying "fallen in the service of his country" although really it was an accident that could have happened if he had been driving to the grocery store. And through old eyes, noticing that the rosebush has spread over the front steps.

As if, driving down this road, she were traveling into the past. She felt this also, sitting beside the hospital bed, holding one pale hand, the skin dry as paper, on which the veins were raised like the roots of an oak tree. Listening to the mother she had not spoken to in years.

"I have to support us now, Pipsqueak. So we're going to live here. Mrs. Payne's going to rent us the housekeeper's cottage, and I'm going to write books."

"What kind of books?"

"Oh, I don't know. I guess I'll have to start writing and see what comes out."

How did it begin? Did she begin it, by telling her mother, over her milk and the oatmeal cookies from the food co-op that tasted like baked sawdust, what she had been doing that day? Or did her mother begin it, by writing the stories? Did she imagine them, Hyacinth, the Thorn King, the Carp in the pond who dreamed, so he said, the future, and the May Queen herself? And, she thinks, pulling into the drive that leads to the housekeeper's cottage, what about Jack Feather? Or did her mother imagine them? And did their imaginations bring them into being, or were they always there to be found?

She slams the car door and brushes crumbs from her pants. Here it is, all here, for what it is worth, the housekeeper's cottage, with its three small rooms, and the ruins of Payne House. The rain has almost stopped, although she can feel a drop run down the back of her neck. And, not for the first time, she has doubts.

"One room was my mother's, one was mine, and one was the kitchen, where we took our baths in a plastic tub. We had a toaster oven and a Crock-pot to make soup, and a small refrigerator, the kind you see in hotels. One day, I remember having soup for breakfast, lunch, and dinner. Of course, when the electricity was turned off, none of them worked. Once, we lived for a week on oatmeal cookies." The interviewer laughed, and she laughed with him. When they moved to California, she went to school. Why doesn't she remember going to school in Payton? She bought lunch every day, meatloaf and mashed potatoes and soggy green beans. Sometimes the principal gave her lunch money. She was happier than when the Thorn King had crowned her with honeysuckle. "Young Pip," he had said, "I pronounce you a Maid of the May. Serve the May Queen well."

That was in *Pip Meets the May Queen.* And then she stops—standing at the edge of the pond—because the time has come to think about what she has done.

What she has done is give up *The Pendletons*, every weekday at two o'clock, Eastern Standard Time, before the afternoon talk shows. She has given up being Jessica Pendleton, the scheming daughter of Bruce Pendleton, whose attractive but troublesome family dominates the social and criminal worlds of Pinehurst.

"How did your mother influence your acting career?"

She did not answer, "By teaching me the importance of money." Last week, even a fan of *The Pendletons* recognized her as Pip.

She has given up the house in the hills, with a pool in the backyard. Given up Edward, but then he gave her up first, for a producer. He wanted, so badly, to do prime time. A cop show or even a sitcom, respectable television. "I hope you understand, Phil," he said. And she did understand, somehow. Has she ever been in love with anyone—except Jack Feather?

What has she gained? She remembers her mother's cold hand pulling her down, so she can hear her whisper, in a voice like sandpaper, "I always knew they were real."

But does she, Philippa, know it? That is why she has come back, why she has bought Payne House from the Payne who inherited it, a Manhattan lawyer with no use for the family estate. Why she is standing here now, by the pond, where the irises are about to bloom. So she can remember.

The moment when, in *Pip and the Fairies*, she trips over something lying on the ground.

> *"Oh," said a voice. When Pip looked up she saw a girl, about her own age, in a white dress, with hair as green as grass. "You've found it, and now it's yours, and I'll never be able to return it before he finds out!"*
>
> *"What is it?" asked Pip, holding up what she had tripped over: a piece of brown leather, rather like a purse.*
>
> *"It's Jack Feather's Wallet of Dreams, which he doesn't know I've taken. I was just going to look at the dreams—their wings are so lovely in the sunlight—and then return it. But 'What You Find You May Keep.' That's the law." And the girl wept bitterly into her hands.*
>
> *"But I don't want it," said Pip. "I'd like to look at the dreams, if they're as nice as you say they are, but I certainly don't want to keep them. Who is Jack Feather, and how can we return his wallet?"*

"How considerate you are," said the girl. "Let me kiss you on both cheeks—that's the fairy way. Then you'll be able to walk through the door in the wall, and we'll return the wallet together. You can call me Hyacinth."

Why couldn't she walk through the door by herself? *Pip wondered. It seemed an ordinary enough door, opening from one of the overgrown rooms to another. And what was the fairy way? She was just starting to wonder why the girl in the white dress had green hair when Hyacinth opened the door and pulled her through.*

On the other side was a country she had never seen before. A forest stretched away into the distance, until it reached a river that shone like a snake in the sunlight, and then again until it reached the mountains.

Standing under the trees at the edge of the forest was a boy, not much taller than she was, in trousers made of gray fur, with a birch-bark hat on his head. As soon as he saw them, he said, "Hyacinth, if you don't give me my Wallet of Dreams in the clap of a hummingbird's wing, I'll turn you into a snail and present you to Mother Hedgehog, who'll stick you into her supper pot!"

—From *Pip and the Fairies*, by Susan Lawson

How clearly the memories are coming back to her now, of fishing at night with Jack Feather, searching for the Wishing Stone with Hyacinth and Thimble, listening to stories at Mother Hedgehog's house while eating her toadstool omelet. There was always an emphasis on food, perhaps a reflection of the toaster and Crock-pot that so invariably turned out toast and soup. The May Queen's cake, for example, or Jeremy Toad's cricket cutlets, which neither she nor Hyacinth could bear to eat.

"I hope you like crickets," said Jeremy Toad. Pip and Hyacinth looked at one another in distress. "Eat What You Are Offered," was the Thorn King's law. Would they dare to break it? That was in *Jeremy Toad's Birthday Party.*

She can see, really, where it all came from.

"I think the feud between the Thorn King and the May Queen represented her anger at my father's death. It was an accident, of course. But she blamed him for leaving her, for going to Vietnam. She wanted him to be a conscientious objector. Especially with no money and a daughter to care for. I don't think she ever got over that anger."

"But the Thorn King and the May Queen were reconciled."

"Only by one of Pip's wishes. The other—let me see if I remember. It was a fine wool shawl for Thimble so she would never be cold again."

"Weren't there three? What was the third wish?"

"Oh, that was the one Pip kept for herself. I don't think my mother ever revealed it. Probably something to do with Jack Feather. She—I—was rather in love with him, you know."

The third wish had been about the electric bill, and it had come true several days later when the advance from the publisher arrived.

Here it is, the room where she found Jack Feather's wallet. Once, in *Pip Meets the Thorn King*, he allowed her to look into it. She saw herself, but considerably older, in a dress that sparkled like stars. Years later, she recognized it as the dress she would wear to the Daytime Emmys.

And now what? Because there is the door, and after all the Carp did tell her, in *Pip Says Goodbye*, "You will come back some day."

But if she opens the door now, will she see the fields behind Payne House, which are mown for hay in September? That is the question around which everything revolves. Has she been a fool, to give up California, and the house with the pool, and a steady paycheck?

"What happened, Pip?" her mother asked her, lying in the hospital bed, her head wrapped in the scarf without which it looked as fragile as an eggshell. "You were such an imaginative child. What made you care so much about money?"

"You did," she wanted to and could not say. And now she has taken that money out of the bank to buy Payne House.

If she opens the door and sees only the unmown fields, it will have been for nothing. No, not nothing. There is Payne House, after all. And her memories. What will she do, now she is no longer Jessica Pendleton? Perhaps she will write, like her mother. There is a certain irony in that.

The rain on the grass begins to soak through her shoes. She should remember not to wear city shoes in the country.

But it's no use standing here. That is, she has always told herself, the difference between her and her mother: she can face facts.

Philippa grasps the doorknob, breathes in once, quickly, and opens the door.

"I've been waiting forever and a day," said Hyacinth, yawning. She had fallen asleep beneath an oak tree, and while she slept the squirrels who lived in the tree had made her a blanket of leaves.

"I promised I would come back if I could," said Pip, "and now I have."

"I'm as glad as can be," said Hyacinth. "The Thorn King's been so sad since you went away. When I tell him you're back, he'll prepare a feast just for you."

"Will Jack Feather be there?" asked Pip.

"I don't know," said Hyacinth, looking uncomfortable. "He went away to the mountains, and hasn't come back. I didn't want to tell you yet, but—the May Queen's disappeared! Jack Feather went to look for her with Jeremy Toad, and now they've disappeared too."

"Then we'll have to go find them," said Pip.

—From *Pip Returns to Fairyland*, by Philippa Lawson

Joe Hill's first book, ***20th Century Ghosts*** *(PS Publishing), which showcases fourteen of his short stories, was recently nominated for the Bram Stoker Award for Best Collection. He is the 2006 winner of the William Crawford Award for outstanding new fantasy writer. His first novel,* ***Heart-Shaped Box*** *(William Morrow), is due in 2007. Learn more at* ***www.joehill fiction.com.***

"Although a lot of the stories in my collection are works of fantasy or outright surrealism, they're always deeply rooted in ordinary, every day life. So even though you're making this one reckless leap of the imagination, there's still solid footing below, a world of the real to come back down into. You're never very far from what you know. 'My Father's Mask' is maybe the one story I've written that isn't like that. This one runs right up to the cliff, and over, and keeps going, like the roadrunner in one of those Warner Brothers cartoons. I guess the trick is you won't fall if you don't look down."

My Father's Mask
Joe Hill

On the drive to Big Cat Lake, we played a game. It was my mother's idea. It was dusk by the time we reached the state highway, and when there was no light left in the sky, except for a splash of cold, pale brilliance in the west, she told me they were looking for me.

"They're playing card people," she said. "Queens and kings. They're so flat they can slip themselves under doors. They'll be coming from the other direction, from the lake. Searching for us. Trying to head us off. Get out of sight whenever someone comes the other way. We can't protect you from them—not on the road. Quick, get down. Here comes one of them now."

I stretched out across the backseat and watched the headlights of an approaching car race across the ceiling. Whether I was playing along, or just stretching out to get comfortable, I wasn't sure. I was in a funk. I had been hoping for a sleepover at my friend Luke Redhill's, ping-pong and late night TV with Luke (and Luke's leggy older sister Jane, and her lush-haired friend Melinda), but had come home from school to find suitcases in the driveway and my father loading the car. That was the first I heard we were spending the night at my grandfather's cabin on Big Cat Lake. I couldn't be angry at my parents for not letting me in on their plans in advance, because they probably hadn't made plans in advance. It was very likely they had decided to go up to Big Cat Lake over lunch. My parents didn't have plans. They had impulses and a thirteen-year-old son and they saw no reason to ever let the latter upset the former.

"Why can't you protect me?" I asked.

My mother said, "Because there are some things a mother's love and a father's courage can't keep you safe from. Besides, who could fight them? You know about playing card people. How they all go around with little golden hatchets and little silver swords. Have you ever noticed how well armed most good hands of poker are?"

"No accident the first card game everyone learns is War," my father said, driving with one wrist slung across the wheel. "They're all variations on the same plot. Metaphorical kings fighting over the world's limited supplies of wenches and money."

My mother regarded me seriously over the back of her seat, her eyes luminous in the dark.

"We're in trouble, Jack," she said. "We're in terrible trouble."

"Okay," I said.

"It's been building for a while. We kept it from you at first, because we didn't want to scare you. But you have to know. It's right for you to know. We're—well, you see—we don't have any money anymore. It's the playing card people. They've been working against us, poisoning investments, tying assets up in red tape. They've been spreading the most awful rumors about your father at work. I don't want to upset you with the crude details. They make menacing phone calls. They call me up in the middle of the day and talk about the awful things they're going to do to me. To you. To all of us."

"They put something in the clam sauce the other night, and gave me wicked runs," my father said. "I thought I was going to die. And our dry cleaning came back with funny white stains on it. That was them too."

My mother laughed. I've heard that dogs have six kind of barks, each with a specific meaning: *intruder, let's play, I need to pee*. My mother had a certain number of laughs, each with an unmistakable meaning and identity, all of them wonderful. This laugh, convulsive and unpolished, was the way she responded to dirty jokes; also to accusations, to being caught making mischief.

I laughed with her, sitting up, my stomach unknotting. She had been so wide-eyed and solemn, for a moment I had started to forget she was making it all up.

My mother leaned toward my father and ran her finger over his lips, miming the closing of a zipper.

"You let me tell it," she said. "I forbid you to talk anymore."

"If we're in so much financial trouble, I could go and live with Luke for a while," I said. *And Jane*, I thought. "I wouldn't want to be a burden on the family."

She looked back at me again. "The money I'm not worried about. There's an appraiser coming by tomorrow. There are some wonderful old things in that house, things your grandfather left us. We're going to see about selling them."

My grandfather, Upton, had died the year before, in a way no one liked to discuss, a death that had no place in his life, a horror movie conclusion tacked on to a blowsy, Capra-esque comedy. He was in New York, where he kept a condo on the fifth floor of a brownstone on the Upper East Side, one of many places he owned. He called the elevator and stepped through the doors when they opened—but there was no elevator there, and he fell four stories. The fall did not kill him. He lived for another day, at the bottom of the elevator shaft. The elevator was old and slow and complained loudly whenever it had to move, not unlike most of the building's residents. No one heard him screaming.

"Why don't we sell the Big Cat Lake house?" I asked. "Then we'd be rolling in the loot."

"Oh, we couldn't do that. It isn't ours. It's held in trust for all of us, me, you, Aunt Blake, the Greenly twins. And even if it did belong to us, we couldn't sell it. It's always been in our family."

For the first time since getting into the car, I thought I understood why we were really going to Big Cat Lake. I saw at last that my weekend plans had been sacrificed on the altar of interior decoration. My mother loved to decorate. She loved picking out curtains, stained glass lamp-shades, unique iron knobs for the cabinets. Someone had put her in charge of redecorating the cabin on Big Cat Lake—or, more likely, she had put herself in charge—and she meant to begin by getting rid of all the clutter.

I felt like a chump for letting her distract me from my bad mood with one of her games.

"I wanted to spend the night with Luke," I said.

My mother directed a sly, knowing look at me from beneath half-lowered eyelids, and I felt a sudden scalp-prickle of unease. It was a look that made me wonder what she knew and if she had guessed the true reasons for my friendship with Luke Redhill, a rude but good-natured nose-picker I considered intellectually beneath me.

"You wouldn't be safe there. The playing card people would've got you," she said, her tone both gleeful and rather too-coy.

I looked at the ceiling of the car. "Okay."

We rode for a while in silence.

"Why are they after me?" I asked, even though by then I was sick of it, wanted done with the game.

"It's all because we're so incredibly superlucky. No one ought to be as lucky as us. They hate the idea that anyone is getting a free ride. But it would all even out if they got ahold of you. I don't care how lucky you've been, if you lose a kid, the good times are over."

We were lucky, of course, maybe even superlucky, and it wasn't just that we were well off, like everyone in our extended family of trust-fund ne'er-do-wells. My father had more time for me than other fathers had for their boys. He went to work after I left for school, and was usually home by the time I got back, and if I didn't have anything else going on, we'd drive to the golf course to whack a few. My mother was beautiful, still young, just thirty-five, with a natural instinct for mischief that had made her a hit with my friends. I suspected several of the kids I hung out with, Luke Redhill included, had cast her in a variety of masturbatory fantasies, and that indeed, their attraction to her explained most of their fondness for me.

"And why is Big Cat Lake so safe?" I said.

"Who said it's safe?"

"Then why are we going there?"

She turned away from me. "So we can have a nice cozy fire in the fireplace, and sleep late, and eat egg pancake, and spend the morning in our pajamas. Even if we are in fear for our lives, that's no reason to be miserable all weekend."

She put her hand on the back of my father's neck and played with his hair. Then she stiffened, and her fingernails sank into the skin just below his hairline.

"Jack," she said to me. She was looking past my father, through the driver's side window, at something out in the dark. "Get down Jack get down."

We were on route 16, a long straight highway, with a narrow grass median between the two lanes. A car was parked on a turnaround between the lanes, and as we went by it, its headlights snapped on. I turned my head and stared into them for a moment before sinking down out of sight. The car—a sleek silver Jaguar—turned onto the road and accelerated after us.

"I told you not to let them see you," my mother said. "Go faster, Henry. Get away from them."

Our car picked up speed, rushing through the darkness. I squeezed my fingers into the seat, sitting up on my knees to peek out the rear window. The other car stayed exactly the same distance behind us no matter how fast we went, clutching the curves of the road with a quiet, menacing assurance. Sometimes my breath would catch in my throat for a few moments before I remembered to breathe. Road signs whipped past, gone too quickly to be read.

The Jag followed for three miles, before it swung into the parking lot of a roadside diner. When I turned around in my seat my mother was lighting a cigarette with the pulsing orange ring of the dashboard lighter. My father hummed softly to himself, easing up on the gas. He swung his head a little from side to side, keeping time to a melody I didn't recognize.

I ran through the dark, with the wind knifing at me and my head down, not looking where I was going. My mother was right behind me, the both of us rushing for the porch. No light lit the front of the cottage by the water. My father had switched car and headlights off, and the house was in the woods, at the end of a rutted dirt road where there were no streetlamps. Just beyond the house I caught a glimpse of the lake, a hole in the world, filled with a heaving darkness.

My mother let us in and went around switching on lights. The cabin was built around a single great room with a lodge-house ceiling, bare rafters showing, log walls with red bark peeling off them. To the left of the door was a dresser, the mirror on the back hidden behind a pair of black veils. Wandering, my hands pulled into the sleeves of my jacket for warmth, I approached the dresser. Through the semi transparent curtains I saw a dim, roughly-formed figure, my own obscured reflection, coming to meet me in the mirror. I felt a tickle of unease at the sight of the reflected me, a featureless shadow skulking behind black silk, someone I didn't know. I pushed the curtain back, but saw only myself, cheeks stung into redness by the wind.

I was about to step away when I noticed the masks. The mirror was supported by two delicate posts, and a few masks hung from the top of each, the sort, like the Lone Ranger's, that only cover the eyes and a little of the nose. One had whiskers and glittery spackle on it and would make the wearer look like a jeweled mouse. Another was of rich black velvet, and would have been appropriate dress for a courtesan on her way to an Edwardian masquerade.

The whole cottage had been artfully decorated in masks. They dangled from doorknobs and the backs of chairs. A great crimson mask glared furiously down from the mantle above the hearth, a surreal demon made out of lacquered paiper-maché, with a hooked beak and feathers around the eyes—just the thing to wear if you had been cast as the Red Death in an Edgar Allan Poe revival.

The most unsettling of them hung from a lock on one of the windows. It was made of some distorted but clear plastic, and looked like a man's face molded out of an impossibly thin piece of ice. It was hard to see, dangling in front of the glass, and I twitched nervously when I spotted it from the corner of my eye. For an instant I thought there was a man, spectral and barely-there, hovering on the porch, gaping in at me.

The front door crashed open and my father came in dragging luggage. At the same time, my mother spoke from behind me.

"When we were young, just kids, your father and I used to sneak off to this place to get away from everyone. Wait. Wait, I know. Let's play a game. You have until we leave to guess which room you were conceived in."

She liked to try and disgust me now and then with intimate, unasked-for revelations about herself and my father. I frowned and gave what I hoped was a scolding look, and she laughed again, and we were both satisfied, having played ourselves perfectly.

"Why are there curtains over all the mirrors?"

"I don't know," she said. "Maybe whoever stayed here last hung them up as a way to remember your grandfather. In Jewish tradition, after someone dies, the mourners cover the mirrors, as a warning against vanity."

"But we aren't Jewish," I said.

"It's a nice tradition though. All of us could stand to spend less time thinking about ourselves."

"What's with all the masks?"

"Every vacation home ought to have a few masks lying around. What if you want a vacation from your own face? I get awfully sick of being the same person day in, day out. What do you think of that one, do you like it?"

I was absent-mindedly fingering the glassy, blank-featured mask hanging from the window. When she brought my attention to what I was doing, I pulled my hand back. A chill crawled along the thickening flesh of my forearms.

"You should put it on," she said, her voice breathy and eager. "You should see how you look in it."

"It's awful," I said.

"Are you going to be okay sleeping in your own room? You could sleep in bed with us. That's what you did the last time you were here. Although you were much younger then."

"That's all right. I wouldn't want to get in the way, in case you feel like conceiving someone else."

"Be careful what you wish for," she said. "History repeats."

The only furniture in my small room was a camp cot dressed in sheets that smelled of mothballs and a wardrobe against one wall, with paisley drapes pulled across the mirror on the back. A half-face mask hung from the curtain rod. It was made of green silk leaves, sewn together and ornamented with emerald sequins, and I liked it until I turned the light off. In the gloom, the leaves looked like the horny scales of some lizard-faced thing, with dark gaping sockets where the eyes belonged. I switched the light back on and got up long enough to turn it face-to the wall.

Trees grew against the house and sometimes a limb batted the side of the cottage, making a knocking sound that always brought me awake with the idea someone was at the bedroom door. I woke, dozed, and woke again. The wind built to a thin shriek and from somewhere outside came a steady, metallic ping-ping-ping, as if a wheel were turning in the gale. I went to the window to look, not expecting to see anything. The moon was up, though, and as the trees blew, moonlight raced across the ground, through the darkness, like schools of those little silver fish that live in deep water and glow in the dark.

A bicycle leaned against a tree, an antique with a giant front wheel, and a rear wheel almost comically too small. The front wheel turned continuously, ping-ping-ping. A boy came across the grass toward it, a chubby boy with fair hair, in a white nightgown, and at the sight of him I felt an instinctive rush of dread. He took the handlebars of the bike, then cocked his head as if at a sound, and I mewed, shrank back from the glass. He turned and stared at me with silver eyes and silver teeth, dimples in his fat cupid cheeks, and I sprang awake in my mothball-smelling bed, making unhappy sounds of fear in my throat.

When morning came, and I finally struggled up out of sleep for the last time, I found myself in the master bedroom, under heaped quilts, with the sun slanting across my face. The impression of my mother's head still dented the pillow beside me. I didn't remember rushing there in the dark and was glad. At thirteen, I was still a little kid, but I had my pride.

I lay like a salamander on a rock—sun-dazed and awake without being conscious—until I heard someone pull a zipper on the other side of the room. I peered around and saw my father, opening the suitcase on top of the bureau. Some subtle rustling of the quilts caught his attention, and he turned his head to look at me.

He was naked. The morning sunshine bronzed his short, compact body. He wore the clear plastic mask that had been hanging in the window of the great room, the night before. It squashed the features beneath, flattening them out of their recognizable shapes. He stared at me blankly, as if he hadn't known I was lying there in the bed, or perhaps as if he didn't know me at all. The thick length of his penis rested on a cushion of gingery hair. I had seen him naked often enough before, but with the mask on he was someone different, and his nakedness was disconcerting. He looked at me and did not speak—and that was disconcerting too.

I opened my mouth to say hello and good morning, but there was a wheeze in my chest. The thought crossed my mind that he was, really and not metaphorically, a person I didn't know. I couldn't hold his stare, looked away, then slipped from under the quilts and went into the great room, willing myself not to run.

A pot clanked in the kitchen. Water hissed from a faucet. I followed the sounds to my mother, who was at the sink, filling a tea kettle. She heard the pad of my feet, and glanced back over her shoulder. The sight of her stopped me in my tracks. She had on a black kitten mask, edged in rhinestones, and with glistening whiskers. She was not naked, but wore a MILLER LITE T-Shirt that came to her hips. Her legs, though, were bare, and when she leaned over the sink to shut off the water I saw a flash of strappy black panties. I was reassured by the fact that she had grinned to see me, and not just stared at me as if we had never met.

"Egg pancake in the oven," she said.

"Why are you and dad wearing masks?"

"It's Halloween isn't it?"

"No," I said. "Try next Thursday."

"Any law against starting early?" she asked. Then she paused by the stove, an oven mitt on one hand, and shot another look at me. "Actually. *Actually.*"

"Here it comes. The truck is backing up. The back end is rising. The bullshit is about to come sliding out."

"In this place it's always Halloween. It's called Masquerade House. That's our secret name for it. It's one of the rules of the cottage, while you're staying here you have to wear a mask. It's always been that way."

"I can wait until Halloween."

She pulled a pan out of the oven and cut me a piece of egg pancake, poured me a cup of tea. Then she sat down across from me to watch me eat.

"You have to wear a mask. The playing card people saw you last night. They'll be coming now. You have to put a mask on so they won't recognize you."

"Why wouldn't they recognize me? I recognize you."

"You think you do," she said, her long-lashed eyes vivid and humorous. "Playing card people wouldn't know you behind a mask. It's their Achilles heel. They take everything at face value. They're very one-dimensional thinkers."

"Ha ha," I said. "When's the appraiser coming?"

"Sometime. Later. I don't really know. I'm not sure there even is an appraiser. I might've made that up."

"I've only been awake twenty minutes and I'm already bored. Couldn't you guys have found a babysitter for me and come up here for your weird mask-wearing, baby-making weekend by yourselves?" As soon as I said it, I felt myself starting to blush, but I was pleased that I had it in me to needle her about their masks and her black underwear and the burlesque game they had going that they thought I was too young to understand.

She said, "I'd rather have you along. Now you won't be getting into trouble with that girl."

The heat in my cheeks deepened, the way coals will when someone sighs over them. "What girl?"

"I'm not sure which girl. It's either Jane Redhill or her friend. Probably her friend. The person you always go over to Luke's house hoping to see."

Luke was the one who liked her friend, Melinda; I liked Jane. Still, my mother had guessed close enough to unsettle me. Her smile broadened at my stricken silence.

"She is a pert little cutie, isn't she? Jane's friend? I guess they both are. The friend, though, seems more your type. What's her name? Melinda? The way she goes around in her baggy farmer overalls. I bet she spends her afternoons reading in a treehouse she built with her father. I bet she baits her own worms and plays football with the boys."

"Luke is hot for her."

"So it's Jane."

"Who said it has to be either of them?"

"There must be some reason you hang around with Luke. Besides Luke." Then she said, "Jane came by selling magazine subscriptions to benefit her church a few days ago. She seems like a very wholesome young thing. Very community minded. I wish I thought she had a sense of humor. When you're a little older, you should cold cock Luke Redhill and drop him in the old quarry. That Melinda will fall right into your arms. The two of you can mourn for him together. Grief can be very romantic." She took my empty plate and got up. "Find a mask. Play along."

She put my plate in the sink and went out. I finished a glass of juice and meandered into the great room after her. I glanced at the master bedroom, just as she was pushing the door shut behind her. The man who I took for my father still wore his disfiguring mask of ice, and had pulled on a pair of jeans. For a moment our eyes met, his gaze dispassionate and unfamiliar. He put a possessive hand on my mother's hip. The door closed and they were gone.

In the other bedroom, I sat on the edge of my bed and stuck my feet into my sneakers. The wind whined under the eaves. I felt glum and out of sorts, wanted to be home, had no idea what to do with myself. As I stood, I happened to glance at the green mask made of sewn silk leaves, turned once again to face the room. I pulled it down, rubbed it between thumb and forefinger, trying out the slippery smoothness of it. Almost as an afterthought, I put it on.

My mother was in the living room, fresh from the shower.

"It's you," she said. "Very Dionysian. Very Pan. We should get a towel. You could walk around in a little toga."

"That would be fun. Until hypothermia set in."

"It is drafty in here, isn't it? We need a fire. One of us has to go into the forest and collect an armful of dead wood."

"Boy, I wonder who that's going to be."

"Wait. We'll make it into a game. It'll be exciting."

"I'm sure. Nothing livens up a morning like tramping around in the cold foraging for sticks."

"Listen. Don't wander from the forest path. Out there in the woods, nothing is real except for the path. Children who drift away from it never find their way back. Also—this is the most important thing—don't let anyone see you, unless they come masked. Anyone in a mask is hiding out from the playing card people, just like us."

"If the woods are so dangerous for children, maybe I ought to stay here and you or Dad can go play pick up sticks. Is he ever coming out of the bedroom?"

But she was shaking her head. "Grown-ups can't go into the forest at all. Not even the trail is safe for someone my age. I can't even see the trail. Once you get as old as me it disappears from sight. I only know about it because your father and I used to take walks on it, when we came up here as teenagers. Only the young can find their way through all the wonders and illusions in the deep dark woods."

Outside was drab and cold beneath the pigeon-colored sky. I went around the back of the house, to see if there was a woodpile. On my way past the master bedroom, my father thumped on the glass. I went to the window to see what he wanted, and was surprised by my own reflection, superimposed over his face. I was still wearing the mask of silk leaves, had for a moment forgotten about it.

He pulled the top half of the window down and leaned out, his own face squashed by its shell of clear plastic, his wintry blue eyes a little blank. "Where are you going?"

"I'm going to check out the woods, I guess. Mom wants me to collect sticks for a fire."

He hung his arms over the top of the window and stared into the yard. He watched some rust colored leaves trip end-over-end across the grass. "I wish I was going."

"Then come."

He glanced up at me, and smiled, for the first time all day. "No. Not right now. Tell you what. You go on, and maybe I'll meet you out there in a while."

"Okay."

"It's funny. As soon as you leave this place, you forget how—pure it is. What the air smells like." He looked at the grass and the lake for another moment, then turned his head, caught my eye. "You forget other things too. Jack, listen, I don't want you to forget about—"

The door opened behind him, on the far side of the room. My father fell silent. My mother stood in the doorway. She was in her jeans and sweater, playing with the wide buckle of her belt.

"Boys," she said. "What are we talking about?"

My father didn't glance back at her, but went on staring at me, and beneath his new face of melted crystal, I thought I saw a look of chagrin, as if he'd been caught doing something faintly embarrassing; cheating at solitaire maybe. I remembered, then, her drawing her fingers across his lips, closing an imaginary zipper, the night before. My head went queer and light. I had the sudden idea I was seeing another part of some unwholesome game playing out between them, the less of which I knew, the happier I'd be.

"Nothing," I said. "I was just telling Dad I was going for a walk. And now I'm going. For my walk." Backing away from the window as I spoke.

My mother coughed. My father slowly pushed the top half of the window shut, his gaze still level with mine. He turned the lock—then pressed his palm to the glass, in a gesture of goodbye. When he lowered his hand, a steamy imprint of it remained, a ghost hand that shrank in on itself and vanished. My father drew down the shade.

I forgot about gathering sticks almost as soon as I set out. I had by then decided that my parents only wanted me out of the house so they could have the place to themselves, a thought that made me peevish. At the head of the trail I pulled off my mask of silk leaves and hung it on a branch.

I walked with my head down and my hands shoved into the pockets of my coat. For a while the path ran parallel to the lake, visible beyond the hemlocks in slivers of frigid-looking blue. I was too busy thinking that if they wanted to be perverted and un-parent-like, they should've figured a way to come up to Big Cat Lake without me, to notice the path turning and leading away from the water. I didn't look up until I heard the sound coming toward me along the trail: a steely whirring, the creak of a metal frame under stress. Directly ahead, the path divided to go around a boulder, the size and rough shape of a half-buried coffin stood on end. Beyond the boulder, the path came back together and wound away into the pines.

I was alarmed, I don't know why. It was something about the way the wind rose just then, so the trees flailed at the sky. It was the frantic way the leaves scurried about my ankles, as if in a sudden hurry to get off the trail. Without thinking, I sat down behind the boulder, back to the stone, hugging my knees to my chest.

A moment later the boy on the antique bike—the boy I thought I had dreamed—rode past on my left, without so much as a glance my way. He was dressed in the nightgown he had been wearing the night before. A harness of white straps held a pair of modest white-feathered wings to his back. Maybe he had had them on the first time I saw him and I hadn't noticed them in the dark. As he rattled past, I had a brief look at his dimpled cheeks and blond bangs, features set in an expression of serene confidence. His gaze was cool, distant. Seeking. I watched him expertly guide his Charlie-Chaplin-cycle between stones and roots, around a curve, and out of sight.

If I hadn't seen him in the night, I might have thought he was a boy on his way to a costume party, although it was too cold to be out gallivanting in a nightgown. I wanted to be back at the cabin, out of the wind, safe with my parents. I was in dread of the trees, waving and shushing around me.

But when I moved, it was to continue in the direction I had been heading, glancing often over my shoulder to make sure the bicyclist wasn't coming up behind me. I didn't have the nerve to walk back along the trail, knowing that the boy on the antique bike was somewhere out there, between myself and the cabin.

I hurried along, hoping to find a road, or one of the other summer houses along the lake, eager to be anywhere but in the woods. Anywhere turned out to be less than ten minutes walk from the coffin-shaped rock. It was clearly marked—a weathered plank, with the words 'ANY-WHERE' painted on it, was nailed to the trunk of a pine—a bare patch in the woods where people had once camped. A few charred sticks sat in the bottom of a blackened firepit. Someone, children maybe, had built a lean-to between a pair of boulders. The boulders were about the same height, tilting in toward one another, and a sheet of plywood had been set across the top of them. A log had been pulled across the opening that faced the clearing, providing both a place for people to sit by a fire, and a barrier that had to be climbed over to enter the shelter.

I stood at the ruin of the ancient campfire, trying to get my bearings. Two trails on the far side of the camp led away. There was little difference between them, both narrow ruts gouged out in the brush, and no clue as to where either of them might lead.

"Where are you trying to go?" said a girl on my left, her voice pitched to a good-humored hush.

I leaped, took a half-step away, looked around. She was leaning out of the shelter, hands on the log. I hadn't seen her in the shadows of the lean-to. She was black-haired, a little older than myself—sixteen maybe—and I had a sense she was pretty. It was hard to be sure. She wore a black sequined mask, with a fan of ostrich feathers standing up from one side. Just behind her, further back in the dark, was a boy, the upper half of his face hidden behind a smooth plastic mask the color of milk.

"I'm looking for my way back," I said.

"Back where?" asked the girl.

The boy kneeling behind her took a measured look at her outthrust bottom in her faded jeans. She was, consciously or not, wiggling her hips a little from side-to-side.

"My family has a summer place near here. I was wondering if one of those two trails would take me there."

"You could go back the way you came," she said, but mischievously, as if she already knew I was afraid to double back.

"I'd rather not," I said.

"What brought you all the way out here?" asked the boy.

"My mother sent me to collect wood for the fire."

He snorted. "Sounds like the beginning of a fairy tale." The girl cast a disapproving look back at him, which he ignored. "One of the bad ones. Your parents can't feed you anymore, so they send you off to get lost in the woods. Eventually someone gets eaten by a witch for dinner. Baked into a pie. Be careful it's not you."

"Do you want to play cards with us?" the girl asked, and held up a deck.

"I just want to get home. I don't want my parents worried."

"Sit and play with us," she said. "We'll play a hand for answers. The winner gets to ask each of the losers a question, and no matter what, they have to tell the truth. So if you beat me, you could ask me how to get home without seeing the boy on the old bicycle, and I'd have to tell you."

Which meant she had seen him and somehow guessed the rest. She looked pleased with herself, enjoyed letting me know I was easy to figure out. I considered for a moment, then nodded.

"What are you playing?" I asked.

"It's a kind of poker. It's called Cold Hands, because it's the only card game you can play when it's this cold."

The boy shook his head. "This is one of these games where she makes up the rules as she goes along." His voice, which had an adolescent crack in it, was nevertheless familiar to me.

I crossed to the log and she retreated on her knees, sliding back into the dark space under the plywood roof to make room for me. She was talking all the time, shuffling her worn deck of cards.

"It isn't hard. I deal five cards to each player, face-up. When I'm done, whoever has the best poker hand wins. That probably sounds too simple, but then there are a lot of funny little house rules. If you smile during the game, the player sitting to your left can swap one of his cards for one of yours. If you can build a house with the first three cards you get dealt, and if the other players can't blow it down in one breath, you get to look through the deck and pick out whatever you want for your fourth card. If you draw a black forfeit, the other players throw stones at you until you're dead. If you have any questions, keep them to yourself. Only the winner gets to ask questions. Anyone who asks a question while the game is in play loses instantly. Okay? Let's start."

My first card was a Lazy Jack. I knew because it said so across the bottom, and because it showed a picture of a golden-haired jack lounging on silk pillows, while a harem girl filed his toenails. It wasn't until the girl handed me my second card—the three of rings—that I mentally registered the thing she had said about the black forfeit.

"Excuse me," I started. "But what's a—"

She raised her eyebrows, looked at me seriously.

"Nevermind," I said.

The boy made a little sound in his throat. The girl cried out, "He smiled! Now you can trade one of your cards for one of his!"

"I did not!"

"You did," she said. "I saw it. Take his queen and give him your jack."

I gave him the Lazy Jack and took the Queen of Sheets away from him. It showed a nude girl asleep on a carved four-poster, amid the tangle of her bedclothes. She had straight brown hair, and strong, handsome features, and bore a resemblance to Jane's friend, Melinda. After that I was dealt the King of Pennyfarthings, a red-bearded fellow, carrying a sack of coins that was splitting and beginning to spill. I was pretty sure the girl in the black mask had dealt him to me from the bottom of the deck. She saw I saw and shot me a cool, challenging look.

When we each had three cards, we took a break and tried to build houses the others couldn't blow down, but none of them would stand. Afterward I was dealt the Queen of Chains and a card with the rules of Cribbage printed on it. I almost asked if it was in the deck by accident, then thought better of it. No one drew a black forfeit. I don't even know what one is.

"Jack wins!" shouted the girl, which unnerved me a little, since I had never introduced myself. "Jack is the winner!" She flung herself against me and hugged me fiercely. When she straightened up, she was pushing my winning cards into the pocket of my jacket. "Here, you should keep your winning hand. To remember the fun we had. It doesn't matter. This old deck is missing a bunch of cards anyway. I just knew you'd win!"

"Sure she did," said the boy. "First she makes up a game with rules only she can understand, then she cheats so it comes out how she likes."

She laughed, unpolished, convulsive laughter, and I felt cold on the nape of my neck. But really, I think I already knew by then, even before she laughed, who I was playing cards with.

"The secret to avoiding unhappy losses is to only play games you make up yourself," she said. "Now. Go ahead, Jack. Ask anything you like. It's your right."

"How do I get home without going back the way I came?"

"That's easy. Take the path closest to the 'any-where' sign, which will take you anywhere you want to go. That's why it says anywhere. Just be sure the cabin is really where you want to go, or you might not get there."

"Right. Thank you. It was a good game. I didn't understand it, but I had fun playing." And I scrambled out over the log.

I hadn't gone far, before she called out to me. When I looked back, she and the boy were side-by-side, leaning over the log and staring out at me.

"Don't forget," she said. "You get to ask him a question too."

"Do I know you?" I said, making a gesture to include both of them.

"No," he said. "You don't really know either of us."

There was a Jag parked in the driveway behind my parents' car. The interior was polished cherry, and the seats looked as if they had never been sat on. It might have just rolled off the dealership floor. By then it was late in the day, the light slanting in from the west, cutting through the tops of the trees. It didn't seem like it could be so late.

I thumped up the stairs, but before I could reach the door to go in, it opened, and my mother stepped out, still wearing the black sex-kitten mask.

"Your mask," she said. "What'd you do with it?"

"Ditched it," I said. I didn't tell her I hung it on a tree branch because I was embarrassed to be seen in it. I wished I had it now, although I couldn't have said why.

She threw an anxious look back at the door, then crouched in front of me.

"I knew. I was watching for you. Put this on." She offered me my father's mask of clear plastic.

I stared at it a moment, remembering the way I recoiled from it when I first saw it, and how it had squashed my father's features into something cold and menacing. But when I slipped it on my face, it fit well enough. It carried a faint fragrance of my father, coffee and the sea-spray odor of his aftershave. I found it reassuring to have him so close to me.

My mother said, "We're getting out of here in a few minutes. Going home. Just as soon as the appraiser is done looking around. Come on. Come in. It's almost over."

I followed her inside, then stopped just through the door. My father sat on the couch, shirtless and barefoot. His body looked as if it had been marked up by a surgeon for an operation. Dotted lines and arrows showed the location of liver, spleen and bowels. His eyes were pointed toward the floor, his face blank.

"Dad?" I asked.

His gaze rose, flitted from my mother to me and back. His expression remained bland and unrevealing.

"Sh," my mother said. "Daddy's busy."

I heard heels cracking across the bare planks to my right, and glanced across the room, as the appraiser came out of the master bedroom. I had assumed the appraiser would be a man, but it was a middle-aged woman in a tweed jacket, with some white showing in her wavy yellow hair. She had austere, imperial features, the high cheekbones and expressive, arching eyebrows of English nobility.

"See anything you like?" my mother asked.

"You have some wonderful pieces," the appraiser said. Her gaze drifted to my father's bare shoulders.

"Well," my mother said. "Don't mind me." She gave the back of my arm a soft pinch, and slipped around me, whispered out of the side of her mouth, "Hold the fort, kiddo. I'll be right back."

My mother showed the appraiser a small, strictly polite smile, before easing into the master bedroom and out of sight, leaving the three of us alone.

"I was sorry when I heard Upton died," the appraiser said. "Do you miss him?"

The question was so unexpected and direct it startled me; or maybe it was her tone, which was not sympathetic, but sounded to my ears too-curious, eager for a little grief.

"I guess. We weren't so close," I said. "I think he had a pretty good life, though."

"Of course he did," she said.

"I'd be happy if things worked out half as well for me."

"Of course they will," she said, and put a hand on the back of my father's neck and began rubbing it fondly.

It was such a casually intimate gesture, I felt a sick intestinal pang at the sight. I let my gaze drift away—had to look away—and happened to glance at the mirror on the back of the dresser. The curtains were parted slightly, and in the reflection I saw a playing card woman standing behind my father, the queen of spades, her eyes of ink haughty and distant, her black robes painted onto her body. I wrenched my gaze from the looking-glass in alarm, and glanced back at the couch. My father was smiling in a dreamy kind of way, leaning back into the hands now massaging his shoulders. The appraiser regarded me from beneath half-lowered eyelids.

"That isn't your face," she said to me. "No one has a face like that. A face made out of ice. What are you hiding?"

My father stiffened, and his smile faded. He sat up and forward, slipping his shoulders out of her grip.

"You've seen everything," my father said to the woman behind him. "Do you know what you want?"

"I'd start with everything in this room," she said, putting her hand gently on his shoulder again. She toyed with a curl of his hair for a moment. "I can have everything, can't I?"

My mother came out of the bedroom, lugging a pair of suitcases, one in each hand. She glanced at the appraiser with her hand on my father's neck, and huffed a bemused little laugh—a laugh that went huh and which seemed to mean more or less just that—and picked up the suitcases again, marched with them toward the door.

"It's all up for grabs," my father said. "We're ready to deal."

"Who isn't?" said the appraiser.

My mother set one of the suitcases in front of me, and nodded that I should take it. I followed her onto the porch, and then looked back. The appraiser was leaning over the back of the couch, and my father's head was tipped back, and her mouth was on his. My mother reached past me and closed the door.

We walked through the gathering twilight to the car. The boy in the white gown sat on the lawn, his bicycle on the grass beside him. He was skinning a dead rabbit with a piece of horn, its stomach open and steaming. He glanced at us as we went by and grinned, showing teeth pink with blood. My mother put a motherly arm around my shoulders.

After she was in the car, she took off her mask and threw it on the backseat. I left mine on. When I inhaled deeply I could smell my father.

"What are we doing?" I asked. "Isn't he coming?"

"No," she said, and started the car. "He's staying here."

"How will he get home?"

She turned a sideways look upon me, and smiled sympathetically. Outside, the sky was a blue-almost-black, and the clouds were a scalding shade of crimson, but in the car it was already night. I turned in my seat, sat up on my knees, to watch the cottage disappear through the trees.

"Let's play a game," my mother said. "Let's pretend you never really knew your father. He went away before you were born. We can make up fun little stories about him. He has a Semper Fi tattoo from his days in the marines, and another one, a blue anchor, that's from—" her voice faltered, as she came up suddenly short on inspiration.

"From when he worked on a deep-sea oil rig."

She laughed. "Right. And we'll pretend the road is magic. The Amnesia Highway. By the time we're home, we'll both believe the story is true, that he really did leave before you were born. Everything else will seem like a dream, those dreams as real as memories. The made-up story will probably be better than the real thing anyway. I mean, he loved your bones, and he wanted everything for you, but can you remember one interesting thing he ever did?"

I had to admit I couldn't.

"Can you even remember what he did for a living?"

I had to admit I didn't. Insurance?

"Isn't this a good game?" she asked. "Speaking of games. Do you still have your deal?"

"My deal?" I asked, then remembered, and touched the pocket of my jacket.

"You want to hold onto it. That's some winning hand. King of Pennyfarthings. Queen of Sheets. You got it all, boy. I'm telling you, when we get home, you give that Melinda a call." She laughed again, and then affectionately patted her tummy. "Good days ahead, kid. For both of us."

I shrugged.

"You can take the mask off, you know," my mother said. "Unless you like wearing it. Do you like wearing it?"

I reached up for the sun visor, turned it down, and opened the mirror. The lights around the mirror switched on. I studied my new face of ice, and the face beneath, a malformed, human blank.

"Sure," I said. "It's me."

*Gavin J. Grant stories have appeared in **Polyphony** and **The Third Alternative** and on **Strange Horizons** and **SCIFICTION**. He co-edits the zine **Lady Churchill's Rosebud Wristlet** with Kelly Link and runs Small Beer Press. He lives in Northampton, MA.*

Heads Down, Thumbs Up
Gavin J. Grant

Mrs. Black repeated her question, but then the border wobbled over us again. She sighed. There was a knock at the door, and the school secretary came in.

"Yes, yes," said Mrs. Black before the secretary could say anything. "I know, I know."

She turned to us. "Boys and girls. Two minutes of heads down, thumbs up."

She went to the sink at the back of the classroom and wet her handkerchief. She touched the tops of our heads as she passed, a diagonal line of us whose hair stood up on the backs of our necks. I wanted to be touched. She took her hankie to the blackboard and stretched up to the top corner and wiped her name away. Her name was Ms. Sterling now. I sneaked a look at Jeanine. She'd never learned to sculpt the letter r out from the other sounds. She had her head down, but her eyes were open. She was staring at her math book (we'd have to use the other set now) and her face was slowly turning red. She hated it, too, the change.

Ms. Sterling said something, and everyone sat up. She said it again, and now she was looking at me but I hadn't been listening, and now she was using a different language.

"Ardgrur-; rjinnsfller?" she asked.

And then I knew what she meant, the other language coming over me like the dirty water spreading across the painting table when I knocked over my paint cup. I hoped it wouldn't last. I liked our other country; the stories were better. In this one the witch always escapes and sometimes she even marries the children's father. Ms. Sterling cried sometimes in the art supply cupboard after reading these stories. But she won't be allowed to tell the other ones anymore. That's what happened to Ms. Frobisher, our teacher when we were last this country. She was ancient, and she always forgot who we were.

After school, dad was late and I told myself the story where the witch got put in the oven. I liked singing the song the brother and sister sang when they gathered apples and herbs to bake with her. Once, when I was in the first class, we got a story where the witch ate all the children. We all cried.

Dad was late because he waited for Mum to come home before coming to get me. Neither of them ask about school. I didn't want to tell them anything anyway. I heard my dad tell Edward's dad I'm a chatterbox. I curl up in my seat and watch the men out on the road painting the white lines light blue.

Dad drove even slower than usual. Mum started talking about how hard it was to sign in for her new job at the library. She wants him to speed up, but I know she'll never actually ask him. Dad jumps when she puts her hand on his leg. Dad's rubbish in this country. I wish the border would go back.

Next day Jeanine doesn't come in. But neither does Bobbie or Bobby or Brian. Someone at the back sends a note forward, but I don't take it. Alison digs her nails into my leg and I jump like my dad in the car. Ms. Sterling notices, and I have to stand in the corner. Alison should be laughing, but she's not. There's something wrong with her eyes, they're too big or something. Her dad's in the other country's army. I wonder if he's dead yet.

Last time the border came over we saw dead people everywhere. They said they'd been Pee Oh Double Yous, but we knew they were dead. They appeared after school. They were gray and cold and wanted to hold us. Edward said they were zombies. We all knew zombies wanted to crack our heads open and suck our brains out. We ran and ran. I didn't know where I was when I stopped. I'd run up a hill, and all the dead people ("Wait. It's me. Your Uncle Billy.") couldn't follow because they were too tired. There were lots of houses up there, and they all looked the same. I thought I knew someone from school who lived there, Caroline, but I didn't know which house she lived in. I don't remember getting home. Sometimes I think I went back to the wrong house. "Where's Sarah?" I asked when I got home. I remember Mum and Dad looking at each other. They thought I couldn't understand the look, but I did. I always understand adults. I wonder if they were ever children: if they don't remember how easy they are to understand.

When we get home I ask dad why adults don't know children understand. But he says, "Don't, shh. Just . . . just pretend, okay?"

"I don't want to," I say.

"When I was young," he says, and he picks me up, sits me on his knees. "When I was young, we didn't have adults."

I know this game. He used to do this a lot when I was younger. But I still scream when he opens his knees to drop me. He holds my arms, and I hang there for a second, pulling my legs up so that my feet don't touch the ground.

"We all lived together. Boys and girls. There were hundreds and hundreds of us," and he pulls me back onto his knees. "You wouldn't have liked it," he says.

I know this story. There are birds nailed to a barn. Cats and squirrels for dinner. There are scary adults who try to get into the children's big house, and sometimes they do and they take some of the children away. Sometimes the adults disappear and Dad gets a look in his eye. I don't like him then. Then there's his friend Ranald who went away (like Bobby and Bobbie? I wonder), and something Dad said once made me wonder if actually he got eaten.

When Dad tells stories, he changes. He likes to play and roll about and then later he makes dinner. I like that and try and get him to tell more stories. For dinner he usually makes scrambled eggs in rolls, and he can't stop smiling when he uses lots and lots of butter and cheese. Mum would make sausages to go with eggs, but after story time Dad won't eat meat until the next day; or maybe the next week.

He drops me through his knees again, and this time I spring back up immediately. He lets go my hands, catches my waist, throws me in the air; I can feel his smile on my back. He stands up really fast and catches me and throws me still further up. Suddenly I realize who he is and what he's done. In this country he's sad because in this country he was cruel and he isn't going to catch me. I start screaming.

He plucks me from the air. "What's wrong?" he asks, and there are ugly lines all over his face. He's breathing fast. "Are you okay? Did I hurt you?"

I catch my breath, but I can't look at him. Mum comes running in. Dad shrugs his shoulders at her, and even as I cling to him, she peels me off and carries me over to her chair. She's colder than he is and has harder edges.

Dad usually finishes stories by saying, "I had many friends then. I met your mother there. We were very lucky."

Ms. Sterling is replaced. "Just for two weeks, class," says the headmistress. Once we had a man for headmistress—he wanted to be called headmaster. We didn't like him, and when the border passed over again he ran away. We were so happy. It was like Saturday, and summer, and that holiday they have in autumn on that side, all in one.

Our new teacher says, "My name is Ms. Matchless. However," and she bends her cracking knees, and then her gray hair and heavy glasses are right down in front of us, "you," and she tickles under Berenice's chin, "you can call me Joanna."

Listening to her, I realize the cake, the apple, the hard black and white liquorice mints, any and all of these will be enough to make me climb into the oven. Ms. Matchless stands, smiles at us.

"Now," she says, beaming, "let's go out to the garden. Who can tell me what we've been growing in the school garden?"

I have always stayed away from the garden. I like drawing. I was going to be an artist, and whenever the border changed I was going to paint new murals in the school halls, but now I throw my hand in the air and tomatoes and cabbages are all I ever want to grow.

Dad's got a beard and he goes to sleep earlier than me now. He makes me laugh, and sometimes I go in to kiss him and tuck him in. He is half-asleep and calls me Ranald, but I'm used to that here. He hopes the border will move back soon. I hope so, too, but I don't want Ms. Matchless to leave.

Ms. Matchless has been our teacher for five weeks. The headmistress stopped visiting our class in the second week, when she saw we weren't upset about Ms. Sterling. But then she started coming again, and now she helps Ms. Matchless every afternoon. She never did that before. She laughs when Ms. Matchless laughs. I wish she wouldn't come.

Ms. Matchless tells us all about our country. Some of us remember our anthem. I don't. We never sing it at home, except when people come over for dinner. I don't like this anthem. The other song is better, but I know not to say that. Ms. Matchless—I don't call her Joanna, no one does—has a very sharp ear and can tell who's singing. I'm learning the words, and I sing very loud. I have a good, high voice although I know it won't last. Dad has a deep voice and likes to sing with me when we walk. We hold hands, and sometimes he swings me around, even though we both know I'm too big.

Ms. Matchless says that our country has one of the biggest forests in the world. She points to it on the map and says she grew up there. We are quiet. There is no forest near us, and we are imagining what it would be like to grow up in a cottage deep in the woods.

"There is nothing as beautiful as the Long Forest," Ms. Matchless says softly.

"Miss, please, miss." I am standing and waving my hand, and she smiles at me.

"Yes?"

I fall back in my chair. "Please, miss, can we go there? Can we see the forest?"

She looks surprised and pleased. Maybe I'll get a green circle on my report card.

"Well, that is an interesting idea! Who else wants to visit the forest?"

Everyone waves their hands in the air. Something hits me in the back of the head, hard enough to sting. I glance back, but all I can see are waving hands and smiling faces.

I am going away for a whole week, and we still haven't told Dad. I've never gone anywhere for a week. Once we drove for hours and then went on a ferry to visit my grandparents, my mum's mum and dad. It smelled of bitter mint and mothballs, and I hated it. There was a lot of shouting at night. I didn't like sleeping in-between my parents. Mum wanted to leave the next day, and Dad wanted to stay forever. I wish I wasn't going on this trip.

I'd waited until Dad went to bed before giving Mum the release form and asking for the trip money.

When she read the form, I didn't like the way she looked at me. "You suggested this?" she'd asked, and I saw Ms. Matchless had put in an extra note just for Mum.

I didn't have anything to say. Mum signed the form and said not to tell Dad just yet.

Now, when I am brushing my teeth, she says, "We'll just tell him tomorrow." But in the morning, Dad has left for work before I get up.

In front of the school there is a big white luxury coach with its engine running with a handwritten sign in the driver's window, *Ms. Matchless, The Long Forest,* and I forget about Dad until lunchtime, when the bus stops and we eat our packed lunches. Mum made mine last night, and my sandwiches are hard around the edges. But I swap my apple for Alison's orange and then we sit next to each other and I think maybe I have a girlfriend.

We don't reach the forest until the next day. We stop for the night at a youth hostel and sleep in two big, dark rooms. The driver sleeps in the boys' room in the bed nearest the door. I lie awake until after he comes in and goes to sleep. I am too frightened to go to the toilet in the night, but I don't wet myself. Early in the morning there is a knock on the door. The driver is still asleep, so I run over and open it. Ms. Matchless smiles at me and kisses me on the cheek. I rush past her to the toilet. When I get back, I find that Lucas needed the toilet, too, but couldn't hold it. I listen to the other boys and I'm very, very happy I held it.

This morning we can see the dark line of the forest, but it is still very far away. I tell Alison ghost stories, and even though it's daytime lots of people get scared because of me. Ms. Matchless walks up the bus and tells me to stop or tonight the witch of the forest will take me away. I can't help but grin, and she does, too. She has false teeth, and they are very white. I've seen her move them around during quiet time at school when we put our heads down on our desks and she marks our homework. The others are still scared from my stories, and I am happy. Maybe I will stay at Ms. Matchless's house in the forest and never go home.

She sits down next to me, and I have to squeeze over beside Alison. No one else can see, so I hold Alison's hand.

When everyone is quiet, Ms. Matchless tells us that there are trees in the Long Forest that are not found anywhere else in the world. They go straight up for hundreds of feet then weave their branches together so that it is very dark below. She says that lots of people live in the forest—some in houses far above the ground—but there is no way to count them all. She says there are more ways into the forest than out. Alison shivers, and I squeeze her hand.

"It's because there's a big city," I burst out. "The capital." Ms. Matchless nods at me but watches the others. I have read far ahead in my textbook, and I know all about the capital and how all the people left the forest towns.

"There are two million people. It has two airports, two big stadiums and lots of small ones, and the parliament buildings, which are very beautiful on the inside because they are made from wood from the Long Forest."

Alison nods her head, and other people do, too. I am smarter in this country. If we stay here, maybe I will be a teacher when I grow up.

Then the bus goes into the forest and it is almost as dark as night because we are driving under the tallest trees we have ever seen. Everyone is quiet. We drive for two hours under the trees, and all the time we are going up.

The forest is like another country. Even the cars are different. Alison gets bored, so there is some seat swapping and me and Edward sit together and count cars. He knows more of them than me, but I have a girlfriend, so I don't care.

The capital is huge. The day after we arrive, we go to the parliament, which is boring on the outside—the walls are gray and very, very thick and the windows all have bars. Inside it's like a church. There are glass walls in front of the wooden walls, and I can see where the old wooden walls look thin where lots of people have touched them. Parliament is in session, and a man is speaking when we go to the visitors' balcony. He is not very interesting, but I like his clothes: they have bright buttons and sharp creases I'd like to touch. We all clap when Ms. Matchless claps, and the man waves up at us. We all wave back, and lots of people laugh. Then we have lunch outside in the gardens. There are huge concrete flowerpots and concrete picnic tables all around the parliament.

The rest of the week we walk everywhere. My feet hurt, but I like the city. We stay in another youth hostel but now I know not to drink anything before bed. I am very thirsty in the morning and I drink lots of milk.

One morning Ms. Matchless tells us to bring our bags down after breakfast. We take them outside and find that the bus is waiting for us. We all protest it isn't time to go back, yet but we are shooed onto the bus. Ms. Matchless says we are going farther into the Long Forest, and we are all quiet. Alison sneaks over and makes Edward swap seats. Berenice is unhappy, and Edward will say he has a girlfriend but he doesn't really.

Leaving, it is hard to tell where the city ends and the forest begins, but then we slow down and turn off the expressway onto a narrow, dark road. We are silent and watch the forest, which is different now that we see it up close. The trees grow far apart, but they go back a long, long way. Their trunks are smooth and silvery and look difficult to climb. The forest is hard, dark, frightening, but Ms. Matchless is smiling.

The driver goes even slower, the front of the bus swings almost into the trees when it goes around corners. Occasionally we see empty cars parked beside the road, but we never see houses or people walking.

We stop at a parking lot and I see there is a path up to a big hall or castle. We walk in twos, holding hands. Edward is now very happy. I am, too, but I know where we are and he doesn't. This is where we will live with Ms. Matchless from now on. We will cook and clean, some of us will be gardeners, some of us will be children, and the noisy ones will be dinner.

This house is not like the youth hostels: we do not sleep in big rooms. Us boys are on the second floor and the girls are somewhere up above. Edward, John, Richard, and me are in a room together. There is a window seat, a fireplace, and four small beds. We each have our own bedside cabinet carved with a forest of trees with lots of apples. Little cottages are hidden among the trees, there are mountains in the distance, and everywhere there are tiny, running wolves. I run my fingers over the carving, pretending I am in the forest. I run away from the hall where Ms. Matchless is showing the class how to bake the cakes she loved as a child. I come upon the wolves, and they chase me, but I find it is not so hard to scramble up one of the silver trees. I throw the apples down at the wolves, trying to drive them away. The wolves are very hungry. For years they have wanted the beautiful golden apples but have not been able to reach them. I throw one apple to each wolf, and the wolves gobble them up. Their smiles get bigger and bigger, and then they all howl. I put my hands over my ears and close my eyes. Suddenly there is a lot of laughing. I am surrounded by boys and by girls, too. The girls should not be here. We had been planning to raid the girls' rooms as soon as the lights are out. I think that when I gave the wolves apples, they changed into these children. I am still on my knees, my fingers tracing the carvings.

At dinner we sit on benches at two long tables. They are round underneath, and Ms. Matchless says they are two halves of one huge birchlike tree from the forest. It's not very comfortable, until I sit on one foot: then I can swing my other foot underneath me. We eat and eat and eat. When I am at home, Mum and Dad don't cook like this. I don't know what I'm eating! There is meat and potatoes and mushy orange and green vegetables, but I don't know what type of meat it is. I imagine it's the wolves: that's why it's dark and chewy. Or maybe I am a wolf like the others. I growl as I eat. Even though they are horrid, I eat the vegetables. I like the bread. It's black and crunchy on the outside and chewy on the inside. I see Ms. Matchless put lots and lots of butter and then salt on it, and I do the same.

After dinner Ms. Matchless says she is going to give us a tour of the house.

I put my hand up. "Is this your house?" I ask.

She is already leading us out of the dining room and she only shakes her head.

There are dusty old paintings on each side of the hallway. Pointing up to the first one, Ms. Matchless says, "This is Edward Doubleaxe."

Edward is grinning so much I wonder if his head will fall off. Ms. Matchless is smiling at him in a way I don't recognize. Later, at home, whenever I think of Edward, I remember this smile.

"Doubleaxe was the first man to rule the whole forest. He burned down a village to build his castle here by the river. Later, during the coup in which he killed his father, Doubleaxe's son burned the castle to the ground and built another but that was much later. There have been many castles here, but Doubleaxe's was the first.

"Doubleaxe was handsome, but his nose was so large he only allowed painters to paint him from the front. Once, a painter tried to paint a portrait of Doubleaxe and his wife with the light coming from the side so that there would be the slightest hint of a shadow of his nose." She smiled at us. "Doubleaxe was not a man who enjoyed being laughed at. This is not that painting."

Behind Ms. Matchless the others are laughing at Edward and using their hands to make pointy beaks. "Beaky, Beaky," Berenice whispers.

The way home was much harder. We did not have the bus. We had to walk. The Long Forest was dark and, at the end, when the trees grew farther apart, the bushes were hard to push through. There were gray wolves, black bears. I was glad I was not the oldest boy, the second brother, or the youngest girl, who would get the prince but had to do all the dirty work first. I thought of my father and his friend, Ranald, and after the mushrooms, acorns, and the leaves that made me sick were gone, I ate what I had to eat. We walked and we walked and Ms. Matchless always walked behind us.

During the day, we couldn't see the sun. I saw Beaky once, but he did not see me. He was a scout, he said, and tried to keep in front of us. We could all smell him, and we tried to stay away from him.

Alison stayed away from me at first. The boys were weaker, the girls stronger. Ms. Matchless was the strongest of all. Once, when we met two soldiers, she took them out of our sight. She made them scream. She limped when she came back, but her eyes were bright. She had tied a khaki shirt around her calf, and as we walked it slowly turned red, brown, black. We liked the soldiers' rations.

She sang songs we'd never heard. She said they were forest songs that didn't belong to any country. This was the first thing I did not understand. I would have hated her for this, but she was my everything: my bare foot stepping in front of my other bare foot; my waking up in the morning, my sidling behind trees to watch her finding food. I learned the songs inside, but I did not sing anymore. I knew now that only girls sang. I will ask my father if Ranald sang. Maybe that was his mistake. I don't want to make any more mistakes.

We got into the forest so easily, but that road is far behind now. My shoes are broken and gone, my trousers torn. I smell like nothing I have ever smelled. I do not like it. I think about Edward Doubleaxe ruling the whole forest and the houses built on top of the first village. Bigger and bigger houses, but always made of wood, and always so easy to burn.

Before we left the big house, after the television stopped, we listened to what the radio said about the border. Ms. Matchless (we never learned her new name; she said she did not have one in this country) said that this border had never crossed the house before, that was why everyone there was so upset.

I spat. I was eleven and I knew what borders did. I could have told them, but no one wanted to listen. I knew they didn't have to go around digging ditches and shouting about parents and blood and our party, their party. They could have changed the flag, washed the windows, and gotten ready for the army's visit. They made me angry. I'm just a boy, I thought. I understand. Why don't they?

Ms. Matchless punches me in the side of the head. It is night, and I have been on guard. Even with her limp I did not notice her. I deserve to be punched harder. I salute, and she walks away. All the soldiers' guns make her walk slower, but she won't let me carry one until much later.

We reach the last border back to our country and find that it has stopped moving. There are guards with guns, big silver and black dogs that look like wolves, and spike-topped fences that run from the road into the forest. We slip back into the forest, and Ms. Matchless leads us along the wire. No one can keep up the borders in the forest, she says.

We wait and cross at night. It is more like swimming. The words buzz and crawl in my mouth, fighting each other. I realize Ms. Matchless is not following us. We have gone back to holding hands, walking in twos, pulling each other along. I am lucky: Alison has left the girls and walks with me. She is very strong. The border makes me want to sing the forest songs, the songs that don't belong to anyone, but I *am* a boy. I am a boy.

We look back and see Ms. Matchless waving. She points her gun at us, and I point the other one at her. Then she salutes, waves, walks tall and strong and limping back into the forest.

Mother and Father are happy to see me. Once I stop eating I will tell them that I am happy to see them, too. Or maybe after I sleep. I do not know when I will sleep. Who will stand guard? I hid the gun in the garden before I knocked on the door. Later, when Mother and Father are asleep, I will get it. Mother and Father think I am just a boy. I am a boy. I understand.

One day, soon after, I climb high up Unionist Bridge and I see Ms. Sterling's little car coming into town. Beaky's voice says "It's a Silver Satellite" in the forest language, but I ignore it. A man in a dark suit is driving, and I know he is Police Army. Ms. Sterling sits in the back and does not see me.

The headmistress brings Ms. Sterling to class the next morning and we all stand and say we are happy to see her. We thank the blurry-faced secretary who has been trying to teach us. Ms. Sterling limps, but on the other leg from Ms. Matchless, and everyone says she has a wooden leg now, to go with her new glass eye. Last year I wouldn't have liked her glass eye because it never moves, but I do now. Sometimes I think it works like a real eye. I wave at it when her real eye is looking the other way, but she never says anything to me. The headmistress nods at her in the hall. We all nod, too. We're children, we know what to do.

Then one day during multiplication tables the border crosses over us again. For a long moment (such a long moment inside), I think it will be something new, some place we've never been before. I am excited and I stop reciting even stop watching for problems.

We'll learn new songs, always wear bright shirts on this day, eat sweet red cakes on a special Wednesday in spring, sour white dumplings on the opposite Wednesday in autumn. The girls will wear their hair long (or maybe I will), and I will grow up tall and blond—my hair has been growing back, but darker than it was before.

Then I feel the old words trying to sink into my teeth, my tongue.

Ms. Sterling says, "Sit down. Heads down until I say," and makes her slow way to the sink to get something to clean the board. Ms. Sterling will be Mrs. Black again, and now we know Ms. Matchless is not coming back. I think of Ms. Matchless limping and hunting and eating in the Long Forest. I wonder if she will go back to where she grew up. Would she stay there in the place with no country, singing the songs from before there were borders? I do not think so. She is too strong. She will leave the forest to fight for the capital. Alison is looking out the window, seeing something I can't. I do not think I am the only one that misses Ms. Matchless.

I am still standing. "Rjihnsfjil;—ardrruwer," I say.

"Shut up," says Mrs. Black. She doesn't touch anyone as she shuffles back from the sink. A thought settles inside me: she is not Ms. Matchless, but she is a girl: she is strong.

She limps by me and punches me on the side of the head just like Ms. Matchless. It is night in my head, and I have let down my guard.

"Foolish boy," she says. She limps to the blackboard, erases her name.

Eugie Foster calls home a mildly-haunted, fey-infested house in Metro Atlanta that she shares with her husband, Matthew, and her pet skunk, Hobkin. She is a winner of the Phobos Award and the Managing Editor of ***Tangent****, and her fiction has been translated into Greek, Hungarian, Polish, and French. She has also been nominated for the British Fantasy, Southeastern Science Fiction, and Pushcart Awards. Her publication credits include stories in* ***Realms of Fantasy, The Third Alternative, Paradox, Cricket, Fantasy Magazine, Cicada,*** *and anthologies* ***Hitting the Skids in Pixeltown, Heroes in Training,*** *and* ***Writers for Relief.***

"Returning My Sister's Face" is a retelling of the classic Edo period Japanese story, "Tokaido Yotsuya Kaidan," a tale that is alleged to be true and that has terrified the Japanese for centuries.

Returning My Sister's Face

Eugie Foster

My earliest memories are of Oiwa in the sunlight, brushing her magnificent hair. Unbound, it trailed to the floor, a waterfall of shimmering black, the same color as a raven's wing. It was Oiwa who picked me up from the dirt with words of comfort and wisdom when my pony threw me off for shouting in his ear.

"Yasuo, do not cry, silly boy," she said as she dried my tears with the hem of her kimono. "And you should not rage at your pony either, but thank him for only tossing you from his back. If you had shouted in my ear like that, I would have bitten you besides."

And it was Oiwa's proud smile I looked for when I won the praise of my sword master. I remember how small she looked, kneeling in her kimono with her hands folded in her lap. But she was always my big sister, even when I towered over her in my samurai armor.

Our father died when I was a boy, felled by the sword of a barbarian from the west. He was a brave warlord. I barely remember him. Oiwa told me how he laughed when he swung me in his arms, proud of how fearless I was as a babe.

With his death, our prosperity ended. Mother grew sick, and people turned away from us, loathe to help those who had so obviously been touched by bad luck, as though it might be contagious. We would have become thieves or beggars if not for Shigekazu—the lord of Yotsuya. He took pity on us and took me in, gave me a swordsman's education, and let us stay in our ancestral home.

To repay him, when I earned my warrior's katana, I became his most loyal captain. I patrolled his borders and kept bandits from abusing his farmers and tradesman.

It was the start of plum blossom season during my seventeenth year when Iyemon arrived. The white and fuchsia petals shed their heavy perfume, and there was anticipation of the upcoming *Ume Matsuri* festival. Iyemon rode to Lord Shigekazu's gate, a masterless samurai, shining in his fine *michiyuki* overcoat, astride a golden stallion. He brought with him his katana and his servant, Kohei, and nothing else.

He went to Shigekazu and petitioned to be allowed to join his guard. In turn, my lord Shigekazu asked me to look after him.

It was strange for me, as Iyemon was a well-grown man, ten years my senior. Yet, I was in the teacher's position. Even so, Iyemon was gracious. He did not chafe when I instructed him as to how we set our watches and shifts, nor did he sneer to spar at bamboo canes with me. Indeed he laughed when I bested him in our first bout, and was as genial in triumph in our second.

He had no kin in the area and no hearth, so I invited him to dinner.

Oiwa was surprised to see three men—Iyemon, Kohei, and myself—walking up the path, but she was sweetly courteous, as I knew she would be. She ran to put more water on for tea and returned with a basin of scented water for us to splash upon our hands and faces.

If I try, I can still remember the flavors from that dinner. Hot soup with tangy seaweed, sticky rice that melted on my tongue, tart *umeboshi* from the plum trees, and sweet bean cakes that could have been clouds of nectar fallen from the heavens.

After the meal, Kohei washed the pots and bowls while Oiwa went to tend our mother. Iyemon and I sat on *tatami* mats and smoked pipes, awash in tranquil harmony.

With the blue smoke wreathing his face, Iyemon cast his eyes down. "Tell me, Yasuo," he said. "Why is your beautiful sister without a husband?"

I was surprised at how forthright he was on this matter of delicacy, but then he was new to Yotsuya and did not know our family's story.

"None will take her," I said. "For though Oiwa is noble, she can bring no dowry to a marriage. Our father died with his riches plundered. What household wealth we had we spent on medicine and doctors for our mother, who languishes with a wasting disease."

"But you have this fine house in the country—"

"We owe all to Lord Shigekazu. Without his mercy and generosity, we would be penniless, cast out into the streets."

"Still, your sister is sweet of face and graceful of temperament. Surely there are men who would take her to wife?"

"She is considered a bad luck woman," I admitted. "She has no suitors."

"Outrageous!" Iyemon declared. Of course, I was not going to disagree.

When Oiwa came from our mother's room, Iyemon rose to his feet and bowed low to her. A soft blush, like the new glow of camellia blossoms on a white bough, filled her face, and she hid behind her fan.

"Lady Oiwa," Iyemon said, "I would be honored if you would walk with me at the *Ume Matsuri* festival. May I call upon you tomorrow?"

My sister's blush deepened, turning the enchanting hue of sunset clouds at midsummer. "I will look forward to it."

The *Ume Matsuri* festival was the traditional start of spring. The plum trees displayed their five-petalled blooms during the month of *Ya Yohi,* while beneath them, maidens and youths strolled together. The maidens wore kimonos to rival the flowers—violet silk embroidered with golden bamboo shoots, apricot sleeves with scarlet chrysanthemum, sea foam brocade with glowing koi painted on them. And the young men wore the maidens like banners upon their arms.

Oiwa did not have much finery, as we had sold her most lavish kimonos long ago. But she had kept one kimono, our great-great grandmother's good luck silk. It was peacock blue brocade with silver pine trees and malachite maple leaves woven through the cloth. With her hair piled high on her head and wooden *geta* sandals on her feet, Oiwa looked like a princess.

Iyemon's eyes widened when he saw her. He bore with him a perfect white plum blossom for her hair, and she let him affix it in her gleaming locks. They walked arm-and-arm together among the plum trees.

Iyemon became a frequent caller, and as the first cherry blossoms began to bud, they announced their *Yui-no* betrothal. Since there was but meager wealth on both sides, the gifts they exchanged were, of necessity, modest. Iyemon gave my sister a white *obi* to use as a belt on her wedding kimono. It was fine silk, embroidered with snow-white phoenixes. In return, Oiwa gave her husband-to-be a black *hakama* she had sewn with her own hands, every stitch a prayer of loyalty and fidelity.

At the wedding ceremony, Oiwa was radiant as the dawn star as she glided through the humble Shinto shrine of our ancestors. We had hired a maid from town to dress her hair with rented *kanzashi* combs and to help her don the traditional *shiro-maku* kimono.

Iyemon was composed, an expression of serenity on his face as he spoke the commitment vows. He looked like a king in his newly made *hakama* robe. Oiwa's hand was steady, without a whisper of tremor, when she lit the customary lamps.

But barely had the taste of the wedding *sake* faded when trouble visited. Our mother, too weak even to attend the ceremony, worsened. We thought death was ready to harvest her, yet she clung with grim tenacity to this world. The newlywed's month of sweetness was cut short, barely begun.

Then Lord Shigekazu received word that Lady Uma, his granddaughter, would be traveling from the city of Edo to visit him on her quest to find a husband. As he had not seen the daughter of his daughter in many years, he was jubilant at the news. He asked me to take a regiment of men to meet her at his border. For the first time, I was loathe to do his bidding.

"Please, Lord Shigekazu," I said. "My mother is very ill. I would prefer to stay near. Will you give me leave to decline this obligation?"

"Obligation?" Lord Shigekazu demanded. "Is it not basic courtesy that the captain I have raised as a grandson should feel honorbound to protect the safety of my only granddaughter? What if there are bandits on the road? Come, Yasuo, your mother has had many a bad turn, surely she will last a fortnight longer?"

"Please, my lord, it is my least desire to defy you, but I also owe duty to she who bore me."

Lord Shigekazu might have said harsher words then, ones that would have made me lose face if I did not bow to his wishes, but Iyemon intervened.

"If my lord would be willing to indulge one so new to his service," he said. "I would be greatly privileged if I could take my brother's place as escort for the Lady Uma."

Lord Shigekazu's brow still creased with darkness, but he allowed the substitution as Iyemon was now my kin, and to refuse him would disgrace both of us. And so the next morning, Iyemon took his golden stallion and a regiment of my most trusted men to the Yotsuya borders.

There was a great storm that night. Rain clattered against the wooden shutters and the fierce wind tipped and twirled the lanterns so their light cast stark shadows and dancing silhouettes. Oiwa and I kneeled by our mother's *tatami* mat, holding her hand and taking turns fanning her brow. She complained of a burning thirst, but her throat was too ragged to swallow the weak tea Oiwa brewed.

Mother's mind flitted like a bird between this world and the next. She rarely knew us, babbling instead as though we were spirits and ancestors long dead. I knew she would leave us soon. They say if someone sees their ancestors in a fever dream, it is not long before they will go to join them.

Oiwa continued to fight against the inexorable. "Mama," she whispered. "Mama, try to drink a little of this green tea. It will cool you."

Mother sat bolt upright and stared at Oiwa. "Where is your face?" she cried.

Oiwa reached a hand to her cheek. "I–it is at the front of my head, where it always is."

"No, only half of it," Mother replied. She glared at me. "I pledge you to return the other half of your sister's face. Swear it, Yasuo!"

Oiwa and I exchanged troubled looks. I do not swear oaths lightly, so I hesitated to promise to some fantasy of fever. But our mother was insistent.

"Swear it, or I will haunt you after I die! Swear!"

Oiwa leaned to me. "There is no harm in giving your word to something that requires no deed. Do not let her final words be a curse."

So I bowed my head over our mother's hand and promised to return Oiwa's missing half-face. I was uneasy, but truthfully, what harm was there in such a promise?

The next thunderbolt brought a sudden gale into the room, crashing open the shutter and blowing out the oil lamp. When we had relit it, our mother was gone, extinguished with the lamp, and unlike it, forever dark.

My sister's ragged sobs filled the room as she clutched our mother's body to her breast. I bowed my head.

Lord Shigekazu's anger with me was somewhat assuaged by the news of Mother's death. Still, I knew he harbored resentment. After her cremation ceremony, he insisted I return to the soldier's barracks.

Though Oiwa was pale and weak with grief, she urged me to go.

"We must not lose Shigekazu's favor," she said. "We owe him a debt we will never be able to repay."

I knew in a mere fortnight Iyemon would return, so I packed my saddlebags and kissed her farewell.

I dined at home when I could escape for an evening so Oiwa would not be alone. She was always glad to see me, but grief haunted her eyes, and where once her cheeks were blushing peaches, they had begun to sink and grow sallow. I saw a strand of white in her lustrous hair, and it saddened me. Oiwa had spent her youth tending our mother. Now her joy had flown with Mother's death. I prayed that Iyemon's devoted attentions would be able to restore her joy, if not her youth.

As though in answer to my prayers, the gods delivered Iyemon at last. And like a sunrise, with him came the Lady Uma. Having spent time in the royal courts, she was like a jeweled butterfly among moths. She wore layers of fine, silk kimonos, twelve of them together, with the sleeve cuffs and collars cut to display each distinctive color—lilac, damson, azure, indigo, emerald, topaz, citrine, garnet, peach, scarlet, magenta, and finally at the last, creamy white—and each one embroidered with a different design in gold thread.

It seemed all the unmarried men in Yotsuya found themselves captivated by the flashing hems of Lady Uma's kimonos and the elusive perfume she wore—jasmine and crushed lily. I, along with half my men, wrote sonnets of love and admiration to her.

But then, more misfortune. Word came of raiders from the west, great men with shaggy faces and beastly apparel, plundering the countryside. I was assigned the duty of quashing their incursion before it became an invasion.

It was with a mournful heart that I left Lady Uma's presence, but I did not dare to protest. I was already low man.

The barbarians were vicious and tenacious. They had set up a rude fortification on the edge of Yotsuya. I knew if I did not disperse them, they would foray deeper in, burning villages and razing fertile farmlands. I organized my men for a siege.

The month of rice planting, *UTzuki*, passed, then the month of rice sprouting, *SaTsuki*. Summer lapsed in a blur of sun and waiting. My soldiers took turns fishing the waters and hunting the forest for our meals. We cooked upwind of the barbarians to torment them with the smell of fresh fish and sweet rice while they were reduced to hard loaves and dry meat.

It was my turn with net and rod. The water laved cool around my knees and I grew lost in thoughts of the perfection of Lady Uma's face with its dusting of rice powder. A great tug on my line nearly pulled me over. I called my men to help bring in the grandfather fish.

We soon saw it was not a fish tangled in my line. It was a most terrible article I had caught—two bodies, nailed to either side of a black door, the prescribed punishment for convicted adulterers. They were purple and bloated. Her face in particular was most terrible to look upon. Half of it seemed to have melted away as though it were wax beside a fire.

I swept away the debris of riverweed from the grisly plank. The woman was wrapped in a peacock blue kimono, the silk ruined by the water. I could make out the memory of silver pine trees and dark green maple leaves outlined on the brocade.

It was Oiwa's festival kimono. Oh, my sister! And sharing her door of disgrace was Iyemon's servant, Kohei. I recognized his face and the *yukata* robe he wore.

I do not know what I screamed then—a curse on my sister, or on the gods, or on myself. I bolted from that place, flung myself upon my stallion, and galloped away.

I rode through rain and sun and night until my steed collapsed beneath me. Then I ran. When my armor and helmet weighed me down, I tossed them aside. I kept only the clothes on my back and my katana, for I would need it to spill the cursed blood from my veins at the altar of my ancestors.

It was night when I stumbled through the gardens of my ancestral home and up the steps of our shrine. I ignited four sticks of incense and lit four candles, the number for death and misfortune. Around me, the icons of the most revered ancestors of my lineage—dukes and warlords and virtuous ladies—watched as I removed my soiled and tattered shirt. I felt their eyes as I knelt and drew my katana.

"Yasuo, do not cry, silly boy." Oiwa stood in the shadow of a bamboo screen, holding a fan over her face. I leaped to my feet, ready to embrace her. But when she came closer, I saw by the light of the four candles that Oiwa had no legs. Where in the darkness I had thought them concealed by night, in the circle of candleshine, I saw she trailed away to a wisp of translucence.

"Oiwa," I whispered, "what has befallen you?"

"Remember the oath you made to our mother?"

"Y-yes."

"I call upon you to honor it." She dropped her fan. What had been dreadful on her poor body, on her visage as a *yurei*, an angry ghost, was even more terrible. One side of her face was sweet and whole, the other melted away. One eye rolled in its socket, yellow and diseased. A crust of tears tracked from it down her sagging cheek. Her once-opulent hair was lank and thin, dirty strands hanging from her torn scalp. Half her mouth was curled down, black and putrid, a wad of spittle hovering at the edge. And the skin on that cheek and that side of her brow was gray and curdled.

I shrieked in horror, and there was only blackness.

I woke in the shrine, the four candles burned away, and the cloying scent of incense hovering in a cloud. Iyemon supported me, dragged me to my feet.

"I thought the voices in the garden were cats fighting or the shriek of night birds," he said. "If I had known you had returned, my brother, I would have run to your side."

"I was fishing," I mumbled, on the edge of delirium. "There was a door. Oiwa and Kohei." I remembered terrible images of Oiwa, her face dripping and her blackened mouth, but no, that was how I saw her on the door, surely?

"That is not how I would have had you learn of it. Come inside. I will tell the sorry tale."

Within, Iyemon poured me a bowl of plum wine which I drank in two gulps. He poured another that I clutched in trembling fingers.

"It was my fault," Iyemon said. "If I had not volunteered to escort Lady Uma to her grandfather's house, perhaps Oiwa would not have gone mad with loneliness."

"What are you saying?"

"I found them together. Oiwa drank poison, some mixture of the garden—suicide. I treated Kohei to the blade of my katana."

"My sister was an honorable woman!"

"I would not have revealed their sin, truly, but—"

"Liar!" I shrieked. "Get out of my house!"

His face, so beseeching a moment before, hardened. "Yasuo, this is now my house. Your mother bequeathed it to Oiwa, and as her husband, I am her beneficiary."

The half-full bowl of wine shattered on the floor. "You are throwing me out?"

Immediately, he was the picture of solicitude. "No, no. Never. I do not blame you for your sister's wantonness. But you must face the truth."

I sank to my knees, sobbing like a child, calling to Oiwa. Iyemon left me alone to preserve what little honor I could still lay claim to.

In the subsequent days, I refused to leave the house, and Iyemon let me brood and weep as I would. He also left me casks of plum wine and bags of opium to ease my grief. Welcoming the blunting of memory, I drank and smoked my days away.

It was during one of these opium-muddled twilights that Oiwa returned.

The peacock blue silk of her kimono was stained by river water, but she protected me from the worst of her terrible appearance. She held a paper fan across the sinister half of her face.

"My face is still half missing," she said.

I scrambled away, cowering in a corner of the room. "What face do you want to recover?" I whimpered. "Your honor or your beauty?"

"Ah, little brother, you have come to the crux of it. Know this, while you have sunk yourself in wine and opium, the nuptial plans rush forward. I will return on their wedding night. Look for me then. See to it my face is restored that night, or I will haunt you forever."

"Oiwa, I'm so sorry."

Her voice softened. "Do not cry, little brother. I have shed enough tears for us both."

Then she was gone, and all the opium cobwebs swept from my mind with her.

It was dark, the sun long fled beneath the horizon. I crept from my chambers, disheveled and bleary. Voices drifted from the sitting room, two men at dinner. I clung to the shadows and listened.

"It was a fortuitous day when you came to Yotsuya." It was Lord Shigekazu.

"I am honored that you say it, my lord," Iyemon replied.

"Come now, surely you can call me 'grandfather'?"

"I would not wish for unseemly haste."

"Tut. Your *Yui-no* to my granddaughter can be announced soon enough. It is well you discovered your wife, that slattern's betrayal, and dealt with her and your servant so decisively. Otherwise the smear on your reputation—"

I did not breathe while I struggled to make sense of their words. Shigekazu as Iyemon's *grandfather*? Iyemon engaged to Lady Uma?

It was the first revelation. The second came after their words penetrated further. Shigekazu had said *dealt with her,* meaning Oiwa. Iyemon had told me my sister had taken poison—dishonorable suicide. But now it seemed more likely Iyemon had dispatched her himself.

A lie. It is well known that falsehoods come in threes. This was the second lie, the first being that Oiwa had been unfaithful. But the third lie I did not yet know.

I slunk back to my chambers. While I poured the last of the wine onto the thirsty rocks outside (for I did not wish to be tempted by the seduction of euphoric forgetfulness), I mused over the question. I was about to scatter the opium to the winds when I paused.

I put on fresh clothing—a short *haori* jacket and *hakama* pants—as befitting a lowly servant. Stealing Iyemon's golden stallion from the stable, I rode to Lord Shigekazu's pavilion.

There, I slipped through the watch corridors and guard niches I knew so well from my time as Shigekazu's captain, until I came to Lady Uma's chambers.

By the light of a muted lamp, I set a porcelain plate by her head and set fire to the opium until a deep, sweet smoke filled the room. In order to keep my own head clear, I wrapped my face with the silk sleeve of one of Uma's kimonos. It also muffled my mouth and thereby my voice, which further served my purposes.

When I was sure she was deep in the opium's thrall, I spoke.

"Uma, Uma," I intoned. "This is your ancestral *kami,* your family's spirit of fertility. If you wish to bear sons, you must honor me."

Uma mumbled and stirred.

"Speak up, Uma, I cannot hear you," I sang.

"What do you want?" Her speech was sluggish. "Let me sleep."

"If you wish for your union to Iyemon to be blessed with sons, you must answer my questions so I can cast your horoscope."

This seemed to pique her interest. "How many sons will I have?" she murmured.

"As many sons as the fortnights of your courtship."

"That is good. We will have many sons."

"Was your courtship so long?"

She laughed, her throat sultry. "He courted me as soon as he saw me on my palfrey, on the very border of Yotsuya."

"As your escort?"

"Even then."

"Was he not married?"

"I suppose so, but it is common knowledge in the Emperor's court that wives are but a passing inconvenience."

Such a place of depravity the Emperor's house must be. "Did you plot with Iyemon to loosen this 'inconvenience'?"

"A noblewoman does not dirty herself with such details. But when his wife and his servant were found forming the double-backed demon, well, I was hardly surprised."

It was enough. I had discovered the third lie. It was Uma herself. Where Oiwa had been pure and innocent, Uma was corrupt and evil. My fingers trembled to wrap around her traitorous throat. I loomed over her, but then I felt an icy touch at my shoulder.

I glanced back, almost upsetting the lamp when I saw Oiwa's *yurei*. Thankfully, she continued to shield her face with her fan, although her single clear eye was baleful.

"In order to bear sons," she said, in imitation of my *kami* voice, "you must marry Iyemon tomorrow."

"We have only just announced our intention to marry to Grandfather today."

"Regardless, you must marry tomorrow or you will be barren forever."

I stared at Oiwa. What was she about?

"Do you understand me, Uma?" she demanded. "You must marry tomorrow!"

"I will, *kami*. I will."

"Do not forget." This last she directed at me, but Uma, with her eyes shut, did not notice the difference.

Oiwa's fan fluttered, an unspoken threat, and she dissolved into the night.

Trembling like a wind-wracked pine tree, I smothered the still-smoldering opium and blew it cool before pouring ashes and plate into the pocket of my *haori* jacket. I made sure to light incense to mask the scent as I skulked out of Uma's room. Making as much haste as I dared, I darted to where I had stashed Iyemon's stallion, and rode him full out, all the way back.

I had him re-stabled, my clean clothes shucked, and the ashes of the opium smeared in my hair while Iyemon and Shigekazu lingered over *sake*. After Shigekazu returned to his pavilion, Iyemon came to my quarters with a jar of wine, which I dutifully drank.

The next morning, Iyemon trotted me out. A man from the town came to shave and dress us. Through this purification, Iyemon continued to ply me with wine. I drank enough to keep my hand steady and my resolve strong, but poured two bowls out for every one I drank.

Iyemon dressed in the black *hakama* Oiwa had given him, a travesty of my sister's devotion.

"Why the finery?" I asked, speaking the words as though through half-numbed lips.

"I am to become engaged to the Lady Uma," Iyemon replied. "As you are my brother, I think you should know before the public announcement. I would prefer to stay single, for my heart lies yet with Oiwa, but Lord Shigekazu insisted. He thought good fortune could be restored to his house by a prosperous match."

The lies tripped so easily off his tongue. "I don't begrudge you happiness, my brother." I giggled like a courtesan, high-pitched and merry, and pretended not to see the look of disgust on my "brother's" face.

When the guests arrived, I played the drunkard for them all, spilling tea and *sake*, and tripping over my own feet.

Shigekazu, especially, was revolted by me. After I groped one of Uma's maidens, he grabbed me and dragged me from the house. It was what I had hoped he would do.

Dropping my dissembling act, I bowed low.

"My lord, I hope you will forgive my display. I needed to speak to you in private."

He was surprised at my sudden lucid speech, but he was not inclined to hear me. He twisted away.

"Wait! My ancestors have warned me. They have given me two things to share with you. If you recognize the signs, will you humor me?"

He turned back, suspicion and distaste marking lines in his brow.

I handed him the plate from his granddaughter's room.

"Why, this is the expensive plate I gave Uma when she arrived. How did you—?"

"Lady Uma will insist that the wedding be held today," I said. "She will not be swayed. This too my ancestors divulged to me. Will you hear me?"

"If Uma insists upon marrying Iyemon today, which I know she will not, then yes, I will."

How Shigekazu's eyes bulged when Uma announced she wished to go to the temple that very day to wed Iyemon. No words could change her mind, and so their *Yui-no* engagement became their wedding party.

And that is how I pressed lord Shigekazu into accompanying me in hiding behind a bamboo screen in their wedding chambers. His patience with me was at its limits, though. It was the height of impropriety for us to be there, but when the bride in her *tsuno kakushi* veil stepped into the room, her face concealed, he was as silent as I could have wished.

Behind her, Iyemon followed, and together they lit the ceremonial lamps.

"Why such haste, my blossom?" Iyemon said. "It goes against the plan we made and looks improper."

"Do you not burn for me after all, my husband?" Through the veil, Uma's voice was muffled and strange. My blood turned chill and slow. It was not Uma's voice at all. I had heard that cadence, that tone every day as a boy, singing and talking and shouting. I would know it in my sleep. It was Oiwa.

My plan had been to force a confession from Iyemon and Uma at blade-point, witnessed by Shigekazu. My sister's *yurei* had other intentions.

Iyemon wrapped his arms around his bride. "How could you ask such a thing?"

"I just wonder if you truly wished to marry me. Were your words of promise lies? Did you instead plan to stay with your wife, Oiwa?"

"Oiwa? That bad luck slut?" Iyemon stepped back. "How could you think that?"

"Perhaps you did not intend for Oiwa to betray you, and were put out by it?"

He caught one of her lily hands. "Come, if it will make you believe my love for you, I will tell you the truth of Oiwa's fate.

"Oiwa did not betray me. She was utterly devoted to me, the simpering cow. You were jealous of her face, you said. She was so sickly after the death of her mother. It was easy to pour poison into her tea. I did it while she watched, calling it medicine. She took it from my hands with such trust. Didn't you hear how the poison I chose disfigured her? Would I have delivered such a caustic potion to anyone I loved?"

"Tell me the symptoms of the poison." Her voice turned harsh. Could Iyemon not hear it?

"It made her ugly, for your enjoyment, my love. It made her hair fall out in great clumps."

The figure of Uma reached under the *tsuno kakushi* and shed a handful of long, black hair with dried blood at their roots.

"What else?"

"Uma, what—?"

"What else!"

"H-her face, one eye grew swollen and infected, weeping pus and tears, while the skin puckered, rotting from within."

"She must have been in great pain."

"She screamed for hours."

Lord Shigekazu looked like the gods themselves had touched him, and they had used a heavy hand.

"It must have felt like a lifetime of suffering," the bride continued.

"Better her lifetime than mine. Come, let us lie together, my beautiful blossom."

He lifted his hands to the *tsuno kakushi*. The thin, white silk slid to the floor. Beneath it, as I had known, was not Uma's pretty face, but Oiwa's terrible one. The white rice powder did not conceal the crust of seeping yellow that oozed from her eye. Nor did it cover the bleak decay of her skin as it sloughed off.

"Come, my husband, kiss me." Oiwa held her arms out to Iyemon. "Embrace me."

Iyemon shrieked and pulled his katana from its sheath. With a single slice, he swept the head off her shoulders. It rolled to where Shigekazu and I spied from behind the bamboo screen.

But it was not Oiwa's face on that severed head, but Uma's.

Shigekazu and I scrambled from cover, away from the grisly remains. Iyemon screamed when he saw us, a cry of rage and madness. He charged at us with his katana upraised. I freed my blade, parried aside his wild strike, and Shigekazu tangled his legs from behind. I knocked his katana from his hand, and together, Shigekazu and I bound him. He gibbered all the while, raving that he saw Oiwa's face in the lantern, her *yurei* in the corner, her shadow behind the bamboo screen. When I glanced at these places, all I saw were lantern, corner, and screen.

Shigekazu sent for the magistrate and told them the whole story, clearing Oiwa of any sin. The magistrate sentenced Iyemon to death for his crimes.

In the days before his execution, Iyemon continued to screech and wail in his tiny cell, mad with terror. His eyes rolled in his head, following unseen specters, unknown horrors, all with Oiwa's face. In the end, the headman's sword was a mercy.

That night, I prayed before the altar of my ancestors.

"Oiwa, my part in restoring your honor is done. Are you pleased?"

There was no sound but the wind.

I did not see her again that night, or any other. Although I have heard stories in the village of a beautiful maiden wearing a peacock blue kimono, walking among the plum trees, singing. They say her face is exquisite, but her song sad.

Jeff VanderMeer is a two-time winner of the World Fantasy Award, and has made the year's best lists of ***Publishers Weekly, The San Francisco Chronicle, The Los Angeles Weekly, Publishers' News,*** *and* ***Amazon.com.*** *His fiction has been shortlisted for* ***Best American Short Stories*** *and appeared in several year's best anthologies. Books by VanderMeer are forthcoming from Bantam, Pan Macmillan, and Tor.*

The Farmer's Cat
Jeff VanderMeer

A long time ago, in Norway, a farmer found he had a big problem with trolls. Every winter, the trolls would smash down the door to his house and make themselves at home for a month. Short or tall, fat or thin, hairy or hairless, it didn't matter—every last one of these trolls was a disaster for the farmer. They ate all of his food, drank all of the water from his well, guzzled down all of his milk (often right from the cow!), broke his furniture, and farted whenever they felt like it.

The farmer could do nothing about this—there were too many trolls. Besides, the leader of the trolls, who went by the name of Mobhead, was a big brute of a troll with enormous claws who emitted a foul smell from all of the creatures he'd eaten raw over the years. Mobhead had a huge, gnarled head that seemed green in one kind of light and purple in another. Next to his head, his body looked shrunken and thin, but despite the way they looked his legs were strong as steel; they had to be or his head would have long since fallen off of his neck.

"Don't you think you'd be more comfortable somewhere else?" the farmer asked Mobhead during the second winter. His wife and children had left him for less troll-infested climes. He had lost a lot of his hair from stress.

"Oh, I don't think so," Mobhead said, cleaning his fangs with a toothpick made from a sharpened chair leg. The chair in question had been made by the farmer's father many years before.

"No," Mobhead said. "We like it here just fine." And farted to punctuate his point.

Behind him, one of the other trolls devoured the family cat, and belched.

The farmer sighed. It was getting hard to keep help, even in the summers, when the trolls kept to their lairs and caves far to the north. The farm's reputation had begun to suffer. A few more years of this and he would have to sell the farm, if any of it was left to sell.

Behind him, one of the trolls attacked a smaller troll. There was a splatter of blood against the far wall, a smell oddly like violets, and then the severed head of the smaller troll rolled to a stop at the farmer's feet. The look on the dead troll's face revealed no hint of surprise.

Nor was there a look of surprise on the farmer's face.

All spring and summer, the farmer thought about what he should do. Whether fairly or unfairly, he was known in those parts for thinking his way out of every problem that had arisen during twenty years of running the farm. But he couldn't fight off the trolls by himself. He couldn't bribe them to leave. It worried him almost as much as the lack of rain in July.

Then, in late summer, a traveling merchant came by the farm. He stopped by twice a year, once with pots, pans, and dried goods and once with livestock and pets. This time, he brought a big, lurching wooden wagon full of animals, pulled by ten of the biggest, strongest horses the farmer had ever seen.

Usually, the farmer bought chickens from the tall, mute merchant, and maybe a goat or two. But this time, the merchant pointed to a cage that held seven squirming, chirping balls of fur. The farmer looked at them for a second, looked away, then looked again, more closely, raising his eyebrows.

"Do you mean to say . . . " the farmer said, looking at the tall, mute merchant. "Are you telling me . . . "

The mute man nodded. The frown of his mouth became, for a moment, a mischievous smile.

The farmer smiled. "I'll take one. One should be enough."

The mute man's smile grew wide and deep.

That winter, the trolls came again, in strength—rowdy, smelly, raucous, and looking for trouble. They pulled out a barrel of his best beer and drank it all down in a matter of minutes. They set fire to his attic and snuffed it only when Mobhead bawled them out for "crapping where you eat, you idiots!"

They noticed the little ball of fur curled up in a basket about an hour after they had smashed down the front door.

"Ere now," said one of the trolls, a foreign troll from England, "Wot's this, wot?"

One of the other trolls—a deformed troll, with a third eye protruding like a tube from its forehead—prodded the ball of fur with one of its big clawed toes. "It's a cat, I think. Just like the last one. Another juicy, lovely cat."

A third troll said, "Save it for later. We've got plenty of time."

The farmer, who had been watching all of this, said to the trolls, "Yes, this is our new cat. But I'd ask that you not eat him. I need him around to catch mice in the summer or when you come back next time, I won't have any grain, and no grain means no beer. It also means lots of other things won't be around for you to eat, like that homemade bread you seem to enjoy so much. In fact, I might not even be around, then, for without grain this farm cannot survive."

The misshapen troll sneered. "A pretty speech, farmer. But don't worry about the mice. We'll eat them all before we leave."

So the farmer went to Mobhead and made Mobhead promise that he and his trolls would leave the cat alone.

"Remember what you said to the trolls who tried to set my attic on fire, O Mighty Mobhead," the farmer said, in the best tradition of flatterers everywhere.

Mobhead thought about it for a second, then said, "Hmmm. I must admit I've grown fond of you, farmer, in the way a wolf is fond of a lamb. And I do want our winter resort to be in good order next time we come charging down out of the frozen north. Therefore, although I have this nagging feeling I might regret this, I will let you keep the cat. But everything else we're going to eat, drink, ruin, or fart on. I just want to make that clear."

The farmer said, "That's fine, so long as I get to keep the cat."

Mobhead said he promised on his dead mothers' eyeteeth, and then he called the other trolls around and told them that the cat was off limits. "You are not to eat the cat. You are not to taunt the cat. You must leave the cat alone."

The farmer smiled a deep and mysterious smile. It was the first smile for him in quite some time. A troll who swore on the eyeteeth of his mothers could never break that promise, no matter what.

And so the farmer got to keep his cat. The next year, when the trolls came barging in, they were well into their rampage before they even saw the cat. When they did, they were a little surprised at how big it had grown. Why, it was almost as big as a dog. And it had such big teeth, too.

"It's one of those Northern cats," the farmer told them. "They grow them big up there. You must know that, since you come from up there. Surely you know that much?"

"Yes, yes," Mobhead said, nodding absent-mindedly, "we know that, farmer," and promptly dove face-first into a large bucket of offal.

But the farmer noticed that the cat made the other trolls nervous. For one thing, it met their gaze and held it, almost as if it weren't an animal, or thought itself their equal. And it didn't really look like a cat, even a Northern cat, to them. Still, the farmer could tell that the other trolls didn't want to say anything to their leader. Mobhead liked to eat the smaller trolls because they were, under all the hair, so succulent, and none of them wanted to give him an excuse for a hasty dinner.

Another year went by. Spring gave on to the long days of summer, and the farmer found some solace in the growth of not only his crops but also his cat. The farmer and his cat would take long walks through the fields, the farmer teaching the cat as much about the farm as possible. And he believed that the cat even appreciated some of it.

Once more, too, fall froze into winter, and once more the trolls came tumbling into the farmer's house, led by Mobhead. Once again, they trashed the place as thoroughly as if they were roadies for some drunken band of Scandanavian lute players.

They had begun their second trashing of the house, pulling down the cabinets, splintering the chairs, when suddenly they heard a growl that turned their blood to ice and set them to gibbering, and at their rear there came the sound of bones being crunched, and as they turned to look and see what was happening, they were met by the sight of some of their friends being hurled at them with great force.

The farmer just stood off to the side, smoking his pipe and chuckling from time to time as his cat took care of the trolls. Sharp were his fangs! Long were his claws! Huge was his frame!

Finally, Mobhead walked up alongside the farmer. He was so shaken, he could hardly hold up his enormous head.

"I could eat you right now, farmer," Mobhead snarled. "That is the largest cat I have ever seen—and it is trying to kill my trolls! Only *I* get to kill my trolls!"

"Nonsense," the farmer said. "My cat only eats mice. Your trolls aren't mice, are they?"

"I eat farmers sometimes," Mobhead said. "How would you like that?"

The farmer took the pipe out of his mouth and frowned. "It really isn't up to me. I don't think Mob-Eater would like that, though."

"Mob-Eater?"

"Yes—that's my name for my cat."

As much as a hairy troll can blanch, Mobhead blanched exactly that much and no more.

"Very well, I won't eat you. But I *will* eat your hideous cat," Mobhead said, although not in a very convincing tone.

The farmer smiled. "Remember your promise."

Mobhead scowled. The farmer knew the creature was thinking about breaking his promise. But if he did, Mobhead would be tormented by nightmares in which his mothers tortured him with words and with deeds. He would lose all taste for food. He would starve.

Even his mighty head would shrivel up. Within a month, Mobhead would be dead . . .

Mobhead snarled in frustration. "We'll be back when your cat is gone, farmer," he said. "And then you'll pay!"

If he'd had a cape instead of a dirty pelt of fur-hair, Mobhead would have whirled it around him as he left, trailing the remains of his thoroughly beaten and half-digested trolls behind him.

"You haven't heard the last of me!" Mobhead yowled as he disappeared into the snow, now red with the pearling of troll blood.

The next winter, Mobhead and his troll band stopped a few feet from the farmer's front door.

"Hey, farmer, are you there?!" Mobhead shouted.

After a moment, the door opened wide and there stood the farmer, a smile on his face.

"Why, Mobhead. How nice to see you. What can I do for you?"

"You can tell me if you still have that damn cat. I've been looking forward to our winter get-away."

The farmer smiled even more, and behind him rose a huge shadow with large yellow eyes and rippling muscles under a thick brown pelt. The claws on the shadow were big as carving knives, and the fangs almost as large.

"Why, yes," the farmer said, "as it so happens I still have Mob-Eater. He's a very good mouser."

Mobhead's shoulders slumped.

It would be a long hard slog back to the frozen north, and only troll to eat along the way. As he turned to go, he kicked a small troll out of his way.

"We'll be back next year," he said over his shoulder. "We'll be back every year until that damn cat is gone."

"Suit yourself," the farmer said, and closed the door.

Once inside, the farmer and the bear laughed.

"Thanks, Mob-Eater," the farmer said. "You looked really fierce."

The bear huffed a deep bear belly laugh, sitting back on its haunches in a huge comfy chair the farmer had made for him.

"I am really fierce, father," the bear said. "But you should have let me chase them. I don't like the taste of troll all that much, but, oh, I do love to chase them."

"Maybe next year," the farmer said. "Maybe next year. But for now, we have chores to do. I need to teach you to milk the cows, for one thing."

"But I hate to milk the cows," the bear said. "You know that."

"Yes, but you still need to know how to do it, son."

"Very well. If you say so."

They waited for a few minutes until the trolls were out of sight, and then they went outside and started doing the farm chores for the day.

Soon, the farmer thought, his wife and children would come home, and everything would be as it was before. Except that now they had a huge talking bear living in their house.

Sometimes folktales didn't end quite the way you thought they would. But they *did* end.

*Mary Rickert's short story collection, **Map of Dreams** will be published by Golden Gryphon Press in the Fall of 2006. About "A Very Little Madness Goes a Long Way," she says, "Sometimes, when searching for story ideas, I give myself an 'assignment.' In this case the assignment was to write an homage to Stephen King."*

A Very Little Madness Goes a Long Way

M. Rickert

She is a young woman, really, though coming upon her like this, standing at the window staring out at the bright California sun and palm trees, her hair pulled back in an innocuous ponytail, her shoulders slightly hunched, her arms wrapped around herself in a desultory manner, as if hugging someone who has become tiresome, she gives the impression of being a sad old woman.

"I thought you'd be happy here," says her husband, who sits at the edge of the bed unlacing his work shoes, his jogging clothes in a heap beside him and his running shoes on the floor by his feet. He isn't rushing exactly, that would be unkind and he is a kind man, but he does have everything ready to go. He wasn't a runner when they lived in Wisconsin. He smiles in spite of her mood, because he isn't much of a runner now either. Who's he kidding? But he likes the heat on his face, neck and limbs. He likes the vastness of the blue sky, marked irregularly by the palm trees single thrusts like fingers. Take that friggin' Wisconsin winters, he thinks when he jogs down Canal and up Avidio Street. He likes the open feeling, so different from their bedroom where she stares out the window like an old woman.

When he's ready, he resists the temptation to bolt from the room. He walks over to her. Places his hand on her shoulder. She sighs. He tries to think of what to say, searching through the ideas as if they were on note cards. I love you. I'm sorry. Everything will be ok. (But he's finally come to understand it might never be.) We could have another child. (He won't make that mistake again.) I love you. I love you. (Does he? Is that what this emotion is? This rooting next to her when he longs to run out of the room and escape into the vast bright world?) "I love you," he says.

She shrugs. It's very slight but he's almost certain that she shrugs. Yet she leans against him, so perhaps he hasn't interpreted that first inflection of muscles right. "Don't you think," she says, "I mean really, I know what you think, but I can't get them out of my head."

"Melinda," he says. Just that. Just her name. But he says it in such a way that she pulls away from him. He lets her. He stands there for a moment and then he shakes his head. If she were paying attention to him she'd see his reflection in the window, shaking his head. But she doesn't see him standing there and she doesn't see him leave. She doesn't see the palm trees, or the bright blue sky, or the blonde woman across the street bringing groceries into the house, or the man in striped shorts watering his lawn, or the children on bikes in their safety helmets pedaling furiously past as though, on some subconscious level, they know what she has brought with her.

Crows. Their sharp black beaks. Beady black eyes. Flap of wings, like the sharp crack of pillowcases and sheets snapped open to make a new bed. For someone else's child. She puts her hands over her eyes and sobs. Her husband, in a white blur she doesn't see, blazes past the window. The children on their bicycles shout at each other. She hears them only vaguely through the harsh cawing of the crows. Thousands and thousands of them. Watching her, with those beady black eyes, devoid.

"What you need to do is get involved in something else for awhile," her best friend, Stella says when she calls. "Have you thought of knitting?"

"I'm going to write about them."

"Who?"

"The crows."

Stella moans. Well, it's not exactly a moan, it's a sigh moan combination, that's what Melinda thinks, and she's been noticing that a lot lately, in the people around her. "You know, I've been thinking," Stella says, "of taking a little vacation. Melinda?"

"I know people think I'm nuts now."

"Nobody thinks you're nuts. It's just, listen how 'bout I come out there?"

"That crow spoke to me."

There it is again, that combination moan sigh, perhaps with a small sob or gasp at the end.

"I know you don't believe me. Nobody does. Crows can speak. I just want . . . " But she doesn't finish the sentence. What she wants is so much. She wants everything. What she's been given is this.

"I'm going to look into some flights, ok? I'll let you know what I find out."

"What? Oh, sure," Melinda says, not really certain what she's agreeing to. All she hears is "flight" and suddenly she is watching them again, thousands and thousands of crows flapping wings and rising only to land swiftly with their cawing sharp cries so loud she can hear them clearly through the closed windows, and all those thousands of miles, and even through time back to that day when she turned from her daughter's bed to stare out the window at those harbingers of death assembled across from the Children's Hospital. No one seemed to notice or understand their significance. Their cold eyes didn't even consider her or the child buried in the clean white sheets and hospital neat folds of a death they came to carry, the same way they picked through the garbage cans, and the lawn, and on one particularly gruesome day which Melinda still remembers by the strange combination of sweat and cold she felt, as they dove and fought over the corpse of one of their own, a dead crow they pulled apart with their sharp beaks and ate, flying into the trees and screaming at each other and her daughter moaned or sighed, she made a sound, Melinda turned to her, and knew, by the beautiful light that emanated there, a shiny bright thing in the dark, what would happen soon and who was to blame.

Later, when the crows fell from the sky, plummeting like rocks and landing in yards and playgrounds, and church parking lots it didn't make her feel better, the way she had thought it would.

Even now, sometimes, she looks to the sky and thinks she sees a black spot hovering above her, destined to spiral down in a swirl of wings and dead weight.

His name is Corvus. His parents, hippies who really did wear flowers in their hair and lived in a bus, had intended to name all their children after birds. He has a sister named Robin and a brother named Jay but he doesn't see or hear from them much. The one he hears from is Melinda, born "just at the edge of my change," as his mother liked to say, during her short second marriage to a carpet salesman from Iowa who died when Melinda was still a baby of something like failure to breathe, or some such malarkey of words, which Corvus can't completely recall. Something stupid like that. Something beauracratic to get the paperwork through when all it really meant was that they didn't know why he died but he did.

Corvus is the one who flew to the cornfield state to comfort his mother when no one else would and even now Melinda, who is a grown woman with her own life and the sad story of her child's death, seems to confuse him with her father though he doesn't think he looks like anyone's dad with his black leather jacket and his pierced ear and the tattoos of a snake, a naked lady, and on his back right shoulder, a raven, which he'd done out of deference to his name (though ravens and blackbirds, are not the same) years before his kid sister went nuts about crows. So when she calls him from California where they moved to "try to make a fresh start" and says she is going to write a book about crows, "about the things they say and do," he rubs his brow and must have made a sound because she says, "I just wish everyone would quit moaning about me," which causes him to pretend he wasn't moaning at all and act excited and say how he's been thinking of coming out to visit her and that husband of hers, whose name he can never remember. What is it again? Not Jack but something normal and ordinary. Safe.

Is Corvus the only one who realizes the truth about Melinda? She should have changed her name by now to something extraordinary like Universa. He understands why their mother did what she did and gave her a pretty, but basically normal name. But Melinda is a grown woman now. Shouldn't she know the truth? Corvus shakes his head as he begins to sort through piles of black clothes. What's happening to Melinda, Corvus thinks, can best be described by a term used for the poor and unloved. Though Melinda is neither she still suffers from it. "Failure to thrive." She has no idea how extraordinary she is. She's surrounded herself with bland normalcy. Well all right, maybe that's not fair, maybe ordinary people have amazing lives, he wouldn't know, when he sees them, in shopping malls, and coffee shops, or even just driving, they tend to wear the same expression, which is partly how he identifies them, it isn't an expression of much, neither satisfaction, nor despair, and certainly not harmony. It's like a mask they all wear. And Melinda has it too. But the thing is, Corvus thinks as he copies Melinda's new address onto a sheet of paper and tucks it into his wallet, she'll suffocate in that mask, just like her father, like a murder with no witnesses and no blood.

"I can't believe you invited him without talking to me about it first."

"Well, he is my brother."

"He never even remembers my name."

"So, tell him."

"What?"

"It's not like . . . it's not . . . Just tell him."

"I've told him a hundred times."

"You can't possibly. Stella is coming out too. What?"

"I thought we moved here to get away from everyone."

"Not me."

"Where are we going to put them?"

"Stella can sleep in my office and Corvus can sleep on the couch. Ok? Ok?"

The thing he hasn't told her about is the crow. It's just one crow, not thousands and thousands of them. It's one crow and he isn't even certain if it's the same one. How's he supposed to know? They all look alike to him. But this crow, well, he knows this is silly, but he thinks it's following him. He first noticed it back in Wisconsin. When the crows started falling from the sky, suddenly paralyzed from the poison. It wasn't unusual to notice a crow then. Circumstances had sort of created a hyper awareness surrounding them. But this crow always seemed to be looking at him, in that sideways manner of birds. Of course he figured he was imagining it. But then they moved here and he started seeing it again. Just one crow staring at him sideways as he jogged past, watching him when he got into his car in the mornings, standing on the lawn outside the office when he left work. It creeped him out. But he sure wasn't going to tell Melinda, or anyone about it.

Just as he didn't tell anyone about his daughter. People meant well, he knew, but it was nice to not have to deal with sudden kind words and gestures, which, in the end, were woefully inadequate. It was nice to be treated like a regular man and not like someone mortally wounded. That's why he didn't want them coming. Well, ok, and he didn't like either of them very much. They were both strange people. He couldn't understand what Melinda got from them that she couldn't get from him.

Corvus isn't surprised to be directed to the side for a terrorist evaluation. They already have his shoes. He takes off his jacket and belt. Raises his arms and turns for the wand. It's silly, really, how they keep trying to change that day in the past by doing the things now they wish they had done then. Corvus is surprised to feel the tear form and relieved when he's nodded on before it falls, as it does, when he leans over to tie his shoe. How can anyone not have compassion for them? They are so awkward, so earnest, so desperate, and increasingly, so alone. Shut off from the rest of existence, shut off from what would sustain them, by their own fear. He looks at the people waiting in the terminal with him, young families, an old man, some business suit men and women, a kid playing a little computer game, a baby crying, a young girl. When he takes a deep breath he can smell their human scent, marked as it is by the powerful fear motivator, laced with sweat, indigestion, onion, garlic, perfumes and lotions, and that vague odor of love.

Corvus stands in line and follows them into the plane. He knows there is irony in this, but he made a promise years ago and he intends to keep it. Because he's going to break the other one. He's going to tell Melinda what their mother told him.

He turns sideways to move down the narrow aisle. He senses the seated passengers eyeing him suspiciously. As if evil could be measured by black clothes and long hair. Like children, he thinks, who truly believe they can recognize a bad guy. When he gets to his seat number he nods at the bald man who looks up at him, and taking in his size, stands in the aisle to let him through. Corvus scrunches into the window seat. He snaps the buckle shut and closes his eyes until the plane takes off. Then he opens them to look at the clouds. How will he tell her? "We are angels."

"What?" the bald man says.

Corvus looks at him, startled. Had he spoken out loud?

"Were you talking to me?"

Corvus shakes his head.

The man frowns and pretends to read his magazine but Corvus can sense his awareness on him. He readjusts his weight, lowers his seat back, and closes his eyes.

When they land Corvus gets off the plane, just like the rest of them and while most passengers have noticed him, and marked him in their minds, only one passenger has recognized him as someone who knows exactly what he is, only one passenger follows him.

"It wasn't murder," Stella says rubbing Melinda's back as she weeps while Joe, who Stella assumes is handling all this the best he can, in his own odd way, runs in circles around the house.

"I mean I was filled with hate. That's the thing," Melinda sobs. "I pretended like it was about reason and logic. But it wasn't. It was just about hate."

"Something had to be done," Stella says, trying to choose her words carefully because the fact is, she'd really been against it all along.

Melinda stops crying. She sits there, staring out the window and biting her fingernail. "Did I tell you one spoke to me?"

"Uh-huh."

"Do you believe me?"

Stella has stood naked in the four directions. She has pledged herself to the earth and the elements. She believes in a lot of things people think are nuts but even she has trouble believing this.

"What did it say?" she asks.

"You don't believe me, do you?"

"Of course I believe you," Stella says, relieved to find this is true. She doesn't add the explanation; I believe you believe it. She doesn't think she needs to.

"Murderer."

"What?"

"That's what the crow said."

She didn't do anything at all for about two weeks after her daughter died. Slept, mostly. Joe had taken time off too. He slept in late and ate the sympathy food people kept sending over; cheesy casseroles, meatloaf, chocolate cake, banana bread, potato salad, and brownies in front of the TV where he muttered invectives at talk shows. Then, one day, he got up right in the middle of a show titled "I'm in love with my mother's husband" or something like that (Melinda could hear it from the bedroom) shut it off, got dressed and went to work. After that the house was very quiet.

Melinda was surprised to find that sleep was like a drug she could always afford. Sure, sometimes she woke up and stared at the flowered border of her walls but if she didn't move around too much, or open her eyes too wide she could sink right back into that place where sometimes she found her daughter still alive.

But one day she woke up to the horrible noise of a crow laughing at her. She got out of bed and walked across the room to the window. The ugly bird was on their lawn. Suddenly, it flew up and perched on top of the swing set. If she had a gun she would have shot it. Instead, she ran out into the yard in her pajamas, shouting. That's when it spoke to her. That single evil word, before it raised those great wings and with one last laugh, flew away. Melinda collapsed, just like the bad witch in the Wizard of Oz, she sank to her knees in her white nightgown and if she could have melted she would have.

When she got up she went into the house, took a shower, put on sweats and a T-shirt, sat down at the kitchen table and began writing letters. To the newspapers, the hospital, the PTA, animal control, the local TV news stations. This city was in danger. Didn't what happened to her daughter prove it? It was an invasion. A possible plague. She started a campaign against the crows. Now, after all this time, she sees her motivation. She can only wonder what got into everyone else. Because the plan was absurd really.

The city council passed the measure with only a vegetarian and a liberal dissenting. They fed them bread laced with poison. That's why birds fell out of the sky the way they did. Suddenly paralyzed, they plummeted to the ground. Their corpses littered sidewalks, parking lots and yards. Once, when Melinda was driving to the post office one plummeted right onto the hood of her car; its black claws splayed and stiff, its wings spread out like a hard cross.

That night, after Corvus doesn't arrive when he said he would, and Stella is asleep on the futon in Melinda's office and Joe is snoring in their bed, Melinda puts on her sneakers and stands in her front yard. They didn't really have a backyard here, just a deck and a strange tree she hasn't identified yet, spindly-limbed, a fruit tree of some sort. She stands in the front yard and waits for it to happen. After awhile, beneath the white moon glow and the scatter of stars, she begins to rise, she floats up about three or four inches and then, gently, like soft dust, she lands.

She doesn't know what this is all about. She only knows it began happening when things got really bad. She wonders if things are getting really bad again.

Corvus is still alive when the creature removes his jacket, his rings, and the knotted string bracelet Melinda's daughter made for him. He's alive to hear it say, "Clearly a hybrid."

Corvus watches it search through his pockets. When he finds the wallet, he tosses out the money, the credit cards, the driver's license and the library card. He almost tosses the wallet too but then the paper with Melinda's address on it slips out. Suddenly its beady eyes focus on his.

"No," Corvus gasps.

The creature smiles.

Corvus looks down and sees a man splayed, the shape of his limbs at odd angles, but bloodless. Standing beside him is someone wearing Corvus's jacket who turns and looks up at him.

It's like looking at a mirror, only something's not right. The man raises his hand. He is wearing Corvus's rings. He turns and walks away.

Corvus looks down at the body that remains, his eyes ripped out, as though by scavengers. Corvus doesn't have time to mourn. He follows the creature who waves down a taxi and tells the driver Melinda's address.

"Corvus," she says and she opens her arms to hug the creature but she is glowing with a silver sheen, as if she were the moon, it burns him and it takes all his power not to writhe with pain as he walks right past her open arms, pretending he hasn't seen them. He turns at the door to smile at her but everything about her hurts him; even the house contains her glow, even the doorknob.

She stands there, in her nightgown and sneakers, her long hair hanging down, so ordinary looking, so easy, a puzzled expression on her face. Clearly, she has no idea.

"It's not me," Corvus shouts but of course it comes out faint, having to travel all the distance from death to the living.

"Corvus?" she says.

The creature can't help it. He's terrified of her. Even at this distance, he burns. "I've been sick," he says, suddenly remembering humans and their fear of illness.

Melinda frowns.

The creature smiles. He should have a plan, that's the thing. But he doesn't. He's never needed one before. "Let's go inside," he says, though the house burns him too. Buying time, he thinks, is this what that expression means?

When they go inside a man stands there in boxers and a T-shirt. He puts out his hand. But the creature sees her glow there; he slips his hand into the pocket of the leather jacket.

"He's been sick," Melinda says.

Joe nods. To be polite. But the guy is worse than he remembered. There's even a faint odor coming off of him. Like sauerkraut.

"Do you want popcorn?" Melinda can't help it. Whenever she's around Corvus, she's fourteen again. When he used to visit they'd watch the late movie and eat popcorn.

"I think I'll just go to bed," the creature says, trying to form a plan. But he's finding it increasingly difficult to concentrate and he's worried that he'll lose the disguise if he's not careful, which would not be a problem with the man who looks half asleep but he's not sure what would happen with her.

When Melinda brings the creature the sheets and a pillow she looks at his face closely. He looks so different, she thinks, though she can't quite decide why until finally, she sees it. "I never noticed before," she says.

"What?"

"How much you look like a crow."

Behind them, Joe groans.

The creature can't figure out how to get around it, he has to take the pillow and sheets from her or she will just stand there and stare at him, but after he does so he turns away, he is in agony.

"I can help you make it," Melinda says.

"No. I'm going to sit up for awhile."

"I'll stay with you. I'll make popcorn."

"I don't like popcorn," the creature says, remembering the strange feel of it in his mouth, once, years ago when he went to a movie with a young woman who was later found raped and murdered. Not by him, of course. He didn't do petty crime. Right away he knows this might be a mistake. He smiles at her again, that baring of teeth. She just looks at him. He raises his hand in a wave.

She doesn't even try to kiss him goodnight. She is surprised to find that she doesn't really want to. Joe falls asleep right away. But Melinda lies there and tries to figure out what's happening. She has trouble concentrating; her mind keeps drifting back to that night, so long ago. When their mother told them she was an angel.

They tried not to laugh but it was impossible not to. Melinda ended up spitting Dr. Pepper in a spray while tiny white flakes of popcorn flew from Corvus's mouth.

"I'm serious," their mother said.

"I'm sorry, mom. We're sorry," they said.

She stood there in her blaze of red curls and the purple and green kimono and for a minute Melinda thought maybe she was telling the truth, the kimono sleeves sort of looked like wings, and she was the most beautiful mother in the school. Really. Even though she was so old.

Afterwards, the three of them sat on the couch eating popcorn and watching a movie about aliens with long green arms and slits for eyes and the invasion of the world until Melinda fell asleep with her head in her mother's lap, which smelled like dark chocolate. She had the vague impression that Corvus and their mother spoke then, whispering about angels and demons and wings but she was never sure if this was something she actually overheard, or something she dreamed.

It's Saturday and Joe likes to sleep late on the weekend so Melinda gets up and tries to be quiet as she walks across the room. She's tired and she can't shake the feeling she's had, since Corvus arrived, of something not being right.

When she walks past the window they begin cawing. She pulls back the drapes. The room blazes with morning sun and the crows' sharp cries. Hundred of them assembled in her yard, screaming, with their little throats and pointed tongues, the sharp beaks open like her daughter who said, "Mom?"

"Jesus Christ," Joe says, "oh Jesus Christ." He comes to stand behind her and wrap her in his arms but Melinda doesn't move or soften into his embrace. She stands there, frozen stiff as a corpse while the crows scream. With a sob she pushes past Joe and runs out of the room. She wants Corvus. But he isn't in the living room, or the bedroom either, or the kitchen or anywhere in the house.

Stella finds Melinda standing in the living room, staring out the window at the crows. It must be the angle of the sun, Stella thinks, because Melinda is glowing a bright halo of light all around her body and just like that, with the noise of sheets snapping on a clothesline, the crows rise in flight. Melinda turns and Stella gasps at the odd illusion, the glowing woman surrounded by wings.

"Corvus came," Melinda says, "but he's already gone."

"He'll be back," Stella says, though she really has no way of knowing.

"I don't think so," Melinda says, no longer glowing or surrounded by wings.

Joe comes into the room dressed in his jogging clothes. He says good morning to Stella and gives Melinda a kiss on the cheek. "Corvus is gone," she says.

He suppresses a grin. "Probably just went for a walk." But this is absurd. Corvus is not the kind to go for a walk in the California sun. He is more about shadows and dark rooms. If he is gone, sure, it's weird, but also the sort of thing, Joe thinks, that he's always been capable of. He sighs.

"You can go," Melinda says. "Go. Run."

He thinks of asking her if she is sure but he doesn't want to press his luck.

After he leaves, Stella says, "Are you really worried about Corvus?"

"Something strange is happening," Melinda says. "I feel like I'm in The Birds."

"In them?"

"You know, that movie."

Joe can't help it; every time he leaves the house he feels like he's escaping a great darkness, he feels like he's running away. He loves the hard concrete beneath his feet, the sun shining on his face and limbs. Hell, he even loves the damn birds. When he's running he feels almost whole again. He can feel his muscles and the sweat on his skin. He feels like a man with a body, instead of the husk he's been. God, he misses her. He misses her too but there's no use trying to talk to Melinda about it because she owns all the sorrow. Well, all right, he thinks as he turns down Avidio Street, that's not fair, but it's been hard enough keeping himself together through all this, and he's not sure how to help her. His feet pound the concrete but he doesn't feel weighted at all, he feels bright, alive, almost winged. He doesn't know what's going to happen to Melinda or to their marriage, but he's already decided, he's going to survive. He's going to learn how to be happy again.

The creature can't believe his luck when her husband runs out of the house like a man making his escape. He watches him and thinks it's just so perfect. He can't destroy her, she's just that powerful, something he understands is both a curse and, he hates to use the word, a blessing, but he can ruin her, oh yes, he can ruin her by ruining everything she loves and believes in.

"Corvus," Joe says, panting and grinning, as if he'd been running to find him. "Melinda was worried about you."

"Come here," the creature says, "I want to show you something."

Joe doesn't know why he's never liked him. That's something the running has helped him with. Afterwards, for fifteen, twenty minutes even, once for almost an hour, he feels like he can love again. As though he drank a witch's potion. This time it's landed on Corvus. Joe follows him down a side street and into a narrow California alley lined with concrete walls, roses and wind chimes.

The creature walks up to Joe who stands there, smiling affably, just for the fun of it, he lets the disguise fall. He watches Joe's face change. Just when he would scream, the creature reaches in, extinguishing the noise, and the light.

"You know what probably happened," Stella says, "they probably ran into each other, went out for coffee together."

Melinda looks at Stella and nods. How can she explain? Evil exists. It stalks her for a reason.

"It's a beautiful day, you should go outside and play."

"I don't wanna."

"Your father and I got you that nice new swing set and you never play on it."

"I hate playing outside."

"Oh, you do not."

"It's buggy. And the grass itches my ankles."

"What are you going to do?"

"I dunno. Sit, I guess."

"I want you to go outside."

"I don't wanna."

"It'll be good for you. You go outside for a while so I can finish my work and then we'll go get ice cream."

"Can't I just stay in the house? I'll be quiet."

"I want you to get some fresh air."

For a while Melinda stood at the window and watched her, lazily swinging and talking to herself. She looked perfectly happy. Safe. But when she came back inside she was probably already dying, though neither of them knew it yet. They went for ice cream. Hers melted so fast she may already have had a fever, "Mom?" she said and Melinda saved her the way she always had, by licking the dripping scoop until it formed a neat round ball and by then she may already have been turning into a spirit. Melinda remembers the way she looked, all wide eyes shining with fever and light. Though at the time Melinda thought it was just happiness.

Now, Melinda stares out the window. Stella goes into the kitchen, which is brightly lit by the California sun. She tries not to regret coming here. This is to help her friend, after all. But the depression is palpable. In spite of the blue sky and the light, which pours into this little house, Stella feels like she is walking in a thick fog. It presses her body with unwelcome weight. No wonder Joe has taken up running. Stella glances towards the living room. Melinda is still staring out the window. Furtively, she doesn't know why, Stella walks to the front door. She opens it slowly. It makes a slight popping noise but Melinda doesn't seem to notice. Stella opens the door wide. Just as she takes a step towards it, Melinda speaks.

"What?" Stella says.

"I said, where are you going?"

"I just wanted to step outside for a minute. It's so beautiful out. Wanna come?"

"Do you know what's out there?"

Stella looks out the doorway again. She looks at Melinda. "I'll just be a minute."

Melinda doesn't answer.

Stella steps outside and immediately wants to scream or shout. She shuts the door behind her. God, it feels so good to breathe. She doesn't even think about how she's barefoot and wearing boxers and an old T-shirt but if she had thought about it she might have concluded that she's been infected by the California spirit. Melinda, staring out of the window, might have seen what happened to her, except Melinda isn't staring at what exists, but at what she remembers. It takes her a long time to realize Stella isn't coming back either. It's as if, she thinks, they are being swallowed by the light, the beautiful California day. She stands at the window while the neighbors leave their houses in suits and ties, suits and heels, shorts and sandals, carrying briefcases, school bags, coffee mugs, driving SUV's, Volkswagens, skateboards, and bicycles.

"Be careful," Melinda whispers to the glass. No one hears her and really, no one would take her seriously if they did. It's obvious she is someone who isn't all there, something not right about her. And that's what the police think too, when they come by later to tell her they found a body, a jacket, rings, a sheet of paper with her address on it. At first she tells them it's her brother but then they mention the jogging clothes, and she says it's her husband and right away they suspect her of murder, maybe a double homicide.

Then things get really strange. The police officers, the detectives, the coroner, the news reporter, everyone who was at the scene of the crime, though they arrive and leave in separate vehicles, have accidents. Every one of them dies.

When a reporter calls to tell her this, Melinda, who has been crying since she had to identify "the body" suddenly dries up. That's it. She's been crying all day and she cried for months before that and now she's done. Because, at a certain point, she thinks, you have to shut down against all the horror of life.

"Do you have any comment?" the reporter asks.

"The body," she says.

There is a long silence. Melinda isn't sure if he's still there or was ever there. Maybe he's just something she imagined. Maybe everyone was.

"Did you say, 'the body'?"

"The body is heavy," Melinda says.

"The body is heavy?"

"We are . . . "

Again, that silence. Melinda looks out the window and sees the blonde woman arrive home. She gets out of the car and waves to her neighbor, a middle-aged man watering his lawn. He walks over to her and then, in a quick and sudden movement, wraps the garden hose around her neck. She struggles against it, but the man is suddenly amazing in his strength, he pulls the hose tighter, water sprays wildly from the nozzle, the blonde woman kicks but her feet flail in the air, she pulls at the hose, waves her arms in a helpless imitation of its wild gyrations, the stream of water rises and falls, slithering across the blue sky. "My neighbor is strangling my neighbor," Melinda says.

"Right now?"

"Ok. She's dead."

"Did you kill her?"

"No. My neighbor did. Oh, but he's clutching his chest now. A heart attack, I guess."

"Are you saying your neighbors had a fight and killed each other?"

"Uh-oh," Melinda says.

"What now?"

"Children."

"What about the children?"

"Coming down the street. Riding their bicycles."

"Please don't hurt the children."

"What? I would never. Oh, but there they go."

"Where?"

"The car. They're dead."

"Someone hit the children with a car?"

"I suppose. But it didn't look like, wait, here's the driver. She got out of the car. She's covered in blood. She's crying. She's trying to save them. I don't know why. It's obvious, oh, now it's her."

"What?"

Melinda turns away from the window. "Excuse me," she says, "but weren't we talking about something else?"

"The body."

"Oh, that's right. The body is heavy."

"Whose body is heavy? Do you mean your husband's, did you kill him?"

"Kill him?"

"I've done some research. I know about your daughter. Did you kill her as well?"

"It was a mosquito. It bit one of those crows that had it. Then it bit her."

"Yes, well, that's what they said but now, with all that's happened—"

Melinda moves her thumb and presses the button that shuts his voice off. She watches her neighbors running out of their houses, piling into cars with kids, dogs and cats, ferrets, pet pigs, hamsters, while the adults and children talk on cell phones, wave their arms wildly and scream at each other. She hears a helicopter flying overhead and sirens looming nearer. She opens the front door and is assailed by the violent noise, the screams, the terrible noise of the helicopter spiraling down, the sirens veering into sick wails, and she smells the blood metal scent of death. "It's not my fault," she whispers.

It's just like they say, as if a great weight has been lifted from her shoulders. Melinda begins to rise, but this time she doesn't hover, as she always has in the past, she rises higher and higher until she is as high as the palm trees and even higher still.

The creature, shading his eyes against the bright sun, watches her. With a snort he leaves, going in the opposite direction. The mayhem he brought with him, though it remains, does not continue its relentless course. The wounded do not die, but suffer. Crows swoop down and pick at the shiny parts of the dead; watches, rings, silver hair and fillings. A wide-eyed EMT, sloshing through the muck of bloody water, turns off the hose. News crews come and set up their mobile units and food vendors follow. The crows peck at dropped bits of corn dog and discarded fries. The children ride bicycles around the dead, or pick flowers, or go into dark rooms and don't do anything at all. Experts come and say this is recovery. This is the cure.

Melinda soon discovers that she likes to fly so high that she no longer sees anyone, nearer to the sun, unpopulated as it is by human misery.

Sometimes she thinks she won't return but she always does. She understands this is the reason for everything. It took her a whole lifetime to learn how to ascend but it doesn't take her long at all to learn how to dive down again. "We are angels," she whispers to the people. Some of them hear her. Some of them don't.

Christopher Barzak grew up in Ohio, has lived in California and Michigan, and recently returned to the United States after spending the last two years in Japan, teaching English near Tokyo. His stories have appeared in Nerve, Realms of Fantasy, Strange Horizons, Trampoline, The Year's Best Fantasy and Horror, and The Mammoth Book of Best New Horror. His first novel, One for Sorrow, is forthcoming from Bantam Dell books. Chris has new stories appearing in The Coyote Road, So Fey, and Twenty Epics. Recently he completed his second novel, The Love We Share Without Knowing. For the moment he's living and writing in his hometown of Kinsman, Ohio again.

I wrote "The Language of Moths" when I was twenty-four and fell in love with a man for the first time—I'd only been in relationships with women until him—and the way I understood love, sex, family and the world itself changed radically, requiring me to learn a new language, it seemed, to describe not only the uncharted territory I found myself traveling, but my own uncharted interior as well.

The Language of Moths
Christopher Barzak

1. Swallowing Bubbles

The four of them had been traveling for what seemed like forever, the two in the front seat rattling maps like they did newspapers on Sunday mornings. They rode in the wagon, her favorite car, the one with the wood paneling on its doors. The wagon wound through the twisty backroads of the mountains, leaving behind it clouds of dust through which sunlight passed, making the air shimmer like liquid gold. The girl wanted the wagon to stop so she could jump out and run through the golden light behind her. She climbed halfway over the back seat and pushed her face against the rear window, trying to get a better look.

The little old man beside her shouted, "No! No! No! Sit down, you're slobbering all over the glass. Sit down this instant!" He grabbed her around her waist and pulled her back into a sitting position. He pulled a strap across her chest, locking it with a decisive click. The little old man narrowed his eyes; he waved a finger in the girl's face. He said things at her. But as his words left his lips, they became bubbles. Large silver bubbles that shimmied and wobbled in the air. The bubbles filled the car in mere moments. So many words all at once! The girl laughed delightedly. She popped some of the bubbles between her fingers. Others she plucked from the air and swallowed like grapes. She let them sit sweetly on her tongue for a while, before taking them all the way in for good. When the bubbles reached her stomach, they burst into music. The sound of them echoed through her body, reverberating. She rang like a bell. One day, when she swallowed enough bubbles, she might understand what the little old man beside her was saying. All of the time, not just now and then. Maybe she'd even be able to say things back to him. She wondered if her own words would taste as sweet. Like honey, maybe. Or like flowers.

2. Being Selfish

Eliot is watching his mother hang bed sheets from a cord of clothesline she's tied off at two walls facing opposite of each other in their cabin. "To give us all a sense of personal space," she explains. Eliot tells his mother that this cabin is so small, hanging up bed sheets to section off rooms is a futile activity. "Where did you learn that word," his mother asks. "Futile. Who taught you that?"

"At school," Eliot says, paging through an *X-Men* comic book, not bothering to look up.

His mother makes a face that looks impressed. "Maybe public school isn't so bad after all," she says. "Your father was right, as usual."

Eliot doesn't know if his father is right, or even if his father is usually right, as his mother seems to imagine. After all, here they are in the Allegheny Mountains, in Pennsylvania, for God's sake, hundreds of miles away from home. Away from Boston. And for what? For a figment of his father's imagination. For a so-called undiscovered moth his father claims to have seen when he was Eliot's age, fourteen, camping right here in this very cabin. Eliot doesn't believe his father could remember anything that far back, and even if he could, his memory of the event could be completely fictional at this point, an indulgence in nostalgia for a time when his life still seemed open in all directions, flat as a map, unexplored and waiting for him.

Eliot's father is an entomologist. His specialty is lepidoptera, moths and butterflies and what Eliot thinks of as creepy-crawlies, things that spin cocoons around themselves when they're unhappy with their present circumstances and wait inside their shells until either they've changed or the world has, before coming out. Eliot's father is forty-three years old, a once-celebrated researcher on the mating habits of moths found in the Appalachian Mountains. He is also a liar. He lied to his grant committee at the college, telling them in his proposal that he required the funds for this expedition to research the habits of a certain species of moth with which they were all familiar. He didn't mention his undiscovered moth, the one that glowed orange and pink, as he once told Eliot during a reverie, with his eyes looking at something unimaginably distant while he spoke of it. Maybe, Eliot thinks, an absurd adventure like this one is a scientist's version of a mid-life crisis. Instead of chasing after other women, Eliot's father is chasing after a moth that, let's face it, he probably imagined.

"There now, isn't that better?" Eliot's mother stands in the center of the cabin, which she has finished sectioning into four rooms. The cabin is a perfect square with clothesline bisecting the center in both directions, like a plus sign. Eliot owns one corner, and Dawn, his sister, has the one next to his: That makes up one half of the cabin. The other half has been divided into the kitchen and his parents' space. The sheet separating Eliot's corner from his sister's is patterned with blue flowers and tiny teacups. These sheets are Dawn's favorites, and secretly, Eliot's too.

Eliot's mother glances around, smiling vaguely, wiping sweat off of her brow. She's obviously happy with her achievement. After all, she's an academic, a philosopher, unaccustomed to cleaning house and rigging up clotheslines and bed linen. The maid back in Boston—back home, Eliot thinks—Marcy, she helps around the house with domestic things like that. Usually Eliot's mother uses her mind to speculate on how the mind works; not just her own mind—but the mind—the idea of what a mind is. Now she finds herself using her mental prowess to tidy up a ramshackle cabin. Who would have guessed she'd be so capable? So *practical*? Not Eliot. Certainly not herself.

The door to the cabin swings open, flooding the room with bright sunlight that makes Eliot squint. He shields his eyes with one hand, like an officer saluting, to witness the shadowy figure of his father's body filling the doorframe, and his sister Dawn trailing behind.

Dawn is more excited than usual, which has made this trip something less than a vacation. For Eliot's father, Dr. Carroll, it was never a vacation; that was a well-known fact. For Dr. Carroll, this was an expedition, possibly his last chance to inscribe his name in History. But the rest of the family was supposed to "take things easy and enjoy themselves." When Dr. Carroll said that, Eliot had snorted. Dr. Carroll had placed his hands on his hips and glowered. "Why the attitude, Eliot?" he'd asked.

"Take it *easy*?" Eliot repeated in a squeaky-scratchy voice that never failed to surface when he most needed to appear justified and righteous. "How can you expect us to do that with Dawn around?"

Dr. Carroll had stalked away, not answering, which didn't surprise Eliot at all. For most of his life, this is what Eliot has seen whenever he questions his father: his father's back, walking away, leaving a room full of silence.

Dawn pushes past Dr. Carroll and runs over to Eliot's cot. She jumps on the mattress, which squeals on old coils, and throws her arms across the moth-eaten pink quilt. The quilt smells of mold and mildew and something a little like mothballs, as if it had been stored in a cedar chest for a long time. Dawn turns to Eliot, her wide blue eyes set in a face as white and smooth as porcelain, and smiles at him, her blonde hair fanning out on the pillow. Eliot considers her over the top of his comic book, pretending not to have noticed her.

Dawn is autistic. She's seventeen-years-old, three years older than Eliot. But when she's around, Eliot feels as if he's already an old man, forced into an early maturity, responsible for things no fourteen-year-old boy should have to think about. He blames this all on his parents, who often encourage him when he pays attention to Dawn, who often scold him when he wants something for himself. "Being selfish," is what his mother calls that, leaving Eliot dashed to pieces on the rocks of guilt. He feels guilty even now, trying to read the last page of his comic book instead of paying attention to Dawn.

"I'm leaving," Dr. Carroll announces. He's wearing khaki pants with pockets all over them, and a wide-brimmed hat with mosquito netting pulled down over his face. A backpack and sleeping bag are slung on his back. He lifts the mosquito netting and kisses Eliot's mother on her cheek and calls her Dr. Carroll affectionately, then looks at Eliot and says, "You take care of Dawn while I'm away, Eliot. Stay out of trouble."

He walks outside, and all of them—Eliot, Dawn and their mother—move to the doorway. As if magnetized by Dr. Carroll's absence, they try to fill the space he's left. They watch him become smaller and smaller, a shadow, until he reaches the trail that will take him farther into the graying mountains, where his moth awaits.

"Good luck," Eliot's mother whispers, waving goodbye to his back, his nets and pockets. She closes her eyes and says, "Please," to something she cannot name, even though she no longer believes in higher powers, ghosts or gods of any sort.

3. First Words

It was strange for the girl in this place; she hadn't been prepared for it. Suddenly the wagon had come to a stop and they all spilled out. The mother and the father, they seemed so excited. They smiled so hard, their faces split in half. The little old man kept scowling; he was so funny. She patted him on his shoulder and he opened his mouth to make room for one huge silver bubble to escape. She grabbed hold of its silky surface and almost left the ground as it floated upwards, towards the clouds. But it popped, and she rocked back on her heels, laughing. When the bubble popped, it shouted, "Get off!"

The father left soon after. The girl was a little frightened at first. Like maybe the father would never come back? Did the father still love her? These thoughts frightened her more than anything else. But then she watched the little old man chop wood for the fire, his skinny arms struggling each time he lifted the axe above his head, which made her laugh, sweeping the fear out of her like the mother sweeping dirt off the front porch. Swish! Goodbye, fear! Good riddance! She forgot the father because the little old man made her laugh so much.

There were so many trees here, the girl thought she'd break her neck from tilting her head back to see their swaying tops. Also, strange sounds burrowed into her skin, and she shivered a lot. Birds singing, crickets creeking. This little thing no bigger than the nail of her pinky—it had transparent wings and hovered by her ear, buzzing a nasty song. She swatted at it, but it kept returning. It followed her wherever she went. Finally the mother saw it and squashed it in a Kleenex. But as it died, it told the girl, "You've made a horrible mistake. I am not the enemy." Then it coughed, sputtered, and was dead.

The girl thought of the wagon. It was still one of her favorite things in the world. But now she was thinking she wasn't so sure. Maybe there were other things just as special as riding in the wagon with the mother, the father and the little old man. She wished the mother wouldn't have killed the winged creature so quick. She wanted it to tell her more things, but now it was dead and its last words still rang in her ears. When the winged creature spoke, no bubbles came out of its mouth. Words, pure and clear, like cold water, filled her up. The winged creature had more words for her, she just knew it. She knew this without knowing why, and she didn't care. She only cared that the bubbles didn't come between her and the words when the creature spoke to her. One drink of that and she wanted more.

4. The Scream

Before Eliot's father left, he placed him in charge of Dawn, and his mother seems more than willing to follow her husband's orders to the letter, leaving Eliot to look after Dawn while she sits on the front porch of the cabin, or in the kitchen, and writes. Eliot finds his mother's loyalty to his father's declarations an annoying trait, as if she had no say-so about anything when it comes to her children; she simply goes along with whatever his father says. He's watched Dawn every day since his father left, which has been for an entire week. He's taken her on the trails that are clearly marked; they've stared into the shallow depths of a creek where the water was as dark as tea, where red and blue crayfish skittered for cover under rocks. He's introduced Dawn to grasshoppers, which she loved immediately and, to Eliot's amazement, coaxed into a perfect line, making them leap in time together, like figure skaters. He was proud of Dawn for that, and could tell she was too; she looked up at him after the synchronized leap went off without a hitch and clapped her hands for a full minute.

Each day they pick wildflowers together, which, when they return in the late afternoons, hang tattered and limp in Dawn's grip. Still, their mother takes them from Dawn gratefully when they're offered. "Oh, they're beautiful," she says, and puts the ragged daisies and buttercups in empty Coke bottles, filling the cabin with their bittersweet scent.

Eliot never gives his mother flowers. He leaves that pleasure for Dawn. And anyway, he knows something Dawn doesn't: his mother doesn't even like flowers, and Dr. Carroll doesn't even give them to her for Valentine's day or for their wedding anniversary. Eliot has to admit that his mother's graciousness in the face of receiving a gift she doesn't like is a mark of her tact and love for Dawn. He couldn't ever be so nice. He watches his mother and Dawn find "just the right place" for the flowers and thinks, I am a bad person. He thinks this because he's imagined himself far away, not from his present location in the mountains, but far away from his family itself. He's imagined himself in a place of his own, with furniture and a TV set and his own books. In none of these fantasies does his mother or father appear, except for the occasional phone call. He never misses them and he wonders if this means he's a wrong person somehow. Shouldn't children love their parents enough to call every once in a while? Apparently in these fantasies, parents aren't that important.

Dawn isn't a part of these fantasies either. Eliot doesn't even imagine phone calls from her because, really, what would be the use? At most, Dawn might latch onto a phrase and ask him it over and over. She might say, like she once did at his twelfth birthday party, "How old is your cat?" sending all of his friends into fits of laughter.

Eliot doesn't have a cat.

Eliot's mother has begun a new essay, and during the day, she spends her time reading essays and books written by other philosophers and scientists who she thinks has something to say on the subject she's considering. "This one," she tells Eliot one morning, "will be a feminist revision of *Walden*. I think it has great potential."

She's packed her Thoreau, Eliot realizes, irritation suddenly tingling at the base of his neck. He's beginning to suspect that, this summer, he has become the victim of a conspiracy got up by his parents, a conspiracy that will leave him the sole caretaker of Dawn. Within the frame of a few seconds he's turned red and his skin has started to itch. He's close to yelling at his mother. He wants to accuse her of this conspiracy, to call her out, so to speak. To scold her for being selfish. I could do that, he thinks. Scold his parents. He's done it before and he'll do it again. He finds nothing wrong with that; sometimes they deserve to be reprimanded. Why does everyone think that because someone gives birth to you and is older, they inherently deserve your respect? Eliot decided a long time ago that he wouldn't respect his parents unless they respected him. Sometimes this becomes a problem.

Before he unleashes his penned-up tensions, though, his mother stops scribbling and lifts her face from her notebook. She smiles at Eliot and says, "Why don't you go into that village we passed on the way in and make some friends? You've been doing so well with your sister. You deserve a break."

She gives Eliot ten dollars from her purse, which he crumples into a wad in his front pocket. She's releasing him for the day, and though he's still fuming over the conspiracy, he runs at this window of chance. He grabs his bike and trots with it at his side for a minute, before leaping onto its sun-warmed seat. Then he peddles away, down the mountain.

When he thinks he's far enough away, Eliot screams at the top of his lungs, an indecipherable noise that echoes and echoes in this silent, wooded place. The scream hangs over the mountainside like a cloud of black smoke, a stain on the clear sky, following Eliot for the rest of the day. Like some homeless mutt he's been nice to without thinking about the consequences, the scream will follow him forever now, seeking more affection, wanting to be a permanent part of his life.

5. The Butterfly's Question

The girl found the butterflies by accident. They were swarming in a small green field splashed yellow and white and orange from their wings. She ran out to meet them, stretched out her fingertips to touch them, and they flitted onto her arms, dusted her face with pollen, kissed her forehead and said,

"Child, where have you been?"

The butterfly that spoke to her was large, and its wings were a burnt orange color, spider-webbed with black veins. It floated unsteadily in front of her face, cocking its head back and forth as if examining her. No silver bubbles came out of its mouth when it spoke, just like the first winged creature, just like the grasshoppers who performed their leaps, their little tricks just for her pleasure.

"Well?" The butterfly circled her head once.

"I don't know," Dawn said. "It's hard to explain. But there are these people. They take care of me really nice."

"I would expect nothing less," said the butterfly, coming to rest on the back of her wrist. It stayed there for a while, its wings moving back and forth slowly, fanning itself. Finally, it crawled up the length of the girl's arm and came to rest on her shoulder. It whispered in her ear, "Why now? Why have they brought you too us now, so late in your life?"

The girl didn't know how to answer the butterfly. She simply looked down at her bare feet in the high grass and shrugged. "I don't know," she told the butterfly, and nearly started crying. But the butterfly brushed her cheek with its wings and said, "No, no. Don't cry, my love. Everything in its own time. Everything in its own time. Now isn't that right?"

6. Centipede

When Eliot rode into the village his first thought was: What a dump. When they passed through it a week ago, they had driven through without stopping, and he figured his father must have been speeding because he hadn't noticed how sad this so-called village is. It has one miserable main street running through the center, a general store called Mac's, a gas station that serves ice cream inside, and a bar called Murdock's Place. Other than that, the rest of the town is made up of family cemeteries and ramshackle farms. The Amish have a community just a few miles out of town, and the occasional horse-drawn buggy *clop-clops* it way down the main street, carrying inside its bonnet girls wearing dark blue dresses and men with bushy beards and straw hats.

Inside Mac's general store, Eliot is playing *Centipede*, an incredibly archaic arcade game from the 1980s. He has to play the game with an old trackball, which is virtually extinct in the arcade world, and it only has one button to push for laser beam attacks. Ridiculous, thinks Eliot. Uncivilized. This is the end of the world, he thinks, imagining the world to be flat, like the first explorers described it, where, in the furthest outposts of undiscovered country, the natives play *Centipede* and sell ice cream in gas stations, traveling from home to school in horse-drawn buggies. He misses his computer in Boston, which offers far more sophisticated diversions. Games where you actually have to think, he thinks.

The front screen door to Mac's squeals open then bangs shut. Mac, the man behind the counter with the brown wart on his nose and the receding hairline, couldn't have oiled the hinges for ages. Probably not since the place was first built. Eliot looks over his shoulder to catch a glimpse of the tall town boy who just entered, standing at the front counter, talking to Mac. He's pale as milk in the gloom of Mac's dusty store, and his hair looks almost colorless. More like fiber optics than hair, Eliot thinks, clear as plastic filaments. Mac calls the boy Roy, and rings up a tin of chewing tobacco on the cash register. Another piece of pre-history, Eliot thinks. This place doesn't even have price scanners, which have been around for how long? Like more than twenty years at least.

Eliot turns back to his game to find he's been killed because of his carelessness. That's okay, though, because he still has one life left to lose and, anyway, he doesn't have to feel like a failure because the game is so absurd that he doesn't even care anymore. He starts playing again anyway, spinning the trackball in its orbit, but suddenly he feels someone breathing on the back of his neck. He stops moving the trackball. He looks over his shoulder to find Roy standing behind him.

"Watch out!" Roy says, pointing a grease-stained finger at the video screen. Eliot turns back and saves himself by the skin of his teeth. "You almost bought it there," says Roy in a congratulatory manner, as if Eliot has passed some sort of manhood rite in which near-death experiences are a standard. Roy sends a stream of brown spit splashing against the back corner of the arcade game, and Eliot grins without knowing why. He's thinking this kid Roy is a real loser, trashy and yet somehow brave to spit on Mac's property when Mac is only a few steps away. Guys like this are enigmas to Eliot. They frighten him, piss him off for how easy-going they act, fire his imagination in ways that embarrass him. He abhors them; he wants to be more like them; he wants them to want to be more like him; he wants them to tell him they want to be more like him, so he can admit to his own desire for aspects of their own personalities. Shit, he thinks. What the hell is wrong with me? Why do I think these things?

After another minute, Eliot crashes yet another life, and the arcade game bleeps wearily, asking for another quarter for another chance. Eliot turns to Roy and asks, "You want a turn?"

Up close, he can see Roy's eyes are green, and his hair is brown, not colorless. In fact, Eliot decides, in the right light, Roy's hair may even be auburn, reddish-brown, like leaves in autumn.

Roy gives Eliot this dirty grin that makes him appear like he's onto Eliot about something. His lips curl back from his teeth. His nostrils flare, then retract. He's caught the scent of something. "No," he tells Eliot, still grinning. "Why don't we do something else instead?"

Eliot is already nodding. He doesn't know what he's agreed to, but he's willing to sign on the dotted line without reading the small print. It doesn't matter, he's thinking. He's only wondering what Roy's hair will look like outside, out of the dark of Mac's store, out in the sunlight.

7. Do You Understand Me?

The mother came out of nowhere, and the girl looked frantically around the field for a place to hide, as if she'd been caught doing something bad, or was naked, like that man and woman in the garden with the snake. Sometimes, the grandma who babysitted for the mother and the father would tell the girl that story and say, "Dear, you are wiser than all of us. You did not bite that apple." The grandma would pet the girl's hair, as if she were a dog or a cat.

The mother said, "Dawn! What are you doing so far away?

I've been looking for you everywhere! You know you're not supposed to wander." The mother was suddenly upon the girl then, and she grabbed hold of her wrist, tight. "Come on," said the mother. "Let's go back to the cabin. I've got work to do. You can't run off like this. Do you understand me? Dawn! Understand?"

The mother and father were always talking about work. The girl didn't know what work was, but she thought it was probably something like when she had to go to the special school, where the Mrs. Albert made her say, "B is for book, B. B is for bat, B. B is for butterfly, B. Buh, buh, buh." It was a little annoying. But the girl was given a piece of candy each time she repeated the Mrs. Albert correctly. The candy made the buh, buh, buhs worth saying.

The mother tugged on the girl's wrist and they left the field together. The girl struggled against her mother's grip, but could not break it. Behind her, the butterflies all waved their wings goodbye, winking in the high grass and yellow-white flowers like stars in the sky at night. The girl waved back with her free hand, and the butterflies started to fly towards her, as if she'd issued them a command. They ushered the mother and girl out of their field, flapping behind the girl like a banner.

When they reached the cabin, the girl saw that the little old man was back again. Something was funny about him now, but it wasn't the kind of funny that usually made her laugh. Something was different. He didn't look so old anymore maybe, as if all the adulthood had drained out of his normally pinched-looking face. He didn't even scold her when she ran up to him and squealed at him, pointing out the difference to him, in case he hadn't noticed it himself. The little old man didn't seem to be bothered by anything now, not the girl, nor the mother. His eyes looked always somewhere else, far away, like the father's. Off in the distance. The mother asked the little old man, "How was your day?" and the little old man replied, "Great."

This was a shock for the girl. The little old man never sounded so happy. He went into the cabin to take a nap. The girl was curious, so she climbed onto the porch and peered through the window that looked down on the little old man's cot. He was lying on his back, arms crossed behind his head, staring at the ceiling. His face suddenly broke into a smile, and the girl cocked her head, wondering why he would ever do that. Then she realized: He'd found something like she had with the insects, and it made her happy for them both.

The little old man stopped staring at the ceiling. He stared at the girl, his eyes warning signals to keep her distance, but he didn't yell like he usually did. The girl nodded, then backed away from the window slowly. She didn't want to ruin his happiness.

8. Life in the Present Tense

Eliot and Roy are sitting in the rusted-out shell of a 1969 Corvette, once painted red, now rotted away to the browns of rust. The corvette rests in the back of a scrap metal junkyard on the edge of town, which Roy's uncle owns. His uncle closes the place down every afternoon at five o'clock sharp. Now it's nine o'clock at night, and the only light available comes from the moon, and from the orange glow on the cherry of Roy's cigarette.

Eliot is holding a fifth of Jim Beam whiskey in his right hand. The bottle is half empty. He lifts it to his lips and drinks. The whiskey slides down his throat, warm and bitter, and explodes in his stomach, heating his body, flushing his skin bright red. He and Roy started drinking over an hour ago, taking shots, daring each other to take another, then another, until they were both good and drunk. It's the first time for Eliot.

"We need to find something to do," Roy says, exhaling a plume of smoke. "Jeez, this'd be better if we'd at least have a radio or something."

"It's all right," Eliot says, trying to calm Roy down before he works himself up. He and Roy have been hanging out together relentlessly for the past few weeks. Here's one thing Eliot's discovered about Roy: He gets angry over little things fast. Things that aren't really problems. Like not having music in the junkyard while they drink. Roy's never satisfied with what's available. His mind constantly seeks out what could make each moment better than it is, rather than focusing on the moment itself. Roy lives in the future imperfect, Eliot's realized, while Eliot mainly lives in the present tense.

"I hate this town," Roy says, taking the bottle from Eliot. He sips some of the whiskey, then takes a fast and hard gulp. "Ahh," he hisses. He turns to Eliot and smiles, all teeth. His smile is almost perfect, except for one of his front teeth is pushed out a little further than the other, slightly crooked. But it suits him somehow, Eliot thinks.

"I don't know," Eliot shrugs. "I kind of like it here. It's better than being up on that stupid mountain with my parents. They're enough to drive you up a wall."

"Or to drink," says Roy, lifting the bottle again, and they both laugh.

"Yeah," Eliot says, smiling back at Roy. He leans back to rest his head against the seat and looks up through the rusted-out roof of the Corvette, where the stars pour through, reeling and circling above them, as though some invisible force is stirring them up. "It's not like this in Boston," Eliot says. "Most of the time you can't even see the stars because of the city lights."

"In Boston," Roy mimics, his voice whiney and filled with a slight sneer. "All you talk about is Boston. You know, Boston isn't everything. It's the not the only place in the world."

"I know," Eliot says. "I was just trying to say exactly that. You know, how I can't see the stars there like I can here?"

"Oh," Roy says, and looks down into his lap.

Eliot pats him on the shoulder and tells him not to get all sad. "We're having fun," Eliot says. "Everything's great."

Roy agrees and then Eliot goes back to staring at the stars above them. The night air feels cold on his whiskey-warmed skin, and he closes his eyes for a moment to feel the slight breeze on his face. Then he suddenly feels hands cupping his cheeks, the skin rough and grainy, and when Eliot opens his eyes, Roy's face floats before him, serious and intent. Roy leans in and they're lips meet briefly. Something electric uncoils through Eliot's body, like a live wire, dangerous and intense. He feels as if all the gaps and cracks in his being are stretching out to the horizon, filling up with light.

"Are you all right?" Roy asks, and Eliot realizes that he's shaking.

"Yes," Eliot says, so softly and quietly that the word evaporates before it can be heard. He nods instead and, before they kiss again, Roy brushes his thumb over Eliot's cheek and says, "Don't worry. We're friends. It's nothing to worry about, right?"

Eliot can't help but begin worrying, though. He already knows some of the things that will come to pass because of this. He will contemplate suicide, he will contemplate murder, he will hate himself for more reasons than usual—not just because he doesn't want to be away from his family, but because he has turned out to be the sort of boy who kisses other boys, and who wants a son like that? Everything seems like a dream right now, though, so sudden, and maybe it is a dream, nothing more than that. Eliot is prepared to continue sleep-walking.

He nods to answer again, his voice no longer functioning properly. Then Roy presses close again, his breath thick with whiskey and smoke. His body above Eliot blocks out the light from the stars.

9. Sad Alone

In the woods at night, the girl danced to the songs of frogs throating, crickets chirring, wind snaking through leaves, the gurgle of the nearby creek. A happy marriage these sounds made, so the girl danced, surrounded by fireflies and moths.

She could still see the fire through the spaces between the trees, her family's campsite near the cabin, so she was safe. She wasn't doing anything wrong—she was following the rules—so the mother shouldn't come running to pull her back to the fire to sit with her and the father. He was back again, but he didn't seem to be there. Not *really* there, that is. He didn't look at the girl during dinner, only stared into the fire before him, slouching. He didn't open his mouth for any bubbles to come out.

Now that it was night, the little old man was back again. This had become a regular event. In the early evening, after dinner, the little old man would leave, promising to be back before sunset at nine-thirty, or else he'd spend the night with his new friend. This time, though, the little old man had come back with his new friend riding along on a bike beside him, saying, "This is Roy. He'll be spending the night."

The girl missed the little old man when he was gone now, but she didn't dwell on this too much. The little old man no longer glowered at her, no longer gripped her hand too tight like the mother did; he no longer looked angry all the time, so she forgave his absence. He was happy, the girl realized, and in realizing the little old man's happiness and the distance between them that went along with it, she realized her own happiness as well. She didn't miss him enough to be sad about his absence, unlike the father, who made the mother sad when he was gone, who made everyone miss him in a way that made them want to cry or shout in his face.

This moth, the girl thought, stopping her dance for the moment. If she could find this moth, the moth that the father was looking for, perhaps he would come back and be happy, and make the mother happy, and then everyone could be happy together, instead of sad alone. She smiled, proud of her idea, and turned to the fireflies and moths that surrounded her to ask the question:

"Can anyone help me?"

To which the insects all responded at once, their voices a chorus, asking, "What can we do? Are you all right? What? What?"

So the girl began to speak.

10. Each in their Own Place

Dr. Carroll is sitting by the campfire, staring at his two booted feet. Eliot's mother is saying, "This week it will happen. You can't get down on yourself. It's only been a month. You have the rest of the summer still. Don't worry."

Eliot's mother is cooking barbecued beans in a pot over the campfire. The flames lick at the bottom of the pan. Dr. Carroll shakes his head, looking distraught. There are new wrinkles in his forehead, and also around his mouth.

This has been a regular event over the past few weeks, Eliot's father returning briefly for supplies and rest, looking depressed and slightly damaged, growing older-looking before Eliot's eyes. Eliot feels bad for his father, but he'd also like to say, I told you so. That's just too mean, though, he's decided. The Old Eliot would have said that, the New Eliot won't.

The New Eliot is a recent change he's been experiencing, and it's because of Roy. Roy's changed him somehow without trying, and probably without even wanting to make Eliot into someone new in the first place. Eliot supposes this is what happens when you meet a person with whom you can truly communicate. The New Eliot will always try to be nice and not so world-weary. He will not say mean things to his parents or sister. He will love them and think about their needs, because his no longer seem so bad off.

Roy says, "Is it always like this?" He and Eliot are sitting on the swing in the cabin's front porch. The swing's chains squeal above their heads as they rock. This is Roy's first visit to the place. Eliot's tried to keep him away from his family, because even though he's made the choice to be nice, he's still embarrassed by them a little. Also, he'd rather have Roy to himself.

That's another thing that's come between them. It happened a couple of weeks back. Roy and Eliot had been hanging out together, getting into minor trouble. They'd spray-painted their names on an overpass; egged Roy's neighbor's car; toilet-papered the high school Roy attends; drank whiskey until they've puked. It's been a crazy summer, the best Eliot can remember really, and he doesn't want it to ever stop. Usually he goes to computer camp or just sits in front of the TV playing video games until school starts back up. Besides the vandalism and the drunken bouts, Eliot thinks he has fallen in love. Something like that. He and Roy have become like a couple, without using those words, without telling anyone else.

"My father's like Sisyphus," Eliot says, and Roy gives him this puzzled look.

"What did you say?"

"Sisyphus," Eliot repeats. "He was this guy from myth who was doomed by the gods to roll a rock up a mountain, but it keeps rolling back down when he gets to the top, so he has to roll it up again, over and over. Camus says it's the definition of the human condition, that myth. My mother teaches a class on it."

"Oh." Roy shakes his head. "Well, whatever."

That *whatever* is another thing that's come between them. Lately Roy says it whenever he doesn't understand Eliot, and doesn't care to try. It makes Eliot want to punch Roy right in the face. Eliot has taken to saying it as well, to see if it pisses off Roy as much, but whenever he says, "Whatever," Roy doesn't seem to give a damn. He just keeps on talking without noticing Eliot's attempts to make him angry.

The fireflies have come out for the evening, glowing on and off in the night mist. Crickets chirp, rubbing their legs together. An owl calls out its own name in the distance. Dawn is running between trees, her figure a silhouette briefly illuminated by the green glow of the fireflies, a shadow in the woods. Eliot still hasn't introduced her to Roy, and Roy hasn't asked why she acts so strangely, which makes Eliot think maybe he should explain before Roy says something mean about her, not understanding her condition. Dawn irritates Eliot, but he still doesn't want other people saying nasty things about her.

"She's autistic," Eliot says all of a sudden, pre-empting Roy's remarks. He pushes against the porch floorboards to make them swing faster, so Roy can't get off this ride too quick.

Roy doesn't seem shocked, though, or even interested in Dawn's erratic behavior. And why should he be? Eliot thinks. Roy himself has told Eliot much weirder things about his family. He told Eliot that first day, over an ice cream at the gas station, that he lived with his grandparents because his mother was an alcoholic, and his father was who-knows-where. That his mother would fight anyone in town, even Roy when she was drunk. That his grandfather was a member of the Ku Klux Klan, that he had found the white robes and the pointy hood in his grandfather's closet. That his grandmother used to sit him down at night before bed and read to him for a half an hour out of the Bible, and that afterwards she'd tell him he was born in sin, and should pray for forgiveness. It frightens Eliot a little, and makes him shiver, thinking of what it must be like to be Roy. He only hopes Roy's secret-sharing doesn't require an admission of his own private weirdnesses. He's not ready for that.

"Let's go inside," Roy says, putting his feet down flat on the porch.

The swing suddenly comes to a halt. Roy stands and Eliot follows him into the cabin, already knowing what's going to happen. It's a vice of Roy's, fooling around in places where they might get caught.

We won't get caught here, Eliot thinks. His parents are outside by the heat of the fire, involved in their own problems. They won't bother to come inside the cabin now. Roy leads Eliot to the pink-quilted cot and they lay down together, and begin to kiss.

Roy's lips are larger than Eliot's. Eliot feels like his lips aren't big enough. They're too thin and soft, like rose petals. Roy, he thinks, would probably like his lips bigger and rougher, chapped even. He can feel the cracks in Roy's lips, can taste Roy's cigarettes. Roy's stubble scratches Eliot's cheeks in this way that makes him crazy. Then Roy is pulling off Eliot's shirt, kissing Eliot's stomach, unbuttoning Eliot's shorts. Eliot closes his eyes. He mouths the words, *Someone is in love with me.* He is in the habit of mouthing sentences silently when he wants what he is saying to be true.

He feels his shorts being tugged down, then his breath catches in his throat, and he is off, off, off. Far away, his parents argue and his sister runs through the wilderness like a woodland creature, a nymph. Each of them in their private spaces, like the sections his mother made of the cabin when they first arrived. Each of them in their own place.

11. What the Firefly Said

"So," said the firefly, "you're looking for a moth."

The girl nodded. "Yes," she said. "Actually, it's for my father. He's been searching for over a month."

"And what does it look like?" the firefly said, floating in front of her face. "You know, a moth is a moth is a moth. But that's just my opinion."

"This one glows," she said. "An orangey-pink. It has brown and gold streaks on its back, and also it only comes out at night."

"Hmm," said the firefly. "I see. Wait here a moment."

The firefly flew off. The girl watched it for a while, then lost it among the other greenish blips. She sighed, sat down on the ground beneath a pine tree, picking up a few needles covered in sticky sap.

"I'm back," said the firefly, and the girl looked up. It had brought a friend, and they both landed on her lap.

"I know who you're looking for," the other firefly said.

The girl felt a rush of excitement churl in her stomach. Her face flushed with heat. "Really?" she said. "Oh, please, you must help me find it."

"This moth, though," the firefly said, "it's a bit of a loner. There are a few of them I know of, but they don't even talk amongst themselves. I don't understand them. You know, we fireflies, we like to have a good time. We like to party." It chuckled softly and nudged its friend.

"I'll do anything," the girl said. "Please, if only it would make my father happier. He looks paler and thinner each time he comes back."

"Well," the firefly said. "Let me see what I can make happen. I have a lot of connections. We'll see what turns up."

"Thank you," said the girl, "Oh, thank you, thank you."

The fireflies both floated off. She sat under the tree for a while longer, thinking everything would be good now. Her whole family would be happy for once.

Then the mother and the father were calling her name, loud, over and over. She saw them coming towards her, running. The mother pulled her up from the ground and said, "I was so worried, so worried." The father grunted and led them back to the cabin, where the little old man and his new friend were sitting by the campfire.

"I can't do this anymore," said the mother. "I can't keep her in one place. She's always wandering off."

"Just a little longer," said the father. "I can't go back without it. I've been teaching the same classes to an endless stream of students. I can't go back without this."

The mother nodded and rubbed her temples. "I know," she said. "I know."

Then the little old man told his friend, "This is my sister. Her name is Dawn. She doesn't talk much."

The little old man's friend stared at her for a moment. His eyes grew wide; he smiled at her. The little old man's friend said, "Your sister's beautiful," as if he couldn't believe it himself.

12. *Your Sister's Beautiful*

Your sister's beautiful.

Your sister's beautiful.

Your sister's beautiful.

Lying on his cot, staring at the bare rafters of the cabin, imagining Roy hanging by his neck from one of the rafters, his face blue in death, Eliot cannot force Roy's words out of his mind. He's been hearing them over and over since Roy—stupid idiotic trashy no-good thoughtless bastard—said them three nights ago.

Your sister's beautiful.

And me? Eliot thinks. What about me? Why couldn't Roy have said the same thing about Eliot, with whom he's much more involved and supposedly loves enough to take to bed? Eliot is thinking, I should kill him. I should be like one of those people on talk shows, or in novels. I should commit a crime of passion that anyone could understand.

Outside somewhere, Roy is hanging out with Dawn. He's been with Eliot for over a month and never once cared to come up to the cabin until Eliot brought him himself. Now he's come up everyday since that first night, and Eliot has been ignoring him defiantly, walking away when Roy starts to speak, finding opportunities to make Roy feel stupid, talking to his mother about high minded philosophical things in front of Roy. Even if Eliot himself doesn't understand some of the things that comes out of his mother's mouth, he's been around her long enough to pretend like he knows what he's talking about; he knows enough catch-phrases to get by. Whatever works, he's thinking, to make that jerk go away or feel sorry.

Eliot notices that everything is strangely quiet, both inside the cabin and out. He sits up in bed and looks out the window. The campfire is a pile of ashes, still glowing orange and red from last night. His mother is nowhere to be seen, and both Roy and Dawn aren't around either. His father, he thinks, is who-knows-where.

Eliot goes outside and looks around back of the cabin.

Nothing but weeds and a few scrub bushes and saplings grow here.

He walks to the edge of the woods, to where the trails begin, and starts to worry. Dawn. He hasn't been in a state of mind to watch her, and his mother has proved ineffectual at the task. He mouths the words, *My sister is safe and around that tree there, playing with a caterpillar,* and then he goes to check.

Dawn's not behind the tree, and there are no caterpillars in sight. Eliot suddenly clenches his teeth. He hears, somewhere close by, Roy's voice. He can't make out what Roy is saying, but he's talking to someone in that voice of his—the idiotic stupid no-good trashy bastard voice.

Eliot walks in the direction of the voice. He follows a trail until it narrows and dips down into a ravine. There's the creek where he and Dawn watched crayfish for hours. The way water moves, the way it sparkles under light, and reflects the things around it, the trees and Eliot's and Dawn's own faces, can entrance Dawn for hours. The creek holds the image of the world on its surface, the trees and clouds and a sun pinned like a jewel on its narrow, rippled neck. Beneath the creek, under the water, is another world, full of crayfish and snakes and fish no bigger than fingers. Eliot wonders if his mother has included something philosophical about the creek in her feminist revision of *Walden*. He wonders if she's noticed the same things that he notices.

Roy's voice fades, then reappears, like a trick or a prank, and soon Eliot sees him sitting under a tree with Dawn. Roy's talking to her real sweet. Eliot recognizes that voice. He's playing with Dawn's hand, which she keeps pulling away from him. Roy doesn't know Dawn hates to be touched. The only thing she can stand is a tight embrace, and then she won't ever let go. It's a symptom, her doctor has told the family, of her autism.

Now Roy is leaning into Dawn, trying to kiss her, and Dawn pulls her head back. She stands up and starts walking towards the creek. Eliot feels his hands clench, becoming fists. Roy stands up and follows Dawn. He walks in front of her and she squeals in his face. A high-pitched banshee squeal. The squeal, Eliot thinks, of death.

Eliot finds he is running towards them, his fists ready to pummel Roy. He wonders if he can actually do it, he hasn't ever used them before, not like this. Can I do it, he wonders, as Roy turns with a surprised expression on his face.

Yes, he can.

His first punch lands on Roy's cheekbone, right under Roy's eye. The second one glances blandly off of Roy's stomach, making Roy double up and expel a gasp of breath. Then Eliot is screaming at the top of his lungs, "Get out! Get the hell out! Get the hell out!" His voice turns hoarser each time he screams, but he keeps screaming anyway. Roy looks up at Eliot with a red mark on his face. It's already darkening into a bruise that Eliot wishes he could take a picture of and frame. He'd like to hang it on his wall and keep it forever. A reminder of his ignorance.

Roy says, "Whatever. Fucking faggot," and starts to walk away, back up the trail. When he reaches the top of the ravine and walks over it, he disappears from Eliot's sight, and from Eliot's life, forever.

Eliot is breathing heavily, ready to hit Roy again. He's a little surprised at how easy it was, that he has a space inside him that harbors violence. At the same time, he's impressed with himself. He's not sure if he should feel afraid or proud of his actions. He's not sure if he has room for both.

Dawn stands beside him, looking into his face. She's quiet and still for once in her life. She smoothes down the wrinkles in her shorts with the flats of her hands, over and over. He's most likely disturbed her. Or Roy has. Or both of them did. Eliot says, "Come on, let's go back." He doesn't yell at her or yank her wrist. And Dawn follows him up the trail, out of the ravine, back to the cabin.

13. The Assignation

Something woke her late in the night. *Tap, tap, tap.* Something kept tapping, and so she sat up in bed and looked around her. The mother and father were asleep on their cots, the little old man slept on the other side of the sheet separating them. None of them were tapping.

Then she heard it again, and looked over her shoulder. In the window square, two fireflies hovered, blinking out a message. *Outside. Five minutes.*

The girl quietly got out of her cot and stepped into her sandals. She pulled a piece of hair out of her mouth. Peaking around the corner of the sheet, she watched the little old man for a while, his chest rising and falling in steady rhythms of sleep. Earlier that evening, she and the little old man had sat in their respective corners, on their respective cots, and by the light of a lantern, they had made shadow creatures appear on the sheet separating their rooms. Bats and butterflies, and even a dog's head that could open its mouth and bark. She loved the little old man, and wished she could tell him as much.

Then she tiptoed out of the cabin, closing the door behind her carefully. The two fireflies were waiting for her by the smoldering campfire.

"What's the matter?" the girl asked. "Has something happened?"

The fireflies nodded together. One of them said, "We've found your moth. The one you asked about. Orangey-pink glow, gold and brown streaks on its wings? We found him."

"Oh, thank you so much," she told them. "How can I repay you?"

"Wait," the fireflies both said. "He isn't here with us. You'll have to wait. He was busy. A real snob, if you want our opinions. But he said he would drop by tomorrow evening. He asked why you wanted to meet him. We said you were a new fixture here, and wanted to meet all the neighbors."

"That's wonderful," the girl said, liking the idea of her being a fixture here, of being a part of the natural surroundings.

She told the fireflies she would be waiting by the campfire the next evening, and that they could bring the moth to her there. "Won't my father be surprised!" she told the fireflies, and they both shrugged, saying, "It's just a moth, I mean really! What's so special about that?"

You have no idea, she wanted to tell them. But she simply told them thank you, and crept back into the cabin to sleep.

14. Why Now?

When Dr. Carroll returned from his latest outing, he looked ready to fold up and die on the spot. Eliot and Dawn hung back in the shadows of the porch, swinging a little, while their mother sat at the campfire with their father and tried her best to comfort him. There was still no moth, he told her, and he was ready to face up to the possibility that this summer has been a total waste, that his memory of something unique that no one else had ever discovered was probably false.

Eliot decided to make himself and Dawn scarce, so he took her inside the cabin and, lighting a lantern, entertained her with hand shadows thrown against the sheet separating their cots. They fell asleep after a while, and when Eliot wakes the next morning, he finds his mother and father already outside, cooking breakfast over the fire.

"We're going to leave tomorrow," Eliot's father tells him, whisking eggs in a stainless steel bowl.

"Good," says Eliot, rubbing sleep out of his eyes. He yawns, and takes a glass of orange juice his mother offers him. She's been to town already, and has brought back some fresh food and drinks from Mac's. He takes a sip of the orange juice and holds it in his mouth for a moment, savoring the taste.

"Well, I for one have got a lot of work to do when we get back," Eliot's mother says. "A whole summer spent camping, and I haven't prepared anything for my fall classes yet."

Eliot looks at Dawn, who sits on a log on the other side of the fire, eating sausage links with her fingers. He smiles at her, and gives her a wink. Dawn, to his surprise, smiles and winks back.

The day passes with all of them making preparations to leave the next day. They pack the wagon full of their clothes and camping equipment, and then retire at dusk to the fire, where their faces flush yellow and orange from the flames. All four of them stare at each other, or stare at the last pot of beans cooking on the fire. They're tired, all of them. Puffy gray sacs of flesh hang under their eyes. They are a family, Eliot thinks, of zombies. The walking dead. Faces gray, eyes distant, mouths closed. No one speaks.

Soon after they're finished eating, Dawn gets up from her seat and wanders away from the fire. But not so far that her mother and father can't see where she has gone. Finally, when the fireflies have come to life, filling the night air with an apple green glow, Eliot spots it, his father's moth, pinwheeling through the air around Dawn, surrounded by an orangey-pink halo.

"Dad," he says, "Dad, look." And Dr. Carroll turns to see where Eliot is pointing. A strange little noise comes out of his mouth. Almost a squeak. He heaves himself off the log he's crouched on, and stumbles towards Dawn and the moth.

There it is, thinks Eliot. Why now? Why has it decided to make an appearance after all this time, after all this pain? Why now? he wonders, wanting answers that perhaps don't exist. He suspects Dawn has something to do with it, the same way Dawn made the grasshoppers line up together and do synchronized leaps.

Dr. Carroll shouts, "Keep an eye on it, don't let it get away!" and he rushes to the car to dig through the back for a net or a box. He comes jogging back with a clear plastic box that has a screen fitted into the lid and vents on the sides. A few twigs and leafs wait inside of it. He opens the lid, scoops up the moth, and snaps the box shut.

But then Dawn is squealing. She runs over to her father and tries to pry the box out of his hands. What is she doing? Eliot can't understand why she'd do a thing like that. She's beating at her father's chest, saying—what?—saying, "No! No! No! You can't lock it up like that!"

What? Eliot's thinking. He's thinking, What's happening here?

His mother steps between Dawn and Dr. Carroll, grabbing Dawn around her shoulders to pull her in for a hug. Dawn is sobbing now, her shoulders heaving, and she leans into her mother for the hug, and doesn't let go for fifteen minutes at least. Eliot stays by the fire, afraid of what's going on in front of him. He doesn't know what to do or say.

Dr. Carroll says, "What's wrong with her? I can't believe she tried to do that."

Eliot's mother says, "Leave her alone. Just leave her alone, why don't you? Can't you see she's upset?"

Dr. Carroll walks away from them, holding his box with the moth inside it close to his chest. It glows still. The box lights up like a faery lantern. The smile on his father's face tells Eliot exactly what he is holding. This box, says Eliot's father's smile, contains my youth.

15. The Message

It is late now, so late that Eliot has fallen asleep for several hours and then, inexplicably, woke in the night. He doesn't have to pee, and he doesn't feel too hot, or sick. But something is wrong, and it makes him sit up and look around the cabin. His parents are asleep on their cots. The cabin is quiet except for their breathing. He gets out of bed, and once again, the coils of the cot squeal as he removes his weight from them. He pulls back a corner of the sheet separating his room from Dawn's and finds that she is not in her bed. She's not in the cabin at all.

Eliot runs out of the cabin in his bare feet. The grass is dewy, wetting his feet. He doesn't look behind the cabin, or by the fire, or in the nearby field. He runs down the trail to the ravine where he hit Roy, and finds Dawn there, standing by the creek. Mist and fog hover over the water. Dawn stands in the mist surrounded by a swarm of fireflies. She looks like a human Christmas tree with all of those lights blinking around her. She looks like a magic creature. Like a woodland spirit, Eliot thinks.

"Dawn," he says when he reaches her. But Dawn holds out her hand and raises one of her fingers. Wait, she is asking. One moment. Wait.

Eliot stands before her, and suddenly the fireflies drop from the air as if they have all had sudden heart attacks, their lights extinguished. They lay at his feet, crawling around in the grasses. Then, all at the same time, their lights flicker on again, and Eliot finds they have arranged themselves into letters. Spelled out in the grass, glowing green, are the words *Love You, Eliot.*

Eliot looks up to find Dawn's face shining with tears, and he feels his own eyes filling. He steps around the fireflies and hugs Dawn, and whispers that he loves her, too. They stay there for a while, hugging, until Eliot takes Dawn's hand and leads her back to the cabin before their parents wake up.

16. Now

When the Carroll's return home from Pennsylvania, they do their best to return to their lives as they once knew them. Eliot's father, uncanny specimen in hand, sets to work on his new research. His mother resumes classes in the Fall and publishes an essay called "Woman, Nature, Words" in a feminist philosophy journal.

On Mondays, Wednesdays and Fridays, Dawn attends school—she has learned how to say "My name is Dawn Carroll, I am seventeen-years-old, Thank you, You're Welcome, Goodbye, Goodbye, Goodbye." Goodbye is her favorite new word. She sometimes shouts it at the top of her lungs, and Goodbye floats up to the vaulted ceilings at home, spinning this direction and that, searching for an escape route, a way out of the confines of walls and floors and ceilings. Eventually it bursts, and bits of Goodbye, wet and soapy, fall back down onto her face.

Eliot returns to school as well, to high school, where he learns to slouch and to not look up from his feet, and how to evade talking to other people as much as possible. He begins to dress in black clothes and to listen to depressing music—"Is that what they mean by Gothic?" his mother asks him—but he doesn't dignify her question with an answer. His grades flag and falter. "Needs to work harder," his teachers report. Mr. and Mrs. Carroll send him to a psychologist, a Dr. Emery, who sits behind her desk and doesn't say much of anything. She waits in the long silences for Eliot to begin speaking, and once he starts talking, it's difficult to stop.

Eliot tells her everything that happened over the summer, and Dr. Emery nods a lot and continues to offer little in the way of conversation. Dr. Emery advises Eliot to tell his parents whatever he feels he needs to, and that she will try to help them understand. But Eliot isn't ready, not yet at least, and now that he's told someone else what happened, he wants to think about other things for a while. Video games, music, television, even his schoolwork. Things that are comforting and easy. For now it's enough to have Dr. Emery to talk to, someone safe and understanding. For now.

This is the first in a series of people that Eliot finds he can actually talk to. The others will come to him, friends and lovers, scattered throughout the rest of his life. In a few years he won't even be thinking that no one can understand him. He will be leaning back on his pillows and staring at the neon plastic stars he's pasted to his ceiling, in his own apartment a few blocks from where he attends college, and he will be thinking about that night in the ravine, by the creek. He'll remember Dawn lit up by fireflies, and how they arranged themselves into glowing green letters, like the constellation of glowing stars above him, like the stars he watched through the roof of the rusted-out corvette with Roy. He'll think about his sister and how she learned to speak the language of moths, the language of fireflies and crickets. How he had learned the language of love and betrayal, the language of self-hate and mistrust. How much more his sister knew, he realizes later, than he ever did.

When he thinks about Dawn's message, Eliot will be in love with someone who loves him back. This boy that he'll love will be asleep beside him while Eliot stays awake, staring at the stars above, thinking about Dawn's message.

Love You, Eliot, she had instructed the fireflies to spell out.

At the time, Eliot had interpreted Dawn's message to mean she loved him, and of course there's that, too. But when he thinks about it now, in the future, he's not so sure. The "I" of her message was mysteriously missing, but its absence might only have been an informal gesture on Dawn's part. He wonders now if Dawn was saying something entirely different that night. Has he misunderstood her message, or only understood half of it? Meaning is always lost, at least partially, in translation, he thinks.

Love You, Eliot, she had told him, the letters glowing like green embers in the grass.

Now, in the future, this future that he imagined so many years ago, the future in which he lived in his own apartment, with his own television and his own books, the future in which he goes to college and finds himself not as wrong or as weird as he once thought he was, in this future he wonders if Dawn was also giving him a piece of advice.

Love You, Eliot, she had told him.

And he does that. He knows how to do that.

Now.

Sonya Taaffe has a confirmed addiction to myth, folklore, and dead languages. Her poem "Matlacihuatl's Gift" shared first place for the 2003 Rhysling Award, and a respectable amount of her short fiction and poetry was recently collected in ***Postcards from the Province of Hyphens*** *and* ***Singing Innocence and Experience****. She is currently pursuing a Ph.D. in Classics at Yale University.*

S. Ansky's 1920 drama ***The Dybbuk*** *may feature the definitive dybbuk in love, but what happens in these latter days when he comes from the turn of the last century and she doesn't even light candles for Shabbes? Thanks to Michael Zoosman for Menachem. "The Dybbuk in Love" was written primarily to the music of the Klezmatics'* ***Possessed*** *and Jill Tracy's* ***Quintessentially Unreal.***

The Dybbuk in Love
Sonya Taaffe

> And then there are souls, troubled and dark, without a home or a resting place, and these attempt to enter the body of another person, and even these are trying to ascend.
>
> —Tony Kushner, *A Dybbuk or Between Two Worlds*

Sunset through the clouds, air full of ozone and the sweet aftertaste of fallen rain, and she walked home from the bus stop through gleaming, deserted streets, the first time with Brendan.

Side by side all the way back from the library, they had talked quietly, about unimportant things like teaching kindergarten and accounting and the books in Clare's leather-bottomed backpack, while the sky spilled over with rain and the bus' wipers squeaked back and forth across the flooding windshield. Arteries and tributaries of water crawled along along the glass as they moved slowly through traffic, in washes of red and green; the downpour sounded like slow fire kindling everywhere a raindrop hit, matchstrike and conflagration. Against Brendan's knee where it had shed rain all over his khakis, the vast blackboard-colored folds of his umbrella stuck out struts at odd angles: he had offered its shelter to Clare on the library's neoclassical steps, and again when they got down from the bus in the last fading scatter between storm and breaking sun, though she had refused him both times. Now they were crossing a street crowded only with puddles, and Clare looked down between her feet to mark their reflections. No shadows, in this diffuse light; no certainty. Brendan's eyes were whitened blue as old denim, a pale mismatch for the heavy leaves of his hair that he wore drawn back into a fox-colored ponytail; she watched them, and listened carefully to his voice, and prayed to be proven wrong.

The sky had turned a washed-out gold, full of haze, luminous, blinded; unreal as an overexposed photograph, dissolving into a grainy blur of light. Up and down the street, windows that had not been thrown open to the cooling, clearing air were opaque with reflection, blank alabaster slates, like the broken hollows in the asphalt that had filled up and rippled only as Clare and Brendan passed. Rain-slicked still, the gutters and the pavement shone: filmed with light, paved with gold; *goldene medine*. Words she could have bitten from her tongue even for thinking them, because they might so easily not have been hers. *Sheyn vi gold iz zi geven, di grine . . .*

No one's cousin, only child of only children: a spare-boned girl, eyes half a shade lighter than her hazelnut hair hacked short and pushed behind her ears; denim coat that buttoned almost to her knees and a scar across her left eyebrow where a stainless steel ring had been. Her sneakers had worn down to soles flat as ballet slippers, laces mostly unraveled into grit and no-color fuzz. She tilted her head up to Brendan and said back reasonably, "If you think I should be reading Gershon Winkler to half a dozen five-year-olds, you can come in and explain their nightmares to their parents."

His prehistoric umbrella was swung up over his shoulder, cheerful parody of Gene Kelly; she had noticed him in the stacks, rust-tawny hair and suit jackets, before he came up to her this afternoon at the circulation desk and asked why she was always taking out children's books. "I don't see why they'd have nightmares."

"This is why you're the number-cruncher."

For the first time, she saw his mouth warm in a laugh, almost soundless as though he feared someone might interrupt and catch him at it. "Clare," he said, and stopped.

The laughter stayed trapped in small places in his face, the lines around his eyes and the angles of his gingery brows, his lips still crooked slightly to his surprise, her teasing, the conversation that might fork and feather out like crystal into somewhere unexpected. "Clare," he said again, gently. A chill pulsed down her bones. "Will you let me come to you?"

The color of his eyes had not changed, neither their depth nor their focus; his voice was as relaxed and nasal as the first time he had spoken to her in the library. But he was looking through his eyes now, not with them: panes of stonewashed stained glass, and she said, dead-end recognition, "Menachem." Something like ice and brandy sunfished up into her throat, sluice and burn past her heart; she put it from her, as she had weeks ago put away her surprise. Wondering for how long this time, she gave her greeting to this new face. "I was wondering when you'd turn up."

"Constellations follow the Pole Star; I follow you." All his sly chivalry in those words, in this earnest head-cold tenor; her mouth tugged itself traitorously up at the corners, and she wanted to slap Brendan's tender, deadpan face until she jarred him loose. If she could have pulled the long hair and faintly freckled cheekbones aside, stripped down through layers of flesh and facade to the teardrop spirit beneath, she might have done it. But nothing would force him out save a full exorcism, candles and shofar blasts and perhaps not even those, and she did not know a rabbi and a minyan that would not call her crazy. With Brendan's mouth, less an accent than the remembered heft and clamber of another language nudging up underneath this one, he was saying, "There's rain in your hair," and even that spare statement was light and wondering.

She stepped backward, one foot up onto the curb and the other above a grate where a page of draggled newspaper had twisted and stuck. Where the clouds threaded away, the sky was like parchment, backlit; summer twilight would leave this glow lingering below the clouds long after Clare had left Brendan standing in the middle of this rain-glazed street and walked home to her apartment alone, in solitude where no one would surface in a stranger's eyes and speak to her.

"Leave him alone. It's not—do you understand this? It's not fair. To him." Easy enough to tell, once she knew what to look for. Brendan's acquaintance gaze would never track each of her movements with such ardent attention, even her frustration, his inability or refusal to understand that she slammed up against each time: that the world was not made of marionettes and masks, living costumes for a rootless dead man. "To any of them. People always ask me, afterward. They know something happened. So I'm supposed to tell them, *Oh, yeah, a free-thinker from the Pale who died of typhus in 1906 just walked through your head, don't mind him . . . ?*" Too absurd a scenario to lay out straight and she clenched her teeth on the knowledge; he kept her smiles like cheating cards up his sleeve. Or perhaps not cheats at all, face-up on the table and nothing at stake but what he had told her, and that might have been worse. "Some comforter you are."

Some things, a century of death and drifting had not worn away. Menachem's wince was a flicker of heat lightning at the back of Brendan's eyes. But he laughed, still with more sound than the accountant, and shrugged; a complicated movement with the umbrella still braced over his shoulder, jounced behind his head like an eclipse. The puddles were drying out from under their feet, mirrors evaporating into the light-soaked air. His voice was less wistful than wry, fading toward farewell. "I'd never seen you in this light before."

She said, more gently than she had thought, "I know. Neither has Brendan. You have to go."

"I would be with you always, if I could. Through grave-dirt, through ashes, through all the angels of Paradise and all the demons of the Other Side, Clare Tcheresky. When I saw you, I knew you for my beloved, the other half of my *neshome*," a quick spill of words in the language that he had given up before he died, in this country of tenements and music halls and tea-rooms, before Clare's great-grandparents had married or even met. ". . . years, I wondered sometimes if this was Gehenna, if I was wrong. The things I have seen, Clare, waiting for you." Brendan's face was distant with the pain of strange memories, atrocities he had never witnessed and laments he had never heard. Within him, Menachem Schuyler, twenty-seven years old and dead for more than three times that, smiled like a snapped bone and said, "You don't need me. But if I could, I would be your comfort. I would cleave to you like God."

Clare closed her eyes, unable to look anymore at his eyes that were not his eyes, his face that was not his face, his borrowed flesh that she would never touch, even in anger, even to comfort. When she opened them again, only Brendan would meet her gaze: denim-eyed, fox-haired, essential and oblivious; already knitting up the gap in their conversation, muscles and tendons forgetting the movements they had not consciously made, the same collage and patches she had seen over and over throughout this long, haunted month. She whispered, before Brendan could hear her, "I know," and did not know if he took the words with him when he disappeared, swifter than an eddy of smoke or the mimicry of a reflection, her dybbuk.

Sunlight fell through the plate-glass windows onto shelves of pale wood, bright covers and spines, and the tune danced like dust motes and photons, *Shtey dir oyf, mayn gelibter, mayn sheyner, un kum dir,* hummed under Clare's breath as she wrapped up paperbacks of Susan Cooper and Laurence Yep for the fair-haired woman who had come in to buy a birthday present for her nine-year-old daughter, an early and voracious reader. Four days through intermittent showers, a half-moon swelled above the skyline for the midpoint of the month. Still Clare stayed too cautious to relax, dreams like an old reel of film run out and flapping in her mind.

Yesterday's rain had left the sky blue as morning glories when she looked up between the buildings, soft with heat: no puddles underfoot to play tricks of light and shadow as she walked from her stop to The Story Corner, and no Brendan by her side. No Menachem today, like a wick sputtering into light behind the woman's lipsticked smile: nothing yet, and that meant nothing.

Always there when she forgot to look for him, until she was looking all the time; courting her with apologies, with history, with fits and starts and fragments of song. *Friling, nem tsu mayn troyer. Oy, dortn, dortn.* Because of him, Clare had read Aleichem and Singer and Ansky at night in her apartment, piecing together the intricacies of past and possession, what might lie on the other side of a mirror and what might kindle up from the embers of a deathbed desire. Like the song she played over and over again, nine-of-hearts piano and Jill Tracy's voice of dry-sliding silk—*and I'm engaged, and I'm enraged, and I'm enchanted with this little bit of magic I've been shown . . .* Sometimes, when she gave him time enough for the loan of lips and tongue to tell a story, he shared tales of Lilith and Ketev Mriri, *mazzikim* like smoke stains and tricksters who could swindle even Ashmedai, even Metatron. The names of his parents, Zvi and Tsippe. His three sisters who had read Shaykevitsh while their brother read Zola in translation. *You are the only living soul who remembers them now.* Confidences bound to chains between them, a cat's-cradle of need and amazement, amusement and nuisance, and she still should have met him in a cemetery. Even a wedding, seven blessings and the glass stamped underfoot like a reminder of every broken thing, would have suited him more than the subway crush of a hot summer's night, coming home from the fireworks: announcements too garbled to make out in the rattle and rush of darkness past the windows and Clare jammed up against an ESL advertisement and a black woman with the face of an aging Persian cat, sure she had lost her mind. But if she had, then so had every second person she had met since the Fourth of July; so had the universe, to let him slip through.

You are why I am here. She tried not to believe him.

Two or three weeks ago, on a day terrible enough to have come right out of one of the picture books The Story Corner sold—alarm that never went off until she had already woken up and yelled at the placid stoplight-red numerals, humid drizzle and buses running late and her coffee slopped all over her hand—he had slid underneath the day's itinerary that Lila Nicoille was reeling off to her, and said something quiet, meaningless, comforting, and for once she thought he and his name were well matched. He could not slide an arm around her shoulders, no brief brush of solidarity from a ghost; but the words were as strong as a handclasp, unasked and given for no more reason than that she needed them. Then Lila had faltered to a halt, her greenish eyes as blurred and surfacing as though she had been shaken awake from dreaming sleep, and Clare felt only cold where she had imagined Menachem's fingers slotted between hers, nothing in her palm but the ashes of another momentary bridge.

No way to explain to Lila, to this woman with sleek blond braids, what about Clare Tcheresky made the world waver like uneasy sleep, déjà vu, like a ghost walking over memories' grave. No way to explain to Brendan, though she had seen him once in the stacks and once walking down the other side of a rush-hour street and his business card lay like a cue on her windowsill at home, why she would not meet him again—give another person's body and soul over to this wandering stranger, to satisfy her curiosity? She could only withdraw, stay alone, and try not wonder too much about what would happen when the school year began. If one of her new class suddenly raised a small head and said in a bird-pipe of a voice, not *Miss T.*, but *Clare*— There were things she thought she would not forgive him for, no matter how lovestruck, how fascinating, and she did not want to find out what they were.

Across the counter, the woman had fallen silent. A glitter moved across her eyes, and Clare snapped her head up, tensing already for the words that would drive him back.

"Is everything all right?"

That was not Menachem's language, nor Menachem looking back in puzzlement and the faintest rim of suspicion: the woman had only blinked. Her eyes were marked out like a leopard's with mascara, even to the tear-line at the inner corners. Like picture frames for her warmly brown irises; like glasses, which Clare did not know if Menachem had worn. Brendan wore contact lenses. Her eyes were going to hell: staring at small print all day, screens and receipts, staring into strangers' eyes. "Yes," she said, clumsy syllable like a weight against her teeth, tongue-twister misunderstanding, and slid the package of books over into the manicured hands.

When the woman had gone, aloud to the gilt-slanting light and the soft white noise of the fan in the back: "Only looking for the truth." Clare pushed her sliding hair back behind her ears; her laugh was little more than a sharpness of air, a puff to blow away ghosts and wishful thinking. *Shtey dir oyf. Extraordinary.*

That night she dreamed of him, once, when the velour air cooled enough for sleep and there were fewer cars honking in the streetlit haze under her window: that she stepped between slender, scarred-black birches into the cemetery where they had not met, and walked among the graves grown up like trees of granite and sawed-off memories, like stumps. Spade-leafed ivy clustered over the weather-blotched stone, delicately rampant tendrils picking through names that the years had all but rubbed out. When Clare pushed leaves aside, scraped softly with a thumbnail at grey-green blooms of lichen, she still could not read who lay beneath her feet; not in this retrograde alphabet, though the dates, in five thousands, were clear. The sky was pewter overcast, pooled dully above the horizon of the trees, and the wind that came through the rustling edges of forest smelled like autumn already turning in cool earth and shortening days.

"Clare," he said behind her, a voice she had never heard, and she turned knowing who she would see.

If anything, she had still expected a character from old photographs and Yiddish literature, a sallow yeshiva student in his scholar's black and white fringes, a prayer for every occasion calligraphed onto his tongue and no more experience of women than the first, promised glimpse of his arranged bride. Bowed over pages so crowded with commentary upon commentary that the candlelight could scarcely find room to dance pale among the flickering letters, nights spent with the smells of burned-down wax and feather ticking, dreaming of angels that climbed up and down ropes of prayer, demons that drifted like an incense of malice down the darkened wind. But he had studied seams and treadles as intently as *Bereshis* or *Vayikra*, taken trains that trailed cinders like an eye-stinging banner and read yellow-backed novels in the tired evenings, and Paradise had not opened for him like a text of immeasurable light when he died, dry-throated and feverish and stranded in a land farther from anything he recognized than even his ancestors had wandered in exile.

He was not tall; he wore a dark overcoat, a grey-striped scarf hanging over his shoulders like an improvised tallis, and wire-rimmed glasses that slid the nowhere light over themselves like a pair of vacant portholes until he reached up and removed them in a gesture like the slight, deliberate tip of a hat: not the movement of a stranger, and it made her smile. Bare-headed, he had wiry hair the color of stained cherrywood, tousled, the same color as his down-slanting brows; all his face gathered forward, bones like promontories and chisel slips. His eyes were no particular color that Clare could discern.

Among the cracked and moss-freckled headstones, he stood quietly and waited for her; he did not look like a dead man, cloudy with light slipping around the edges of whatever otherworld had torn open to let him through, like a shroud-tangled *Totentanz* refugee with black holes for eyes and his heart gone to dust decades ago, and she wondered what she was seeing. Memories patched like old cloth, maybe, self sewed back together with fear and stubbornness and the blind, grappling desire for life. She did not think he was as truthful as a phonograph recording, a daguerreotype in sepia and silver, more like a poem or a painting; slantwise. He might have been thinking the same, for all the care his eyes took over her—puzzling out her accuracy, her details and her blind spots, the flawed mirrors of her eyes from the inside. What did the dreams of the living look like, from the vantage point of the dead?

Then there was half a step between them, though she was not sure which of them had moved: both, or neither, as the cemetery bent and ebbed around them. The trees were a spilling line of ink, camouflage shadows bleeding into the low sky. With his glasses off, he looked disproportionately vulnerable, lenses less for sight than defense against whomever might look too closely. If she moved close, gazed into his colorless eyes, past the etched-glass shields of the irises and through the pupils, what she might read in the darkness there . . . "Menachem," she murmured, and his name caught at the back of her throat. So ordinary her voice shook, "Put your glasses back on."

For a moment he had the sweet, dazzled smile of the scholar she had pictured, staggered by the newly met face beneath the veil that he lifted and folded back carefully, making sure this was his bride and no other, and then he laughed. The sound was not seminary laughter.

"Clare, oy—" One stride into the wind that blew her hair up about them, dreamcatcher weave on the overcast air, and she felt him solid in her arms: breastbone against breastbone hard enough to jar her teeth through the buffers of cloth and coat, arms around her shoulders in a flinging afterthought; his delight like a spark flying, the crackling miracle of contact, and she hugged him back. He smelled like sweat, printer's ink and starched cloth, the powdery bark and fluttering leaves of the birch trees that she had walked through to meet him. Desire, wonder, curiosity; Clare roped her arms around his back, her chin in the hollow of his shoulder and his wild hair soft and scratching down the side of her neck, and held him fast. Embracing so tightly there was no way to breathe, no space for air, not even vacuum between them, like two halves of the universe body-slammed together and sealed, cleaving—

The wind rose as though the sky had been wrenched away. Clare shouted as a gust punched into her from behind, invisible boulder growling like something starved and let suddenly off its chain, snapped the scarf from around Menachem's neck and flung it at her throat like a wool garrote and it hurt hard as rope, all the whirlwind tearing at them, tearing loose. Thrown aside hard enough that her shoulder hurt from the deadweight jolt of keeping hold of one of his hands, arms jerked straight like cable and she heard a seam in his coat rip, she watched his face go liquid with terror: whatever a dead soul had to fear from a dream. The headstones were folding forward under the wind, peeling back, papery as dry leaves; names and dates and stars of David blown past her in fragments, bits of marble like a scarring handful of rain, even the flat, plate-silver sky starting to bulge and billow like a liquid surface, a mercury upheaval. When he cried out her name, the sound vanished in a smear of chalk-and-charcoal branches and granite that shed letters like rain. His glasses had evaporated like soap bubbles, not even a circle of dampness left behind. He was sliding away into landscape beneath her fingers.

His eyes were the color of nothing, void, before any word was spoken and any light dawned. When she blinked awake, sweat dried to riverbeds of salt on her naked skin, heart like something caged inside her chest and wanting out, even the close darkness of her bedroom felt bright in comparison. Still she wished she could have held him a moment longer, who had clung to her like a lifeline or a holy book; and she wondered, as she watched the sun melt up through the skyline's cracks and pool like burning honey in the streets below, whether she should have let go first.

Six days gone like flashpaper in the heat as August hurtled toward autumn, and she had seen nothing of him, not in strangers or dreams. The cemetery was there behind her eyes when she submerged into sleep, unclipped grass and birches like a palisade of ghosts, but never Menachem; the dreamscape held no more weight than any other random fire of neurons, brainstem spattering off images while her body tossed and settled under sheets that crumpled to her skin when she woke. She was already beginning to forget his articulate, unfamiliar face, the crispness of his hair and the rhythms of his voice, cadences of another place and time. Once or twice she even caught herself, in The Story Corner's little closet of a bathroom, looking over her reflected shoulder for his movements deep in the mirror's silver-backed skim.

Dream as exorcism, wonder-worker subconscious: it should have been so easy.

Preparing for classes, she sorted away books for the year, old paperwork and child psychologies and mnemonic abecedaries, stacking her library returns next to the Japanese ivy until she could take them back. Air that smelled of sun and cement came in warm drifts through the open windows, propped up permanently now that Clare's air conditioner sat out on the sidewalk between a dented Maytag and ripening trash bags, found art for the garbage collectors; music from some neighbor's stereo system like an argument through the wall, bass beats thumping out of sync with The Verve's melancholy guitars and hanging piano chords, "Weeping Willow" set on loop while she worked. Comfort music, and the smile her mouth moved into surprised her;

faded as the phrase's edge turned inward.

Off the top of the nearest pile, she picked up one of the books from the library afternoon with Brendan, considering weight in her hand before she opened it—blue ballpoint underlinings here and there, scrawled notes in the margins, some student's academic graffiti—and read aloud, "*There is heaven and there is earth and there are uncountable worlds throughout the universe but nowhere, anywhere is there a resting place for me.*" It might have been an incantation, save that Menachem did not answer; save that it was not meant for him. Her voice jarred against the rich layers of sound, the dissonant backbeat from next door. Self-consciously, she put the book down, paranoiac's glance around her apartment's shelves and off-white walls as though some observant gaze might be clinging in the corners like dust bunnies or spirits.

Brendan's card was still bleaching on the windowsill, almost two weeks' fine fuzz of dust collected on the stiff paper, black ink slightly raised to her fingertips when she picked it up and the penciled address on the back dented in, to compensate. Swatches of late-morning light, amber diluted through a sieve of clouds, moved over her hands and wrists as she leaned over the straight-backed chair to her laptop; paused the music, *Beside me*, pulled up her e-mail and started to type.

Full evening down over the skyscrapers, a milky orange pollution of light low in the sky like a revenant of sunset, by the time her doorbell buzzed; Brendan looked almost as startled standing in her doorway as she felt opening the door to him, so many days later than it should have been. Out of his suits and ties, grey T-shirt with some university crest and slogan across the chest and a worn-out blue windbreaker instead, he might have passed for one of the students that she had walked past a few hours ago at the library, younger and less seamless, Menachem without his glasses. Some shy welcome handed back and forth between them, too much space between replies, unhandy as an arranged date; he was still smiling, bright strands of hair streaked across his forehead with sweat and four flights of stairs, and Clare gestured him into the apartment with a wave that almost became a handshake, a panoramic introduction instead.

As she stepped past him to lock up the door, deadbolt snap and she always had to bump the door hard with her hip, she caught the odd half-movement he made toward her, slight stoop and lean, arrested: as if he had been expecting something more, an embrace or a kiss, Judas peck on the cheek before she led him in to the sacrifice. But he was no Messiah, anointed in the line of David; there were no terrors and wonders attendant upon him, only halogen and shaded lamplight as he looked absently across her bookshelves, the stacks of CDs glittering on either side of her laptop, back at Clare coming in from the little hallway and she thought her heartbeat was louder than her bare feet on the floor.

Shnirele, perele, gilderne fon: Chasidic tune she had not learned from Menachem, nothing he would ever have chanted and swayed to in his lifetime. She wanted to blame him anyway, as it ran through her head; nonsense accompaniment to her voice raised over the burr of the little fan on the bare-boards floor of her bedroom, behind the door half swung shut and her name in street-vendor's dragon lettering over the lintel. "I didn't see you when I took the books back this afternoon."

"Believe it or not," he answered, "I don't spend that much time at the library. Just that week, really. I needed some statistics." Wary camaraderie, testing whether they could simply pick up where they had left off or whether this was a different conversation altogether, if that mattered, "I guess I just got lucky."

She had to smile at that, at him, dodging any reply as he picked up a paperback of *The Day Jimmy's Boa Ate the Wash* and flipped through the meticulous, ridiculous illustrations. Lights peppered the night outside her window, streetlights and storefront glare and windows flicked to sudden brightness or snapped off to black, binary markers for each private life; sixty-watt eyes opening and closing, as on the wings of the Angel of Death. There was a tightness in her throat that she swallowed, that did not ease. Hands on the chair's slatted back, she observed, "You don't have your umbrella."

Not quite an apology, waiting to see where these lines were leading, "No."

"It was a really scary umbrella."

The same near-silent laugh that she remembered, before Brendan said dryly, "Thank you," and she thought in one burning second that he should have known better than to come here. On her threshold, he should have shied away, not stepped across the scuffed hardwood strip and almost knocked one worn oxford against the nearest milk crate of paperbacks: some twitch of memory, pole stars and shrugging with his arms full of umbrella, should have warned him off.

Never mind that Clare had known no one who had flashbacks from Menachem, leftover remains of possession like an acid trip. She rarely saw again those people whom he had put on and taken off, unless she could not avoid them. Strangers made briefly familiar and not themselves, their secret that she carried and they might never guess: she never dared. If Brendan had any recollection of a dybbuk swimming like smoke in his blood, he should have run from Clare's apartment as though she were fire or radiation, a daughter of Lilith beckoning from beyond his reflection, trawling for his soul. But he was standing next to her desk, perusing children's books in the sticky breeze through the windows, and Clare did not want to know what he remembered from ten days ago, whether he remembered anything; and why he was still here, if he did.

Before she could find out, she called softly, "Brendan," and when he glanced up from Dr. Seuss, no catch in her throat this time, "Menachem Schuyler."

Bewilderment rose in Brendan's face, but no following curiosity. The dybbuk was there instead.

Always before, he had stepped sideways into being when Clare was not looking; now she kept her eyes on Brendan and saw how Menachem moved into him, like a tide, an inhalation, filling him out; rounding into life beneath his skin, his flesh gravid with remembrance. His features did not press up through Brendan's, skull underneath the face's mask of meat, but all its expressions were abruptly his own. She held on to the dog-eared, dreaming memory of his face seen under a tarnished-metal sky, and said quietly, inadequate sound for all of what lay between them, "Hey."

Menachem said, "I dreamed of you."

A sharp, stupid pang closed off her throat for a moment. He had always taken the world for granted, for his own. Half rebuttal, half curiosity, "The dead don't dream."

"The dead have nothing to do *but* dream."

"Don't make me feel sorry for you." Barely six weeks and already she might have known him all her life, to order him around so dryly and familiarly: childhood friends, an old married couple, and her next sentence stopped. Menachem was watching her through frayed-blue eyes, taller in a stranger's bones than she had dreamed him. Brendan stood with *Fox in Socks* in his hand and was not Brendan, and she had made him so. She had always known that there was too little room in the world.

No other way, no reassurance in that knowledge, and she said finally, "I dreamed of you," and shook her head, as though she were the one possessed; nothing loosened, nothing realigned. "He'll never speak to me again," as lightly as though it did not matter at all, another possibility chopped short as starkly as a life by fever and louse-nipped chills; shove friendship under the earth and leave it there, a picture book for a headstone, an umbrella laid like flowers over the grave. "I liked him."

He put down the book that Brendan had picked up, soft slap of hardcover cardboard against desktop, like a fingersnap. His voice was pinched off somewhere in his nose, hushed and sympathetic; no comfort, and perhaps none intended. "I know."

"Our parents never promised us to each other, Menachem," the name like the flick of a rein, the way his gaze pulled instantly to hers, a handful of jumbled letters to make him animate and rapt. "No pact before we were born. There's no rabbinical court in this world that will rule you my destined bridegroom. This isn't Ansky, this isn't even Tony Kushner. I can't write a good ending for this . . . " Too easily, she could recollect the particular scent of him, salt and iron gall and cigarette-paper flakes of bark, as she took a breath that still left her chest tight; barely a flavor in the warm night air, the phantom of a familiar smell. Halfway across the room, Brendan would have smelled like a newer century, Head & Shoulders rather than yellow soap, no chalk smudges on the shoulders of his coat. She said, inconsequentially, "I wasn't sure you'd come."

"You called me." A thousand declarations she had heard from him before, promises as impossible and persistent as his presence; now he said only, "I wouldn't stay away." Then he smiled, as she had never yet seen Brendan smile and now never would, and added, "I've never seen your apartment before. You have so many books, my sisters would have needed a month to get through them all," and Clare hurt too much to know what for.

"Don't." Cars were honking in the street below her window, hoarse voices raised in argument; maybe shouting would have been simpler than this whisper that backed up in her throat, fell past her lips softer than tears. "I can't look at these faces anymore. I'm trying to imagine what you look like, looking out, but there's nothing to see. You're here; you're not *here*. There's no one I can—find."

His voice was as soft, breath over Brendan's vocal cords; the faint rise of a question waiting to be rebuffed. "But you held me."

"In a dream." She made a small sound, too barbed for a laugh. "Forget everyone else, I can't even keep you out of my head."

He blinked. Faint shadows on the walls changed as he took one step toward her, stopped himself, stranded in the middle of the room away from shelves, desk, doorways, Clare; apart. "I didn't come to you," Menachem said carefully. With great gentleness, no cards on the table, "You came to me."

Clare stared at him. He stared back, Brendan's eyebrows tilted uncertainly, hesitant. Maybe she should have felt punched in the stomach, floor knocked out from under her feet; but there was no shock, only an empty place opening up where words should have been, blank as rain-blinded glass. Denial was automatic in her mouth, *That can't be true*, but she was not sure that she knew what *true* looked like anymore. He had never lied to her. She had always been waiting for him to try.

Brendan's hand lifted, folded its fingers suddenly closed and his mouth pulled to one side in the wry sketch of a smile; Menachem, she realized, had been reaching to adjust his glasses, a nervous habit more than ninety years too late. "When I'm not . . . with you," he started, choosing words as delicately as stepping stones, laying out for a living soul the mechanics of possession, occupancy, that they never discussed, "it's what I said, Clare, it's dreaming. Or it's a nightmare. For a soul to be without a body, without a world . . . I don't think I even believed in souls when I was alive," and this shrug she remembered from an afternoon of fading storm-light and streets cobbled with rain. "But I am not alive. And maybe I know better, maybe I know nothing; I know that I was in the place like a snuffed-out candle, where angels take no notice and even demons have better things to do, and you were there. In a graveyard, but there. With me.

"Clare, if there's one thing I want in this world, in any world, it's not to have died—I wanted so much more life, isn't that what all the dead say?" If she should have assented, argued, she had no idea; she listened, and did not look away. "But I would have died an old man before I ever met you. I wonder if that would have made you happier."

Clare smiled a little, though it was not a joke. *Do you love me?* Four words tangible and thorny enough on her tongue that for a moment she thought she had actually asked them, the chill and sting of sweat across her body in the seconds before he answered, and a high school musical flashed through her mind instead. Golde's squawk of disbelief, *Do I what?* and the scathing dismissal of her advisor in college, *took Tevye and made him into a chorus line—tra-la-la-la-la, pogroms ain't that bad!* One of her own great-grandfathers had lost a brother in a maelstrom of shouting students and iron-shod hooves, taken a saber cut across his temple that he carried like a badge through two marriages, past quarantine in Holland and all the way to his New Jersey grave. Those same politics had no more than grazed Menachem, set him alight with ideas, left him for the angel of tenement bedclothes to destroy. Broken branches on the Tree of Life. She wondered if it looked like a birch sometimes.

He was close enough now that if she reached out her arms, she could have held him as in dreams, in the flesh. He had kept the distance between them; she had moved, bare heel down onto the varnished pine as hard as onto folded cloth and something inside that crunched, snapped, would cut if carelessly unwrapped. Menachem was silent, no dares or teasing, cleverness proffered to coax her into laughter, her smiles that had paved the way for him in this alien, unpromised land; quiet, as he had been in rare moments when she saw through more layers than that day's borrowed skin, as he had waited in the cemetery that existed nowhere but the fragile regions of dream. She could send him away now and he would never return, she knew this as though it had been inscribed on the inside of her skin, precise and fiery hand engraving on the level of cells and DNA, deep as belief. She needed no name holier than his own, nothing more mystic than the will not to want; and wherever the soul of Menachem ben Zvi v'Tsippe fled, it would be none of Clare Tcheresky's concern.

She said, knowing it had never been the turning point, this decision made long ago and the dream only its signatory, smoke from the fire that was every soul, "I should never have touched you."

Menachem's cheerful slyness moved over Brendan's lines and freckles, resettled into a twist of sadness around the corners of his smile. Perhaps he had said these words before, perhaps never; no matter. "You still haven't."

This step she could not take back; the glass broken once and for all. "Then come here," Clare said, "come to me." As softly as though the words might summon a storm, make one of them vanish like a drying tear, she sang, "*Dortn vel ikh gebn mayn libshaft tsu dir,*" and turned her hand palm-up.

Brendan's fingers did not close around hers, the dybbuk like an armature within his body, moving him; if he had reached to embrace her, she would have stepped back and screamed like a siren and maybe never stopped. But behind the pupilled lenses of his eyes, a color that was no color swirled, faded, bloomed outward and Brendan fell to his knees, painful double-barreled smack of bone against flooring and she would have reached out to catch him, but nothingness still spilled from him in streams and veils, flesh on flesh too easy a betrayal, and she had only room for one in her arms right now.

Like trying to gather an armful of smoke, overflowing, reaching out to pull down a cloud: all vision and no weight. No chill against her skin, nothing like body heat, only the steady bleed that she watched disappear when it touched her outstretched arms, her fingers spread wide and her unguarded chest and throat, one skein even drifting against her face so that she saw through it, for less time than it took her to release the breath she had held, into a dull gleam of clouds and pewter, a crumble of ambiguous darkness like soot. Tattered glimpses of what lay between dreams, those of the living and those of the dead, and she would never close her eyes on only one world again. On hands and knees now, Brendan coughed, hoarse and racking, and his body jerked as though all the muscles were climbing away from one another under skin and cotton and nylon; tarantella of sinew and flesh that chattered Clare's teeth, fingers buried in a lightning bolt and not enough sense to pull away, but the last nothing haze was soaking into her hand and gone.

Dimly, through sheetrock and posters, she heard music starting up, the same electronic slam from this afternoon. After all the buildup, what a finish: walking three apartments down the corridor whose doors were all painted the same monotonous sage-green as the banisters and stairs that cored the building, and walking back again without ever asking them to turn down the noise, the endless party that always seemed to be happening behind 5G's door once the sun went down; one ordinary night, with dybbuk. Her head felt no different, if dizzy, her fingers flexed and folded like her own; only someone might have hung lead weights from all her joints when she was not looking, so that she sat down abruptly on the floor beside Brendan, one hand out behind her for balance and the back of her knuckles brushed against the rumpled sleeve of his windbreaker. No danger, now. When she looked over and down at his long, sprawled form, merciful blackout or the next best thing, Clare realized that she was still looking for the little giveaways of gaze and movement and inhabitance, tell-tale pointers to the presence beneath his skin. She had never considered what it might be like to look for them in herself.

She parted her lips to speak Menachem's name, closed them instead. Beside her, Brendan stirred and groaned, "Oh, God," a vague mush of syllables and sense; his face was pressed against her floor, his eyes still shut. Gently, she touched his shoulder and said his name, as odd to the taste as Menachem's might not have been. Still she tried to sort through her thoughts, to find what she would say when he opened his eyes, what comfort or acceptable explanation, this last time with Brendan.

The last few days of the month, as the fragile rind of feather-white moon and the stars she could not see for the city's horizon glow pronounced; coincidence of lunar and Gregorian calendars, and some of the nights had begun to turn cold. Clare had hauled an old quilt from the top shelf of her bedroom closet, periwinkle-blue cloth from her childhood washed down to the color of skimmed milk, and occasionally woke to a sky as wind-scoured and palely electric as autumn. The day before yesterday, she had worked her last shift at The Story Corner, said goodbye to Lila until next summer and turned a small percentage of her paycheck into an Eric Kimmel splurge: some of the stories too old to read to her class in a couple of weeks, most for herself, tradition and innovation wound together as neatly as the braided wax of a candle, an egg-glazed plait of bread.

Cross-legged on her bed, she read two retellings of Hershel Ostropolier aloud to the little pool of lamplight that made slate-colored shadows where the quilt rucked up, yellow and steadier than any dancing flame. She had lit a candle on the windowsill when the sun set, but it had burned down to the bottom of the glass; wax and ashes melted there.

When she leaned over to lay the book down on the jackstraw heap accumulating near the head of her bed, her shadow distorted to follow, sliding bars of dark that teased the corners of her vision, and she made a butterfly shape with her hands against the nearest wall. Out in the other room, *Blood on the Tracks* had finished and *Highway 61 Revisited* come on, Dylan's voice wailing right beside his harmonica, "Like a Rolling Stone." Homeless, nameless, roving: Clare had never been any of these things, but she knew something of how they felt; and she sang along as best as she could find the melody while she stripped off her clothes, black and white Dresden Dolls T-shirt and cutoff jeans, unremarkable underwear and socks all tossed into the same milk crate in the far corner, and stood for a moment in the lamp's frank shine before turning back the covers. Another chill night, wind like silver foil over the roofs, and she would have welcomed some warmth beside her as she tucked her feet up between the cool sheets; but she had chosen, she might sleep cold for the rest of her life, and she was not sorry.

If she pressed her face into the pillow, she could imagine a scent that did not belong to her own hair and skin, her soap that left an aftertaste of vanilla: slight as a well-handled thought, the slipping tug of reminiscence, a memory or a blessing. *Zichrono liv'rachah.* But her eyes were already losing focus, the Hebrew wandering off in her head toward smudges of free association and waking dream; Clare turned over on her side, arm crooked under the pillow under her head, and said softly into the shadow-streaked air, "*Zise khaloymes.*"

A murmur in her ear that no outsider would ever pick up, lover's tinnitus with the accent of a vanished world, Menachem said back in the same language, "Sweet dreams."

Together they reached out and turned off the light.

> My life gets lost inside of you.
>
> —Jill Tracy, "Hour After Hour"

*Tim Pratt used to spend a lot of time at the beach. He writes novels (like **The Strange Adventures of Rangergirl**) and stories and poems, and works as a senior editor at **Locus** . He lives in Oakland, California.*

A sentence about the story: "I used to spend my summers in some of the tackier beachfront areas of the North and South Carolina coasts, and I always thought there was something sinister about the tanned out-of-towners and their private beaches. And don't get me started on the perfidy of seagulls."

Gulls

Tim Pratt

Grady ran bounce-bouncing down the sidewalk, flip-flops flapping, face smeared with summermelted chocosicle, and Harriet swooped down (like a bandersnatch, she thought, like the poem I read to him) and grabbed him before he could jump off the curb.

He didn't struggle, only goggled with mint-green eyes at Monstrous Miniature Golf across the street. That's where he wanted to go, Harriet thought, to bat balls between Frankenstein's legs, to climb on the papier-machè tombstones. There were jagged fake trees (coathanger trees, she thought, all twisted and pointed) with rubber bats hanging like rotten bananas from the branches. Harriet clucked and guided Grady along, past the surf-shops and lemonade stands and not-so-discreet stripclubs. They were looking for a public beach access. Harriet's shoulder bag was swollen with towels and sunscreen and grocery-store-checkout romances, and it thumped against her as she walked.

Her nephew, dear Grady, sweet Grady, wanted to swim. That was all he ever wanted to do, swim or chase sandcrabs. He did that all day at the house, the rented house, crammed with relatives pitching in money to make a vacation possible. They slept six to a room in that house but none of them could have afforded it alone, and they were right on the beach. That didn't help now. Harriet had gone shopping with her three sisters and her nephew Grady, and Grady had stomped and been bored and Harriet offered to take him swimming for the afternoon. Her sisters only talked about children and Harriet had no children so she too was bored. She was nearly forty and worry-lined and fifty weeks a year she typed things she didn't understand and fed her cats. Now two weeks of vacation and she was at the beach, unnerved by bikinis and broken glass, surrounded by her squabbling kin who made her nervous, all but Grady, who was almost a son. Once a man had promised to marry her and give her children, but he was gone and no children though they'd done it enough, the thing that makes children, but not enough or well enough to keep him from leaving her, she supposed.

She sweated under her floppy hat and even through tinted glasses everything flashed neon and gleamed metal. She could hardly believe there was an ocean nearby. She could have been in a beach-town theme park, otherwise in the middle of a baking desert. She giggled at the thought and Grady giggled because laughter made him happy. He was already tanned brown despite the pale promise of his yellow hair, just like his mother's and Harriet's (though his mother seldom laughed and never just to make Grady laugh, what sort of mother was that?). Everywhere metal now and no surf sound, only the whoosh of passing cars (too close, even holding his hand it was too close and she moved him away from the street), no salt smell just exhaust and the fried reek of fast food. Nothing to really speak of beach except the wheeling gulls, like styrofoam gliders overhead, and they flew over other places, inland dumps and sewage treatment plants. The beach is there, she thought, craning her neck to look around buildings and dumpsters; only show me the way.

And then a blue sign, standing up rusty and bullet-holed in a weedy gravel lot, blue with a zigzag diagram of waves and a cartoon picnic table with umbrella. There were no cars in the lot, tiny as it was and jammed between a white hotel and the bar (featuring wet t-shirt contest amateurs only) they'd just passed. "Look, Grady, the beach!" and he streaked but she held his hand and he bounced back like a paddleball. They couldn't really see the beach, but a boardwalk stretched over the grass-covered dune, its steps drifted with fine sand. They crunched over gravel, Grady babbling excitedly about dolphins and mermaids and octopuses and crabs, and clomped over the boardwalk.

Fifty yards of walking before the beach. A high fence of weathered wood ran along the right side, partitioning the beach for the people in the hotel. The fence ran for a distance even into the water before giving up hope of division. Harriet heard happy shouts and laughter from the other side. It was a gleaming white hotel with balconies on the back; she could see the top floors rising over the fence, much better than the ramshackle crammed-in house with rusty showerheads and sand in the mattresses. Same water, she thought, squelching her envy, they get the same beach we do.

But this was a sad little beach. Grady surged like a live wire, pulling away and eager to be in the gray-green water, but she held on and stepped with distaste around broken beer-bottles and chunks of styrofoam. The horizon was infinite and curved but the air stank of fish. She saw a dead jellyfish on the line of the lapping water.

"Lookit the boy with the seagulls!" Grady said, and Harriet lifted her hat-shaded eyes to see a boy down the beach. He held his arms open, playing Messiah to the shorebirds who circled around him and dove at his feet. He had a jumbo-bag of potato chips and he scattered them, feeding the devotion of the birds. There was something horribly hungry about the gulls, dirty white feathers drifting and long beaks darting as they squabbled over fragments of food.

"Why they his friends?" Grady demanded, his jealousy an echo of Harriet's when she looked at the fence, screening off a beach without beer bottles and dead things.

"They'll come to anyone who feeds them," she said, "They're not really his friends, not like the animals in cartoons. They're just hungry." Grady nodded, already forgetting and looking at the water. She tenderly ruffled his short gold hair and wished there were time to teach him about friends, about being careful. He wouldn't understand that some people are true friends, but that some people only want to feed on you.

She spread a towel in the long thin rectangle of shade cast by the fence and told Grady to be careful and mind the undertow and stay in the shallows. He nodded, all impatience and eyeing the water, and bolted at her nod. She smiled after him and rummaged through her bag for sunscreen and her current gaudy romance novel; she knew they were foolish, and told herself she read them only because that is what women alone on the beach do, but secretly she loved them and dreamed.

She looked up to check on Grady and he was deep, dog-paddling deeper. "Grady!" She stood and ran but he was swimming, bumping against the hotel's board fence in the water. He didn't hear. She slipped off her sandals and ran, glad she wore shorts now despite her pale thin legs. Her hat fell away and she barely had her feet wet when Grady disappeared around the fence. Harriet hung, a moment of indecision (like a seagull flying against the wind, suspended), then ran back up the beach. There was a gate in the fence, tacked with a sign that said "NO ENTRY." She tugged and it opened and she ran through.

An impression of clean sand, beach chairs and sleek dark people in bright swimsuits and trunks, a multitude of children, but her eyes were on Grady, swimming back to shore, grinning impish and in no danger of drowning. Curiosity, she thought, every little boy has to see what's on the other side of the fence, never mind the side they're on.

Grady came out and looked around, face aglow with sun and shiny with water, and Harriet took his hand, scolding until his smile faded and his eyes widened and he nodded, solemn as an owl. Grady never meant to be bad, and if you pointed out bad he seldom did it twice. Harriet was satisfied, even if her heart still pounded in her throat from running and fear, the fear (she imagined) of a mother for her child.

She held his hand and walked from the water to find every eye on her. A dozen adults, all so similar in height and color that they must be a hoard of brothers and sisters, all a bit younger than she was. The women were hurrying over, looking concerned, and the men stood in a group around the barbecue grill, the eldest with gray hair holding a spatula. The smell of cooking meat wafted toward her, slightly sweet, she couldn't place it. No smell of dead fish here. She blushed as the women, their oiled bodies firm and cared for beyond the fitness of youth, crowded around. One was older, white-haired, but her face had few lines and her black one-piece swimsuit fit snugly. She was a match for the man at the grill; grandparents to all those children, perhaps? Six wedding rings glittered on six hands, and Harriet supposed these women were married to those men, for all that their husbands looked like blood siblings, too. A similarity of taste, she supposed.

"Is he all right?" white-hair said, smiling a greeting. Grady was looking around them at the gaggle of children, from toddlers to almost-teens, laughing and splashing in the shallows and taking no notice of the interlopers on their beach. Grady was thrumming, wanting to be away with them, but Harriet held on.

"I'm sorry," she said, "I know we shouldn't be here, we'll go." The women exchanged glances with a familiarity that spoke of sisterhood; certainly it was a clan of daughters. But all the men shared the square-jawed features of the gray-haired man (now approaching in a polo shirt, spatula in one hand like a scepter) and they stood nursing beers like brothers.

"You'll do no such thing," white-hair said firmly. The youngest of the others smiled and licked her lips, then looked startled when she met Harriet's eyes. "The boy frightened you, and the beach is awful beyond the fence. Do stay. We'll help you watch the boy."

Grady hooked a finger in his mouth and looked up at the women, who cooed and smiled at him, but Grady seemed only fascinated by the bright colors of their swimsuits.

"We wouldn't want to be trouble," Harriet said, feeling every sag and brittleness of her body, thinking of the broad-shouldered square-faced men and wondering why she'd never found them, why she wasn't oiled and tan and beautiful.

The gray-haired man arrived in time to shake his head and say "No trouble at all, this family makes enough trouble on its own, you won't add to it. You're welcome to stay for dinner. There will be plenty."

He smiled, straight white teeth, and Harriet found herself nodding. Grady sensed the shift and darted toward the children, who greeted him and sucked him into their throng. There must be thirty children, she thought, and glanced at the women again. No sign of stretch-marks, no indications of motherhood, they'd borne perfect children and emerged perfect themselves.

The women hustled her aside giving introductions, establishing relations (though unclearly; three generations of a family on vacation, but which were married, whose children, who belonged to the old couple, and who were in-laws?). The women had long perfect nails and tiny teeth, and Harriet was aware of her own bitten-to-the-quick hands and coffee-stained smile. The women chattered and hardly noticed if Harriet answered. Did they ever ask her name? They certainly never used it. She wondered; why are they being so nice to me? Pity? She thought she heard something, a scream from the children and she turned, but they were only splashing in a knot, playing. She didn't see Grady; his golden hair should have stood out like a beacon in that sea of dark, but there were so many children, he was surely just out of sight, and the women were plucking at her sleeves for attention. The youngest, with her eager eyes, plucked too hard, her fingernails brought a crescent of blood on Harriet's forearm, making her gasp. The girl only licked her lips again and the white-haired woman slapped her daughter (in-law?) hard across the face. She dropped her eyes and murmured and apology. Harriet stared, shocked, but in a moment she was overwhelmed by chattering ministrations, offers of paper towels and exclamations over the small wound.

The white-haired woman smiled graciously, then laughed, looking beyond Harriet to the water. "Those children," she said, "Always snacking when we're about to have dinner."

Harriet turned to look, a tentative smile on her face. The dark children were crouched in a circle, eating something off the sand, reaching down with their hands. One child, very small, sat sullenly away from the rest, tearing at a half-rotted fish with her teeth, shooting glares at her cousins (brothers? sisters?) as she chewed.

"What?" Harriet began, standing, drawing breath to call for Grady. The gray-haired man shouted "These are done! Bring me more meat!" and Harriet smelled the sweet, unidentifiable odor from the grill again.

Why so friendly? She thought. What can they want from me?

The children scattered at the announcement of food, hurrying toward the grill, a flurry of graceful limbs and placid faces. They looked at Harriet as they loped past, wolfish faces and cool dark eyes. What they'd left steamed on the sand, ragged, scattered, wet. She saw a mass of golden hair and a jagged white stick, driftwood or a bone, driven into the sand beside it, but nothing she could call Grady. The gray-haired man called again for more meat, and his wife and daughters began plucking at Harriet's skin, silent now, no more chatter. Harriet didn't make a sound either, only stood, barely feeling the nips become tugs and wrenchings. She watched a cyclone of white gulls descend to fight over what the children had left.

Catherynne M. Valente is the author of ***The Orphan's Tales*** *series, as well as* ***The Labyrinth, Yume no Hon: The Book of Dreams, The Grass-Cutting Sword,*** *and two books of poetry,* ***Apocrypha*** *and* ***Oracles.*** *She lives in Virginia with her husband and two dogs.*

"The Maiden-Tree" came out of both the compelling similarity between the needle of the spindle and the needle of narcotics, and a serious consideration of the effects of the Sleeping Beauty story. What would happen to a body lying motionless for a hundred years? What would happen to a society in which essential tools were outlawed?

The Maiden Tree
Catherynne M. Valente

It is remarkable how like a syringe a spindle can be.

That explains the attraction, of course. A certain kind of sixteen-year-old girl just cannot say no to this sort of thing, and I was just that measure of girl, the one who looks down on the star-caught point of a midnight needle, sticking awkwardly up into the air like some ridiculous miniature of the Alexandrian Lighthouse and breathe: yes. The one who impales herself eagerly on that beacon, places the spindle against her sternum when a perfumed forefinger would be more than enough to do the job, and waits, panting, sweating through her corset-boning, for a terrible rose to blossom in her brain.

Well, we were all silly children once.

They could not get it out. I lie here with the thing still jutting out of my chest like an adrenaline shot, still wispy with flax fine as ash. Eventually the skin closed around it, flakes of dried blood blew gently away, and it and I were one, as if we had grown in the same queen's womb, coughed into the world at the same moment, genius and child, and I had spent those sixteen years before we were properly introduced chasing it like a dog her own bedraggled tail. My little *lar domestici*, my household god, standing over me for all these years, growing out of me, the skin-soil of my prostration, as swollen with my blood as everything else within these moss-clotted walls.

And these are the thoughts of a sleeping woman as she breathes in and out in a haze no less impenetrable than if it had been opiate-bred; these are the thoughts of a corpse kept roseate by the rough symbiosis of spindle and maiden, a possibility never whispered of in all the biology texts she ever knew, or hinted at by the alchemists who whittled sixteen years away burning spinning wheels to lead and ash.

I have been arranged here as lovingly as the best morticians could manage, my hair treated with gold dust so that it would lose none of its luster, even as it tangled and grew wild across the linen, and the parquet floor, up to the window-frames and dove-bare eaves. My lips were painted with the self-same dyes that blush the seraphs' cheeks in chapel frescoes, and injected with linseed oil so that my kiss would remain both scarlet and soft. My skin was varnished to the perfection of milk-pink virginity, violet petals placed beneath my tongue to keep the breath, no matter how thin it might become, fresh. From scalp to arch, I have been tenderly stroked with peacock-feather brushes dipped in formaldehyde (specially treated so as not to offend the nose of any future visitor, of course). The place where my breast joins the spindle has been daubed with witch-hazel and clover-tincture, cleaned as best as could be managed—all this was done with such love, devotion, even, before the briar sprouted beneath the first tower, and the roses put everyone else to sleep with me.

But they were not prepared, and this has become a tomb with but one living Juliet clutching her nosegay of peonies and chrysanthemums against her clavicle, her back aching on a cold stone slab.

You cannot imagine what has happened here.

My father stood behind me at each of the great bonfires—one at midsummer, one at midwinter, every year since my first. He kept me well away while those wide-spoked wheels were piled up like hecatombs in the courtyard, carted in on peasants' backs and in wheelbarrows, bound up in tablecloths and burlap sacks, dragged behind families in knotted nets. I was transfixed when they blazed and crackled, bright as Halloween, up to the sky in skeins of smoke and fire, sending off clouds of sparks like flax-seeds. The wheels spun the heavens like a length of long, black cloth.

Now you will be safe, he whispered, and stroked my golden hair. *Now nothing can hurt you, and you will be my little girl forever and ever, amen.*

But Father, I could not help but think, how will they spin without their wheels? There are less of them every year, and everyone is getting holes in their stockings. The sheep will snarl in their pastures, weighted to the mud by unshorn fleece! Folk will clothe themselves in brambles, and the markets will be so silent, so silent!

Hush, now, he sighed. *Don't think on that. You are safe, that is enough. I have done what was required of me.*

Will they move to the cities? Will they work in the factories under great windows like checkerboards of glass? Will they stitch a thousand breeches an hour, a hundred bonnets a minute?

No, he said, (and oh, his gaze was dead and cold!) *A textile factory is but a spindle with teeth of steel. They, too, will burn before you are a woman grown. Everything, everything, will be ashes but you.*

Oh, I whispered, *I see.*

I see.

And I inclined my head a little, into his great hand.

I remember the blueberries best, I think. How they grew wild beneath my window, and dappled the air with purple.

The roses took them, too.

I lie here, I lie here, and my hands are so carefully tented in prayer, frozen in prayer, but I hear, oh, how I hear, as only the dead can hear. Out of the loamy soil came a little sprig among the fat, dark berries, innocent as oatmeal, and I heard it come wheedling through the earth, sidling up to the stone. They cleared a space for it, watered it with delight, of course, once they ascertained its botanical nature—what could give the sleeping dear sweeter dreams than a rose blooming just here, below her bower?

Nothing, of course.

And it might have been alright, it might really have been nothing but a rose, white or orange or violet, buds sweetly closed up like pursed lips. But it sent out no flowers at all for months, while the gardeners frowned like midwives and buried fish heads in the flowerbed. It grew, upwards and onwards, and it might have been harmless if it had not found its tendrils brushing through my window one night when October was beating the glass in, if it had not crept slowly across the polished floor and grazed—so faintly!—my angelically positioned foot.

It lay against me for a moment, as though it meant only to decorate.

At first I thought it was my mother's voice—and I cannot recall when, in all these years, I recalled that there had been a witch, and a curse, and that curses generally come from witches, who possess more or less female voices of their own. It is so easy for a certain kind of girl to forget the origins of things.

But at first I did not even understand that I was sleeping. I thought it was the natural result of a spindle syringe, that the lovely warm feeling of *seeping* was what my father had meant to hid from me, the niggardly old fool. I lay back on the bed only because my head felt so hot, so hot, full of sound and the weeping of golden meats, and I could not stand, I could not stand any longer. And when I whispered to no one at all that there were all these red, red roses blooming inside me, I thought I was very clever with my turns of phrase, and would have to remember to write that down when I was quite myself again.

I did not feel as though I was falling, but rather that I had failed to fall. I lay there, and lay there, (and now it has become so much my habit to lie that I consider myself a student of the art, an initiate to its mysteries—no mystic with limbs like branches could outlast me) and there was a moment, just before dawn, when I tried to rouse myself to go down and sit at a table which surely held fried eggs and fine brown sausages speckled with bits of apple-peel, and made the inevitable discovery.

Of course I panicked, and thrashed in my scented bed, and shrieked myself into Bedlam—but none of this sounded outside the echoes of my own skull, and soon after my father—his face so haggard!—resigned and so thin, so thin, set his men to preserving my flesh. I was still screaming when they stopped up my mouth with wax, but they heard nothing, and patted my cheek with a refined sort of pity, as though they knew all along I was a bad girl, and would come to some end or another.

At first I thought it was my mother's voice. But something in the way it vibrated within me—well, a mother whispers in one's ear, does she not?

You are so beautiful, little darling, like light bottled and sold.

The spindle said it, I know that now, the spindle stuck in me like a husband, and it sang me through sleep with all these black psalms.

Beautiful, yes, but you cannot really think anyone is coming. Do you know what happens to a body in a hundred years? Some bourgeois second-son will hack through the briar—such labor is needed in a world without spindles, in the world your father made with his holocaust of spinning wheels, and there will be no shortage of starving, threadbare boys willing to brave the thorns for a chance at the goods in the castle—but not you, little lar familiari; he will be looking for the coats off of your aunties' frozen backs, for the shoes in a dozen closets, for the tableware and the tablecloths—oh, especially the tablecloths! He will be looking for curtains and carpets and scraps of damask, your mother's trousseau, your sister's gowns, as much as he can carry—and he will come upon this little room. He will be almost too revolted to enter; the smell of twelve hundred months of menses will wash the hall in red, (it will hardly be a year before you'll flood the wax stopper there), and then the smell of bed-sweat and bed-sores gone to fester, the smell of formaldehyde having long since conquered its pretty mask of flowers. He will hardly be able to open the door for the press of your grotesquely spiraling toenails. You'll be a stinking, freakish, blood-stuck frog pickled in a jar, and he won't see you but for the gold in your hair, and your long, lovely bridal dress which will not have been white for decades.

He'll strip you down as though he meant to be your lover after all. He'll take the dress, and the veils, and the sheets off the bed, he'll shave your hair to stubble and clip your nails for swords, and leave you naked and alone to rot in this tower until the next desperate prince comes through the roses and cuts you up for meat.

Please, please be quiet. I never did anything to you. I only wanted the needle, and the rose.

No one is coming for you. I am all you have, and I love you better and more loyally than all the princes in Araby. Who else would have stayed with you all this while?

Please. I want to sleep.

Aristotle said it was impossible. (Do not be surprised—girls with no natural defense against spindles are always classically educated.) He stroked a beard like lambswool after a March rain and assured a gaggle of rosy-testicled boys that one cannot bury a bed and expect a bed-tree to grow from that large and awkward seed.

But.

You can plant a maiden, oh yes, and watch the maiden-tree flower. And the spindle planted me into a bed, and the bed grew with me. And look, oh, look at us now.

I have wept in my sleep and watered it, but I might have saved the moisture. The rose-briar pushed its way into my heel, sinuously, insistently, as if trying to slide in unnoticed. There was a small, innocent popping noise when it pricked the skin, and left its red mark, predictably like a stigmata. It began a slow wind through the complicated bones of my ankle, and I could feel the leaves sliding against the meat of my calf.

Almost immediately, it detonated a blossom, a monstrous, obscene crimson unfolding on the wall like a spider, and the silence of its breathing clambered into my ear. The petals were crushed by a ceiling of skin, but no matter in a month or two those too will break through, and all my pores will be the roots of roses.

And with this I will tangle you up in me, came the spindle-voice, soft and shattered as a witch who has sold her soul for the magnitude of her spell. The roses came open inside my legs—oh!—the thorns broke through the nails of my toes, and there was red, nothing but red, everywhere.

If you had lived, you would still have had the spindle stuck in you—you cannot really escape it, the bruised fingers and the sheep-sweat smell of wool in your lap. Isn't it better this way? A rose is a rose is a rose is a maiden, maidens are supposed to be roses, and I will make of you a bed for flowers like erupting maidenheads—

Out of my torso the briars came, up around the shaft of the spindle, around my arms like shackles, around my throat, through my hair. I was soil, I was earth, I could not move and my flesh exploded into roses with a perfume like shadows. I screamed; I was silent.

I've saved you, you'll see. I am your spindle; I am your prince; this is my kiss. With this lacerate of flowers, I have taken you out of the world, the blighted, wasted world your beauty has stripped of cloth, the poor, rubbish-strewn landscape that was the country of your birth—it is all gone now, the vineyards and the rolling hills and the corn—

No, no, someone will come and gather me up like a sack of cotton and I will eat blueberries again and drink new milk and you will be nothing but a faint scar between my breasts and he will remark when we are old that it looks something like a star. I will never hear your voice in my bones again, you cannot keep seeding my skin forever—

I can. Whoever said this was a hundred-year sentence and not a whit more? Calendars lie, I lie. I lie inside you no less than a liver or a spleen, I breathe your breath, I rise and fall with your sleeping breast, my needle pulses in you, warm alongside your heart, and this is all there is.

They wound out of the room, splintering the door, down the stair, and it was not some sepulchral perfume that felled the court—no, no, the roses did it, the roses snapped round their calves and whickered a path to their throats. The stems shot past their lips and sent out their petals there like thick cakes, blocking their breath as mine was never blocked, tearing their lungs as mine were never torn. Trails of thin blood trickled out of five hundred mouths, five hundred gasps were stoppered up like water in a jar. The maiden-tree was in its summer, and from its briar-branches hung five hundred bright and bobbing fruits, orange-ladies and lemon-lords, cherry-sculleries and plum-cooks, and an apple-king, and a queen among figs.

I am not for them. I am for you alone.

And they were not prepared, they were not treated with gold and formaldehyde, their bodies grayed on the vine as bodies will do, and I can smell my mother's skin sodden through with mold, and I can smell my sisters rotting.

There is nothing but briars, briars all around, and throttling roses scouring the stone.

Nonsense, darling. I am here.

Please. I am so tired.

Years later, even the bed sprouted, little tendrils of green wandering out of the rain-saturated wood, seeking out more wetness, and finding all that there is to find here—my skin, my blood, my tears. The room which was ample to hold a maiden while she slept off an overdose has become a clot of green, snarled full of woody branches and tender, new shoots. I am enough to water them all, and the spindle is enough to water me. That is the biology of maidenhood.

And so it was that even the bridal bower became rooted in me, and the pillows were blossoms, and the coverlet was bark, and I was the heartwood, still and hard within. Aristotle, Aristotle, with your beard of briars, there are such secret things at work when a bed becomes a tree. I do not fault you for ignorance.

I have had a long time to think.

I am sorry about the needle.

Laird Barron's award nominated work has appeared in ***Sci Fiction, The Magazine of Fantasy & Science Fiction*** *and been reprinted in* ***The Year's Best Fantasy & Horror, Year's Best Fantasy 6*** *and elsewhere. Mr. Barron is an expatriate Alaskan currently at large in Washington State.*

"Proboscis" is set in and around the enigmatic Mima Mounds, a little-known tourist attraction in the hinterlands just south of Olympia, Washington. Over the decades, this rapidly-vanishing geological oddity has spurred its share of campfire tales in the region. It certainly inspired the story to follow."

Proboscis

Laird Barron

1.

After the debacle in British Columbia, we decided to crash the Bluegrass festival. Not we—Cruz. Everybody else just shrugged and said yeah, whatever you say, dude. Like always. Cruz was the alpha-alpha of our motley pack.

We followed the handmade signs onto a dirt road and ended up in a muddy pasture with maybe a thousand other cars and beat-to-hell tourist buses. It was a regular extravaganza—pavilions, a massive stage, floodlights. A bit farther out, they'd built a bonfire, and Dead-Heads were writhing among the cinder-streaked shadows with pagan exuberance. The brisk air swirled heavy scents of marijuana and clove, of electricity and sex.

The amplified ukulele music was giving me a migraine. Too many people smashed together, limbs flailing in paroxysms. Too much white light followed by too much darkness. I'd gone a couple beers over my limit because my face was Novocain-numb and I found myself dancing with some sloe-eyed coed who'd fixed her hair in corn rows. Her shirt said MILK.

She was perhaps a bit prettier than the starlet I'd ruined my marriage with way back in the days of yore, but resembled her in a few details. What were the odds? I didn't even attempt to calculate. A drunken man cheek to cheek with a strange woman under the harvest moon was a tricky proposition.

"Lookin' for somebody, or just rubberneckin'?" The girl had to shout over the hi-fi jug band. Her breath was peppermint and whiskey.

"I lost my friends," I shouted back. A sea of bobbing heads beneath a gulf of night sky and none of them belonged to anyone I knew. Six of us had piled out of two cars and now I was alone. Last of the Mohicans.

The girl grinned and patted my cheek. "You ain't got no friends, Ray-bo."

I tried to ask how she came up with that, but she was squirming and pointing over my shoulder.

"My gawd, look at all those stars, will ya?"

Sure enough the stars were on parade; cold, cruel radiation bleeding across improbable distances. I was more interested in the bikers lurking near the stage and the beer garden. Creepy and mean, spoiling for trouble. I guessed Cruz and Hart would be nearby, copping the vibe, as it were.

The girl asked me what I did and I said I was an actor between jobs. Anything she'd seen? No, probably not. Then I asked her and she said something I didn't quite catch. It was either etymologist or entomologist. There was another thing, impossible to hear. She looked so serious I asked her to repeat it.

"Right through your meninges. Sorta like a siphon."

"What?" I said.

"I guess it's a delicacy. They say it don't hurt much, but I say nuts to that."

"A delicacy?"

She made a face. "I'm goin' to the garden. Want a beer?"

"No, thanks." As it was, my legs were ready to fold. The girl smiled, a wistful imp, and kissed me briefly, chastely. She was swallowed into the masses and I didn't see her again.

After a while I staggered to the car and collapsed. I tried to call Sylvia, wanted to reassure her and Carly that I was okay, but my cell wouldn't cooperate. Couldn't raise my watchdog friend, Rob in LA. He'd be going bonkers too. I might as well have been marooned on a desert island. Modern technology, my ass. I watched the windows shift through a foggy spectrum of pink and yellow. Lulled by the monotone thrum, I slept.

Dreamt of wasp nests and wasps. And rare orchids, coronas tilted towards the awesome bulk of clouds. The flowers were a battery of organic radio telescopes receiving a sibilant communiqué just below my threshold of comprehension.

A mosquito pricked me and when I crushed it, blood ran down my finger, hung from my nail.

2.

Cruz drove. He said, "I wanna see the Mima Mounds."

Hart said, "Who's Mima?" He rubbed the keloid on his beefy neck.

Bulletproof glass let in light from a blob of moon. I slumped in the tricked-out back seat, where our prisoner would've been if we'd managed to bring him home. I stared at the grille partition, the leg irons and the doors with no handles. A crusty vein traced black tributaries on the floorboard. Someone had scratched R+G and a fanciful depiction of Ronald Reagan's penis. This was an old car. It reeked of cigarette smoke, of stale beer, of a million exhalations.

Nobody asked my opinion. I'd melted into the background smear.

The brutes were smacked out of their gourds on junk they'd picked up on the Canadian side at the festival. Hart had tossed the bag of syringes and miscellaneous garbage off a bridge before we crossed the border. That was where we'd parted ways with the other guys—Leon, Rufus and Donnie. Donnie was the one who had gotten nicked by a stray bullet in Donkey Creek, earned himself bragging rights if nothing else. Jersey boys, the lot; they were going to take the high road home, maybe catch the rodeo in Montana.

Sunrise forged a pale seam above the distant mountains. We were rolling through certified boondocks, thumping across rickety wooden bridges that could've been thrown down around the Civil War. On either side of busted up two-lane blacktop were overgrown fields and hills dense with maples and poplar. Scotch broom reared on lean stalks, fire-yellow heads lolling hungrily. Scotch broom was Washington's rebuttal to kudzu. It was quietly everywhere, feeding in the cracks of the earth.

Road signs floated nearly extinct; letters faded, or bullet-raddled, dimmed by pollen and sap. Occasionally, dirt tracks cut through high grass to farmhouses. Cars passed us head-on, but not often, and usually local rigs—camouflage-green flatbeds with winches and trailers, two-tone pickups, decrepit jeeps. Nothing with out-of-state plates. I started thinking we'd missed a turn somewhere along the line. Not that I would've broached the subject. By then I'd learned to keep my mouth shut and let nature take its course.

"Do you even know where the hell they are?" Hart said Hart was sour about the battle royale at the wharf. He figured it would give the bean counters an excuse to waffle about the payout for Piers' capture. I suspected he was correct.

"The Mima Mounds?"

"Yeah."

"Nope." Cruz rolled down the window, squirted beechnut over his shoulder, contributing another racing streak to the paint job. He twisted the radio dial and conjured Johnny Cash confessing that he'd "shot a man in Reno just to watch him die."

"Real man'd swallow," Hart said. "Like Josey Wales."

My cell beeped and I didn't catch Cruz' rejoinder. It was Carly. She'd seen the bust on the news and was worried, had been trying to reach me. The report mentioned shots-fired and a wounded person, and I said yeah, one of our guys got clipped in the ankle, but he was okay, I was okay and the whole thing was over. We'd bagged the bad guy and all was right with the world. I promised to be home in a couple of days and told her to say hi to her mom. A wave of static drowned the connection.

I hadn't mentioned that the Canadians contemplated jailing us for various legal infractions and inciting mayhem. Her mother's blood pressure was already sky-high over what Sylvia called my, "midlife adventure." Hard to blame her—it was my youthful "adventures" that set the torch to our unhappy marriage.

What Sylvia didn't know, couldn't know, because I lacked the grit to bare my soul at this late stage of our separation, was during the fifteen-martini lunch meeting with Hart, he'd showed me a few pictures to seal the deal. A roster of smiling teenage girls that could've been Carly's schoolmates. Hart explained in graphic detail what the bad man liked to do to these kids. Right there it became less of an adventure and more of a mini-crusade. I'd been an absentee father for fifteen years. Here was my chance to play Lancelot.

Cruz said he was hungry enough to eat the ass-end of a rhino and Hart said stop and buy breakfast at the greasy spoon coming up on the left, materializing as if by sorcery, so they pulled in and parked alongside a rusted-out Pontiac on blocks. Hart remembered to open the door for me that time. One glimpse of the diner's filthy windows and the coils of dogshit sprinkled across the unpaved lot convinced me I wasn't exactly keen on going in for the special.

But I did.

The place was stamped 1950s from the long counter with a row of shiny black swivel stools and the too-small window booths, dingy Formica peeling at the edges of the tables, to the bubble-screen tv wedged high up in a corner alcove. The tv was flickering with grainy black and white images of a talk show I didn't recognize and couldn't hear because the volume was turned way down. Mercifully I didn't see myself during the commercials.

I slouched at the counter and waited for the waitress to notice me. Took a while—she was busy flirting with Hart and Cruz, who'd squeezed themselves into a booth, and of course they wasted no time in regaling her with their latest exploits as hardcase bounty hunters. By now it was purely mechanical; rote bravado. They were pale as sheets and running on fumes of adrenaline and junk. Oh, how I dreaded the next twenty-four to thirty-six hours.

Their story was edited for heroic effect. My private version played a little differently.

We finally caught the desperado and his best girl in the Maple Leaf Country. After a bit of "slap and tickle," as Hart put it, we handed the miscreants over to the Canadians, more or less intact. Well, the Canadians more or less took possession of the pair.

The bad man was named Russell Piers, a convicted rapist and kidnaper who'd cut a nasty swath across the great Pacific Northwest and British Columbia. The girl was Penny Aldon, a runaway, an orphan, the details varied, but she wasn't important, didn't even drive; was along for the thrill, according to the reports. They fled to a river town, were loitering wharf-side, munching on a fish basket from one of six jillion Vietnamese vendors when the team descended.

Piers proved something of a Boy Scout—always prepared. He yanked a pistol from his waistband and started blazing, but one of him versus six of us only works in the movies and he went down under a swarm of blackjacks, tasers and fists. I ran the hand-cam, got the whole jittering mess on film.

The film.

That was on my mind, sneaking around my subconscious like a night prowler. There was a moment during the scrum when a shiver of light distorted the scene, or I had a near-fainting spell, or who knows. The men on the sidewalk snapped and snarled, hyenas bringing down a wounded lion. Foam spattered the lens. I swayed, almost tumbled amid the violence. And Piers looked directly at me. Grinned at me. A big dude, even bigger than the troglodytes clinging to him, he had Cruz in a headlock, was ready to crush bones, to ravage flesh, to feast. A beast all right, with long, greasy hair, powerful hands scarred by prison tattoos, gold in his teeth. Inhuman, definitely. He wasn't a lion, though. I didn't know what kingdom he belonged to.

Somebody cold-cocked Piers behind the ear and he switched off, slumped like a manikin that'd been bowled over by the holiday stampede.

Flutter, flutter and all was right with the world, relatively speaking. Except my bones ached and I was experiencing a not-so-mild wave of paranoia that hung on for hours. Never completely dissipated, even here in the sticks at a godforsaken hole in the wall while my associates preened for an audience of one.

Cruz and Hart had starred on Cops and America's Most Wanted; they were celebrity experts. Too loud, the three of them honking and squawking, especially my ex brother-in-law. Hart resembled a hog that decided to put on a dirty shirt and steel toe boots and go on its hind legs. Him being high as a kite wasn't helping. Sylvia tried to warn me, she'd known what her brother was about since they were kids knocking around on the wrong side of Des Moines.

I didn't listen. '*C'mon, Sylvie, there's a book in this. Hell, a Movie of the Week*!' Hart was on the inside of a rather seamy yet wholly marketable industry. He had a friend who had a friend who had a general idea where Mad Dog Piers was running. Money in the bank. See you in a few weeks, hold my calls.

"Watcha want, hon?" The waitress, a strapping lady with a tag spelling Victoria, poured translucent coffee into a cup that suggested the dishwasher wasn't quite up to snuff. Like all pro waitresses she pulled off this trick without looking away from my face. "I know you?" And when I politely smiled and reached for the sugar, she kept coming, frowning now as her brain began to labor. "You somebody? An actor or somethin'?"

I shrugged in defeat. "Uh, yeah. I was in a couple tv movies. Small roles. Long time ago."

Her face animated, a craggy talking tree. "Hey! You were on that comedy, one with the blind guy and his seein' eye dog. Only the guy was a con man or somethin', wasn't really blind and his dog was an alien or somethin', a robot, don't recall. Yeah, I remember you. What happened to that show?"

"Cancelled." I glanced longingly through the screen door to our ugly Chevy.

"Ray does shampoo ads," Hart said. He said something to Cruz and they cracked up.

"Milk of magnesia!" Cruz said. "And 'If you suffer from erectile dysfunction, now there's an answer!'" He delivered the last in a passable radio announcer's voice, although I'd heard him do better. He was hoarse.

The sun went behind a cloud, but Victoria still wanted my autograph, just in case I made a comeback, or got killed in a sensational fashion and then my signature would be worth something. She even dragged Sven the cook out to shake my hand and he did it with the dedication of a zombie following its mistress's instructions before shambling back to whip up eggs and hash for my comrades.

The coffee tasted like bleach.

The talk show ended and the next program opened with a still shot of a field covered by mossy hummocks and blackberry thickets. The black and white imagery threw me. For a moment I didn't register the car parked between mounds was familiar. Our boxy Chevy with the driver-side door hanging ajar, mud-encrusted plates, taillights blinking SOS.

A grey hand reached from inside, slammed the door. A hand? Or something like a hand? A B-movie prosthesis? Too blurry, too fast to be certain.

Victoria changed the channel to All My Children.

3.

Hart drove.

Cruz navigated. He tilted a road map, trying to follow the dots and dashes. Victoria had drawled a convoluted set of directions to the Mima Mounds, a one-star tourist attraction about thirty miles over. Cruise on through Poger Rock and head west. Real easy drive if you took the local shortcuts and suchlike.

Not an unreasonable detour; I-5 wasn't far from the site—we could do the tourist bit and still make the Portland night scene. That was Cruz' sales pitch. Kind of funny, really. I wondered at the man's sudden fixation on geological phenomena. He was a NASCAR and *Soldier of Fortune* magazine -type personality. Hart fit the profile too, for that matter. Damned world was turning upside down.

It was getting hot. Cracks in the windshield dazzled and danced.

The boys debated cattle mutilations and the inarguable complicity of the Federal government regarding the Grey Question and how the moon landing was fake and remember that flick from the 1970s, Capricorn One, goddamned if O.J wasn't one of the astronauts. Freakin' hilarious.

I unpacked the camera, thumbed the playback button, and relived the Donkey Creek fracas. Penny said to me, "Reduviidea—any of a species of large insects that feed on the blood of prey insects and some mammals. They are considered extremely beneficial by agricultural professionals." Her voice was made of tin and lagged behind her lip movements, like a badly dubbed foreign film. She stood on the periphery of the action, scrawny fingers pleating the wispy fabric of a blue sundress. She was smiling. "The indices of primate emotional thresholds indicate the [*click-click*] process is traumatic. However, point oh-two percent vertebrae harvest corresponds to non-[*click-click*] purposes. As an X haplotype you are a primary source of [*click-click*]. Lucky you!"

"Jesus!" I muttered and dropped the camera on the seat. *Are you talkin' to me*? I stared at too many trees while Robert Deniro did his mirror schtick as a low frequency monologue in the corner of my mind. Unlike Deniro, I'd never carried a gun. The guys wouldn't even loan me a taser.

"What?" Cruz said in a tone that suggested he'd almost jumped out of his skin. He glared through the partition, olive features drained to ash. Giant drops of sweat sparkled and dripped from his broad cheeks. The light wrapped his skull, halo of an angry saint. Withdrawals something fierce, I decided.

I shook my head, waited for the magnifying glass of his displeasure to swing back to the road map. When it was safe I hit the playback button. Same scene on the view panel. This time when Penny entered the frame she pointed at me and intoned in a robust, Slavic accent, "Supercalifragilisticexpialidocious is Latin for a death god of a primitive Mediterranean culture. Their civilization was buried in mudslides caused by unusual seismic activity. If you say it loud enough—" I hit the kill button. My stomach roiled with rancid coffee and incipient motion-sickness.

Third time's a charm, right? I played it back again. The entire sequence was erased. Nothing but deep-space black with jags of silvery light at the edges. In the middle, skimming by so swiftly I had to freeze things to get a clear image, was Piers with his lips nuzzling Cruz' ear, and Cruz' face was corpse-slack. And for an instant, a microsecond, the face was Hart's too; one of those three-dee poster illusions where the object changes depending on the angle. Then, more nothingness, and an odd feedback noise that faded in and out, like Gregorian monks chanting a litany in reverse.

Okay. ABC time.

I'd reviewed the footage shortly after the initial capture in Canada. There was nothing unusual about it. We spent a few hours at the police station answering a series of polite yet penetrating questions. I assumed our cameras would be confiscated, but the inspector simply examined our equipment in the presence of a couple suits from a legal office. Eventually the inspector handed everything back with a stern admonishment to leave dangerous criminals to the authorities. Amen to that.

Had a cop tampered with the camera, doctored it in some way? I wasn't a film-maker, didn't know much more than point and shoot and change the batteries when the little red light started blinking. So, yeah, Horatio, it was possible someone had screwed with the recording. Was that likely? The answer was no—not unless they'd also managed to monkey with the television at the diner. More probable one of my associates had spiked the coffee with a miracle agent and I was hallucinating. Seemed out of character for those greedy bastards, even for the sake of a practical joke on their third wheel—dope was expensive and it wasn't like we were expecting a big payday.

The remaining options weren't very appealing.

My cell whined, a dentist's drill in my shirt pocket. It was Rob Fries from his patio office in Gardena Rob was tall, bulky, pink on top and garbed according to his impression of what Miami vice cops might've worn in a bygone era, such as the '80s. Rob also had the notion he was my agent despite the fact I'd fired him ten years ago after he handed me one too-many scripts for laxative testimonials. I almost broke into tears when I heard his voice on the buzzing line. "Man, am I glad you called!" I said loudly enough to elicit another scowl from Cruz.

"Hola, compadre. What a splash y'all made on page 16. '*American Yahoos Run Amok!*' goes the headline, which is a quote of the Calgary rag. Too bad the stupid bastards let our birds fly the coop. Woulda been better press if they fried 'em. Well, they don't have the death penalty, but you get the point. Even so, I see a major motion picture deal in the works. Mucho dinero, Ray, buddy!"

"Fly the coop? What are you talking about?"

"Uh, you haven't heard? Piers and the broad walked. Hell, they probably beat you outta town."

"You better fill me in." Indigestion was eating the lining of my esophagus.

"Real weird story. Some schmuck from Central Casting accidentally turned 'em loose. The paperwork got misfiled or somesuch bullshit. The muckety-mucks are po'd. Blows your mind, don't it?"

"Right," I said in my actor's tone. I fell back on this when my mind was in neutral but etiquette dictated a polite response. Up front, Cruz and Hart were bickering, hadn't caught my exclamation. No way was I going to illuminate them regarding this development—Christ, they'd almost certainly consider pulling a u-turn and speeding back to Canada. The home office would be calling any second now to relay the news; probably had been trying to get through for hours—Hart hated phones, usually kept his stashed in the glovebox.

There was a burst of chittery static. "—returning your call. Keep getting the answering service. You won't believe it—I was having lunch with this chick used to be one of Johnny Carson's secretaries, yeah? And she said her best friend is shacking with an exec who just frickin' adored you in *Clancy & Spot.* Frickin' adored you! I told my gal pal to pass the word you were riding along on this bounty hunter gig, see what shakes loose."

"Oh, thanks, Rob. Which exec?"

"Lemmesee—uh, Harry Buford. Remember him? He floated deals for the *Alpha Team*, some other stuff. Nice as hell. Frickin' adores you, buddy."

"Harry Buford? Looks like the Elephant Man's older, fatter brother, loves pastels and lives in Mexico half the year because he's fond of underage Chicano girls? Did an expose piece on the evils of Hollywood, got himself blackballed? That the guy?"

"Well, yeah. But he's still got an ear to the ground. And he frickin'—"

"Adores me. Got it. Tell your girlfriend we'll all do lunch, or whatever."

"Anywhoo, how you faring with the gorillas?"

"Um, great. We're on our way to see the Mima Mounds."

"What? You on a nature study?"

"Cruz' idea."

"The Mima Mounds. Wow. Never heard of them. Burial grounds, huh?"

"Earth heaves, I guess. They've got them all over the world—Norway, South America, Eastern Washington—I don't know where all. I lost the brochure."

"Cool." The silence hung for a long moment. "Your buddies wanna see some, whatchyacallem—?"

"Glacial deposits."

"They wanna look at some rocks instead of hitting a strip club? No bullshit?"

"Um, yeah."

It was easy to imagine Rob frowning at his flip-flops propped on the patio table while he stirred the ice in his rum and coke and tried to do the math. "Have a swell time, then."

"You do me a favor?"

"Yo, bro'. Hit me."

"Go on the Net and look up X haplotype. Do it right now, if you've got a minute."

"X-whatsis?"

I spelled it and said, "Call me back, okay? If I'm out of area, leave a message with the details."

"Be happy to." There was a pause as he scratched pen to pad. "Some kinda new meds, or what?"

"Or what, I think."

"Uh, huh. Well, I'm just happy the Canucks didn't make you an honorary citizen, eh. I'm dying to hear the scoop."

"I'm dying to dish it. I'm losing my signal, gotta sign off."

He said not to worry, bro', and we disconnected. I worried anyway.

3.

Sure enough, Hart's phone rang a bit later and he exploded in a stream of repetitious profanity and dented the dash with his ham hock of a fist. He was still bubbling when we pulled into Poger Rock for gas and fresh directions. Cruz, on the other hand, accepted the news of Russell Piers' "early parole" with a Zen detachment demonstrably contrary to his nature.

"Screw it. Let's drink," was his official comment.

Poger Rock was sunk in a hollow about fifteen miles south of the state capitol in Olympia. It wasn't impressive—a dozen or so antiquated buildings moldering along the banks of a shallow creek posted with **NO SHOOTING** signs. Everything was peeling, rusting or collapsing toward the center of the earth. Only the elementary school loomed incongruously—a utopian brick and tile structure set back and slightly elevated, fresh paint glowing through the alders and dogwoods. Aliens might have landed and dedicated a monument.

Cruz filled up at a mom and pop gas station with the prehistoric pumps that took an eon to dribble forth their fuel. I bought some jerky and a carton of milk with a past-due expiration date to soothe my churning guts. The lady behind the counter had yellowish hair and wore a button with a fuzzy picture of a toddler in a bib. She smiled nervously as she punched keys and furiously smoked a Pall Mall. Didn't recognize me, thank God.

Cruz pushed through the door, setting off the ding-dong alarm. His gaze jumped all over the place and his chambray shirt was molded to his chest as if he'd been doused with a water hose. He crowded past me, trailing the odor of armpit funk and cheap cologne, grunted at the cashier and shoved his credit card across the counter.

I raised my hand to block the sun when I stepped outside. Hart was leaning on the hood. "We're gonna mosey over to the bar for a couple brewskis." He coughed his smoker's cough, spat in the gravel near a broken jar of marmalade. Bees darted among the wreckage.

"What about the Mima Mounds?"

"They ain't goin' anywhere. 'Sides, it ain't time, yet."

"Time?"

Hart's ferret-pink eyes narrowed and he smiled slightly. He finished his cigarette and lighted another from the smoldering butt. "Cruz says it ain't."

"Well, what does that mean? It 'ain't time'?"

"I dunno, Ray-bo. I dunno fuckall. Why'nchya ask Cruz?"

"Okay." I took a long pull of tepid milk while I considered the latest developments in what was becoming the most bizarre road trip of my life. "How are you feeling?"

"Groovy."

"You look like hell." I could still talk to him, after a fashion, when he was separated from Cruz. And I lied, "Sylvia's worried."

"What's she worried about?"

I shrugged, let it hang. Impossible to read his face, his swollen eyes. In truth, I wasn't sure I completely recognized him, this wasted hulk swaying against the car, features glazed into gargoyle contortions.

Hart nodded wisely, suddenly illuminated regarding a great and abiding mystery of the universe. His smile returned.

I glanced back, saw Cruz' murky shadow drifting in the station window.

"Man, what are we doing out here? We could be in Portland by three." What I wanted to say was, let's jump in the car and shag ass for California. Leave Cruz in the middle of the parking lot holding his pecker and swearing eternal vengeance for all I cared.

"Anxious to get going on your book, huh?"

"If there's a book. I'm not much of a writer. I don't even know if we'll get a movie out of this mess."

"Ain't much of an actor, either." He laughed and slapped my shoulder with an iron paw to show he was just kidding. "Hey, lemme tell'ya. Did'ya know Cruz studied geology at UCLA? He did. Real knowledgeable about glaciers an' rocks. All that good shit. Thought he was gonna work for the oil companies up in Alaska. Make some fat stacks. Ah, but you know how it goes, doncha, Ray-bo?"

"He graduated UCLA?" I tried not to sound astonished. It had been the University of Washington for me. The home of medicine, which wasn't my specialty, according to the proctors. Political science and drama were the last exits.

"Football scholarship. Hard hittin' safety with a nasty attitude. They fuckin' grow on trees in the ghetto."

That explained some things. I was inexplicably relieved.

Cruz emerged, cutting a plug of tobacco with his pocket knife.

"C'mon, H. I'm parched." And precisely as a cowboy would unhitch his horse to ride across the street, he fired the engine and rumbled the one quarter block to Moony's Tavern and parked in a diagonal slot between a hay truck and a station wagon plastered with anti-Democrat, pro-gun bumper stickers.

Hart asked if I planned on joining them and I replied maybe in a while, I wanted to stretch my legs. The idea of entering that sweltering cavern and bellying up to the bar with the lowlife regulars and mine own dear chums made my stomach even more unhappy.

I grabbed my valise from the car and started walking. I walked along the street, past a row of dented mailboxes, rust-red flags erect; an outboard motor repair shop with a dusty police cruiser in front; the Poger Rock Grange, which appeared abandoned because its windows were boarded and where they weren't, kids had broken them with rocks and bottles, and maybe the same kids had drawn 666 and other satanic symbols on the whitewashed planks, or maybe real live Satanists did the deed; Bob's Liquor Mart, which was a corrugated shed with bars on the tiny windows; the Laundromat, full of tired women in oversized tee-shirts, and screeching, dirty-faced kids racing among the machinery while an A.M. radio broadcast a Rush Limbaugh rerun; and a trailer loaded with half-rotted firewood for **75 BUCKS**! I finally sat on a rickety bench under some trees near the lone stoplight, close enough to hear it clunk through its cycle.

I drew a manila envelope from the valise, spread sloppy typed police reports and disjointed photographs beside me. The breeze stirred and I used a rock for a paper weight.

A whole slew of the pictures featured Russell Piers in various poses, mostly mug shots, although a few had been snapped during more pleasant times. There was even one of him and a younger brother standing in front of the Space Needle. The remaining photos were of Piers' latest girlfriend—Penny Aldon, the girl from Allen Town. Skinny, pimply, mouthful of braces. A flower child with a suitably vacuous smirk.

Something cold and nasty turned over in me as I studied the haphazard data, the disheveled photo collection. I felt the pattern, unwholesome as damp cobwebs against my skin. Felt it, yet couldn't put a name to it, couldn't put my finger on it and my heart began pumping dangerously and I looked away, thought of Carly instead, and how I'd forgotten to call her on her seventh birthday because I was in Spain with some friends at a Lipizzaner exhibition. Except, I hadn't forgotten, I was wired for sound from a snort of primo Colombian blow and the thought of dialing that long string of international numbers was too much for my circuits.

Ancient history, as they say. Those days of fast-living and superstar dreams belonged to another man, and he was welcome to them.

Waiting for cars to drive past so I could count them, I had an epiphany. I realized the shabby buildings were cardboard and the people milling here and there at opportune junctures were macaroni and glue. Dull blue construction paper sky and cotton ball clouds. And I wasn't really who I thought of myself as—I was an ant left over from a picnic raid, awaiting some petulant child god to put his boot down on my pathetic diorama existence.

My cell rang and an iceberg calved in my chest.

"Hey, Ray, you got any Indian in ya?" Rob asked.

I mulled that as a brand new Cadillac convertible paused at the light. A pair of yuppie tourists mildly argued about directions—a man behind the wheel in stylish wraparound shades and a polo shirt, and a woman wearing a floppy, wide brimmed hat like the Queen Mum favored. They pretended not to notice me. The woman pointed right and they went right, leisurely, up the hill and beyond. "Comanche," I said. Next was a shiny green van loaded with Asian kids. Sign on the door said THE EVERGREEN STATE COLLEGE. It turned right and so did the one that came after. "About one thirty-second. Am I eligible for some reparation money? Did I inherit a casino?"

"Where the hell did the Comanche sneak in?"

"Great grandma. Tough old bird. Didn't like me much. Sent me a straight razor for Christmas. I was nine."

Rob laughed. "Cra-zee. I did a search and came up with a bunch of listings for genetic research. Lemme check this . . . " he shuffled paper close to the receiver, cleared his throat. "Turns out this X haplogroup has to do with mitochondrial DNA, genes passed down on the maternal side—and an X-haplogroup is a specific subdivision or cluster. The university wags are tryin' to use female lineage to trace tribal migrations and so forth. Something like three percent of Native Americans, Europeans and Basque belong to the X-group. Least, according to the stuff I thought looked reputable. Says here there's lots of controversy about its significance. Usual academic crap. Whatch you were after?"

"I don't know. Thanks, though."

"You okay, bud? You sound kinda odd."

"Shucks, Rob, I've been trapped in a car with two redneck psychos for weeks. Might be getting to me, I'll admit."

"Whoa, sorry. Sylvia called and started going on—"

"Everything's hunky-dory, All right?"

"Cool, bro." Rob's tone said nothing was truly cool, but he wasn't in any position to press the issue. There'd be a serious Q&A when I returned, no doubt about it.

Cruz' dad was Basque, wasn't he? Hart was definitely of good, solid German stock only a couple generations removed from the mother land.

Stop me if you've heard this one—a Spaniard, a German and a Comanche walk into a bar—

After we said goodbye, I dialed my ex and got her machine, caught myself and hung up as it was purring. It occurred to me then, what the pattern was, and I stared dumbly down at the fractured portraits of Penny and Piers as their faces were dappled by sunlight falling through a maze of leaves.

I laughed, bitter.

How in God's name had they ever fooled us into thinking they were people at all? The only things missing from this farce were strings and zippers, a boom mike.

I stuffed the photos and the reports into the valise, stood in the weeds at the edge of the asphalt. My blood still pulsed erratically. Shadows began to crawl deep and blue between the buildings and the trees and in the wake of low-gliding cumulus clouds. Moony's Tavern waited, back there in the golden dust, and Cruz' Chevy before it, stolid as a coffin on the altar.

Something was happening, wasn't it? This thing that was happening, had been happening, could it follow me home if I cut and ran? Would it follow me to Sylvia and Carly?

No way to be certain, no way to tell if I had simply fallen off my rocker—maybe the heat had cooked my brain, maybe I was having a long-overdue nervous breakdown. Maybe, shit. The sinister shape of the world contracted around me, gleamed like the curves of a great killing jar. I heard the lid screwing tight in the endless ultraviolet collisions, the white drone of insects.

I turned right and walked up the hill.

4.

About two hours later, a guy in a vintage farm truck stopped. The truck had cruised by me twice, once going toward town, then on the way back. And here it was again. I hesitated; nobody braked for hitchhikers unless the hitcher was a babe in tight jeans.

I thought of Piers and Penny, their expressions in the video, drinking us with their smiling mouths, marking us. And if that was true, we'd been weighed, measured and marked, what was the implication? Piers and Penny were two from among a swarm. Was it open season?

The driver studied me with unsettling intensity, his beady eyes obscured by thick, black-rimmed glasses. He beckoned.

My legs were tired already and the back of my neck itched with sunburn. Also, what did it matter anyway? If I were doing anything besides playing out the hand, I would've gone into Olympia and caught a southbound Greyhound. I climbed aboard.

George was a retired civil engineer. Looked the part—crewcut, angular face like a piece of rock, wore a dress shirt with a row of clipped pens and a tie flung over his shoulder, and polyester slacks. He kept NPR on the radio at a mumble. Gripped the wheel with both gnarled hands.

Seemed familiar—a figure dredged from memories of scientists and engineers of my grandfather's generation. He could've *been* my grandfather. I didn't study him too closely.

George asked me where I was headed. I said Los Angeles and he gave me a glance that said LA was in the opposite direction. I told him I wanted to visit the Mima Mounds—since I was in the neighborhood.

There was a heavy silence. A vast and unfathomable pressure built in the cab. At last George said, "Why, they're only a couple miles farther on. Do you know anything about them?"

I admitted that I didn't and he said he figured as much. He told me the Mounds were declared a national monument back in the '60s; the subject of scholarly debate and wildly inaccurate hypotheses. He hoped I wouldn't be disappointed—they weren't glamorous compared to real natural wonders such as Niagara Falls, the Grand Canyon or the California Redwoods. The preserve was on the order of five hundred acres, but that was nothing. The Mounds had stretched for miles and miles in the old days. The land grabs of the 1890s reduced the phenomenon to a pocket, surrounded it with rundown farms, pastures and cows. The ruins of America's agrarian era.

I said that it would be impossible to disappoint me.

George turned at a wooden marker with a faded white arrow. A nicely paved single lane wound through temperate rain forest for a mile and looped into a parking lot occupied by the Evergreen vans and a few other vehicles. There was a fence with a gate and beyond that, the vague border of a clearing. Official bulletins were posted every six feet, prohibiting dogs, alcohol and firearms.

"Sure you want me to leave you here?"

"I'll be fine."

George rustled, his clothes chitin sloughing. "X marks the spot."

I didn't regard him, my hand frozen on the door handle, more than slightly afraid the door wouldn't open. Time slowed, got stuck in molasses. "I know a secret, George."

"What kind of secret?" George said, too close, as if he'd leaned in tight.

The hairs stiffened on the nape of my neck. I swallowed and closed my eyes. "I saw a picture in a biology textbook. There was this bug, looked exactly like a piece of bark, and it was barely touching a beetle with its nose. The one that resembled bark was what entomologists call an assassin bug and it was draining the beetle dry. Know how? It poked the beetle with a razor sharp beak thingy—"

"A rostrum, you mean."

"Exactly. A rostrum, or a proboscis, depending on the species. Then the assassin bug injected digestive fluids, think hydrochloric acid, and sucked the beetle's insides out."

"How lovely," George said.

"No struggle, no fuss, just a couple bugs sitting on a branch. So I'm staring at this book and thinking the only reason the beetle got caught was because it fell for the old piece of bark trick, and then I realized that's how lots of predatory bugs operate. They camouflage themselves and sneak up on hapless critters to do their thing."

"Isn't that the way of the universe?"

"And I wondered if that theory only applied to insects."

"What do you suppose?"

"I suspect that theory applies to everything."

Zilch from George. Not even the rasp of his breath.

"Bye, George. Thanks for the ride." I pushed hard to open the door and jumped down; moved away without risking a backward glance. My knees were unsteady. After I passed through the gate and approached a bend in the path, I finally had the nerve to check the parking lot. George's truck was gone.

I kept going, almost falling forward.

The trees thinned to reveal the humpbacked plain from the tv picture. Nearby was a concrete bunker shaped like a squat mushroom—a park information kiosk and observation post. It was papered with articles and diagrams under plexiglass. Throngs of brightly-clad Asian kids buzzed around the kiosk, laughing over the wrinkled flyers, pointing cameras and chattering enthusiastically. A shaggy guy in a hemp sweater, presumably the professor, lectured a couple of wind-burned ladies who obviously ran marathons in their spare time. The ladies were enthralled.

I mounted the stairs to the observation platform and scanned the environs. As George predicted, the view wasn't inspiring. The mounds spread beneath my vantage, none greater than five or six feet in height and largely engulfed in blackberry brambles. Collectively, the hillocks formed a dewdrop hemmed by mixed forest, and toward the narrowing end, a dilapidated trailer court, its structures rendered toys by perspective. The paved footpath coiled unto obscurity.

A radio-controlled airplane whirred in the trailer court airspace. The plane's engine throbbed, a shrill metronome. I squinted against the glare, couldn't discern the operator. My skull ached I slumped, hugged the valise to my chest, pressed my cheek against damp concrete, and drowsed. Shoes scraped along the platform. Voices occasionally floated by. Nobody challenged me, my derelict posture. I hadn't thought they would. Who'd dare disturb the wildlife in this remote enclave?

My sluggish daydreams were phantoms of the field, negatives of its buckled hide and stealthy plants, and the whispered words *Eastern Washington, South America, Norway*. Scientists might speculate about the geological method of the mounds' creation until doomsday. I knew this place and its sisters were unnatural as monoliths hacked from rude stone by primitive hands and stacked like so many dominos in the uninhabited spaces of the globe. What were they? Breeding grounds, feeding grounds, shrines? Or something utterly alien, something utterly incomprehensible to match the blighted fascination that dragged me ever closer and consumed my will to flee.

Hart's call yanked me from the doldrums. He was drunk. "You shoulda stuck around, Ray-bo. We been huntin' everywhere for you. Cruz ain't in a nice mood." The connection was weak, a transmission from the dark side of Pluto. Batteries were dying.

"Where are you?" I rubbed my gummy eyes and stood.

"We're at the goddamned Mounds. Where are *you*?"

I spied a tiny glint of moving metal. The Chevy rolled across the way where the road and the mobile homes intersected. I smiled—Cruz hadn't been looking for me; he'd been trolling around on the wrong side of the park, frustrated because he'd missed the entrance. As I watched, the car slowed and idled in the middle of the road. "I'm here."

The cell phone began to click like a Geiger counter that'd hit the mother lode. Bits of fiddle music pierced the garble.

The car jolted from a savage tromp on the gas and listed ditchward. It accelerated, jounced and bounded into the field, described a haphazard arc in my direction. I had a momentary terror that they'd seen me atop the tower, were coming for me, were planning some unhinged brand of retribution. But no, the distance was too great. I was no more than a speck, if I was anything. Soon, the car lurched behind the slope of intervening hillocks and didn't emerge.

"Hart, are you there?"

The clicking intensified and abruptly chopped off, replaced by smooth, bottomless static. Deep sea squeals and warbles began to filter through. Bees humming. A castrati choir on a gramophone. Giggling. Someone, perhaps Cruz, whispering a Latin prayer. I was grateful when the phone made an electronic protest and expired. I hurled it over the side.

The college crowd had disappeared. Gone too, the professor and his admirers. I might've joined the migration if I hadn't spotted the cab of George's truck mostly hidden by a tree. It was the only rig in the parking lot. I couldn't tell if anyone was behind the wheel.

The sun hung low and fat, reddening as it sank. The breeze had cooled. It plucked at my hair, dried my sweat, chilled me a little. I listened for the roar of the Chevy, buried to the axles in loose dirt, high-centered on a stump; or perhaps they'd abandoned the vehicle. Thus I strained to pick my companions from among the blackberry patches and softly undulating clumps of scotch broom which had invaded this place too.

Quiet.

I went down the stairs and let the path take me. I went as a man in a stupor, my muscles lethargic with dread. The lizard subprocessor in my brain urged me to sprint for the highway, to scuttle into a burrow. It possessed a hint of what waited over the hill, had possibly witnessed this melodrama many times before. I whistled a dirge through clenched teeth and the mounds closed ranks behind me.

Ahead, came the dull clank of a slamming door.

The car was stalled at the foot of a steep slope, its hood buried in a tangle of brush. The windows were dark as a muddy aquarium and festooned with fleshy creepers and algid scum.

I took root a few yards from the car, noting that the engine was dead, yet the vehicle rocked on its springs from some vigorous activity. A rhythmic motion that caused metal to complain. The brake lights stuttered.

Hart's doughy face materialized on the passenger side, bumped against the glass with the dispassion of a pale, exotic fish, and withdrew, descending into a marine trench. His forehead left a starry impact. Someone's palm smacked the rear window, hung there, fingers twitching.

I retreated. Ran, more like. I may have shrieked. Somewhere along the line the valise flew open and its contents spilled—a welter of files, the argyle socks Carly gave me for Father's Day, my toiletries. A handful of photographs pinwheeled in a gust. I dropped the bag. Ungainly, panicked, I didn't get far, tripped and collapsed as the sky blackened and a high-pitched keening erupted from several locations simultaneously. In moments all ambient light had been sucked away; I couldn't see the thorny bush gouging my neck as I wriggled for cover, couldn't make out my own hand before my eyes.

The keening ceased. Peculiar echoes bounced in its wake, gave me the absurd sensation of lying on a sound stage with the kliegs shut off. I received the impression of movement around my hunkered self, although I didn't hear footsteps. I shuddered, pressed my face deeper into musty soil. Ants investigated my pants cuffs.

Cruz called my name from the throat of a distant tunnel. I knew it wasn't him and kept silent. He cursed me and giggled the unpleasant giggle I'd heard on the phone. Hart tried to coax me out, but this imitation was even worse. They went down the entire list and despite everything I was tempted to answer when Carly began crying and hiccupping and begging me to help her, daddy please, in a baby girl voice she hadn't owned for several years. I stuffed my fist in my mouth, held on while the chorus drifted here and there and eventually receded into the buzz and chirr of field life.

The sun flickered on and the world was restored piecemeal—one root, one stump, one hill at a time. My head swam; reminded me of waking from anesthesia.

Dusk was blooming when I crept from the bushes and tasted the air, cocked an ear for predators. The Chevy was there, shimmering in the twilight. Motionless now.

I could've crouched in my blind forever, wild-eyed as a hare run to ground in a ruined shirt and piss-stained slacks. But it was getting cold and I was thirsty, so I slunk across the park at an angle that took me to the road near the trailer court. I went, casting glances over my shoulder for pursuit that never came.

5.

I told a retiree sipping ice tea in a lawn chair that my car had broken down and he let me use his phone to call a taxi. If he witnessed Cruz crash the Chevy into the Mounds, he wasn't saying. The police didn't show while I waited and that said enough about the situation.

The taxi driver was a stolid Samoan who proved not the least bit interested in my frightful appearance or talking. He drove way too fast for comfort, if I'd been in a rational frame of mind, and dropped me at the Greyhound depot in downtown Olympia.

I wandered inside past the rag-tag gaggle of modern gypsies which inevitably haunted these terminals, studied the big board while the ticket agent pursed her lips in distaste. Her expression certified me as one of the unwashed mob.

I picked Seattle at random, bought a ticket. The ticket got me the key to the restroom, where I splashed my welted flesh, combed cat tails from my hair and looked almost human again. Almost. The fluorescent tube crackled and sizzled, threatened to plunge the crummy toilet into darkness, and in the discotheque flashes, my haggard face seemed strange.

The bus arrived an hour late and it was crammed. I shared a seat with a middle-aged woman wearing a shawl and scads of costume jewelry. Her ivory skin was hard and she smelled of chlorine. I didn't imagine she wanted to sit by me, judging from the flare of her nostrils, the crimp of her over-glossed mouth.

Soon the bus was chugging into the wasteland of night and the lights clicked off row by row as passengers succumbed to sleep. Except some guy near the front who left his overhead lamp on to read, and me. I was too exhausted to close my eyes.

I surprised myself by crying.

And the woman surprised me again by murmuring, "Hush, hush, dear. Hush, hush." She patted my trembling shoulder. Her hand lingered.

*Yoon Ha Lee's fiction has appeared in **The Magazine of Fantasy and Science Fiction, Lady Churchill's Rosebud Wristlet, Ideomancer,** and **Shadows of Saturn.** She was born in the Year of the Horse. This story was written for the tigers in her family.*

Eating Hearts
Yoon Ha Lee

They tell many stories in that land surrounded on three sides by ocean, sometimes of foxes with small sharp smiles, sometimes of rats wearing men's clothing. They tell stories of the magician whose tomb was found empty after his death and of bones that beg for proper burial. Sometimes they speak of their first human king, a son of heaven, and his mother, a bear who had become human by meditating in the deepest and most dreadful of caves.

If they mention the bear's companion, it is to describe her pacing in the darkness, unable to sit still, then running out of the cave in shame, unable to become human.

"It's about not seeing," Chuan explained to her just after he brought the meal to the table. "The perfect magician is all-blind, all-unknowing. No sound reaches a wall to wake an echo; no touch bridges distance." He leaned back against the wall where, Horanga imagined, the cloth of his shirt hung over the hollow curve of his back. He lived in a house in the city, by the river, and long ago the sound of fish swimming endlessly in that river would have distracted her from her purpose.

"Then what do you do in this house?" asked Horanga, looking not at his face or his hands, but at the plate between them. The plate was heaped with tender vegetables, slivers of rare meat, and sliced nuts; over the vegetables and meat and nuts, he had drizzled three different sauces in a tapestry of taste.

"A *perfect* magician, I said." He smiled.

It was important to understand exactly what Chuan, this latest maker of magic, said to her. To do that, Horanga had to ask insolent questions, which was easy because a woman who came alone to a man's house had no pretense of virtue. She had walked away from her mother's family long ago to seek magic, and since no one in her mother's family would acknowledge her, she sought the more interesting thing: magicians. She was a striking woman, tall like a tree in the moment before wind and snow bring it down, and she had long loose hair and lips on the verge of promises.

Magicians were permitted their eccentricities and their dalliances. So Chuan had bought her new shoes, although she needed them not, and a new umbrella besides, and put a purse of his own coins into her hand, and invited her into his house. An old bargain.

Horanga looked back up at Chuan's face by way of his poised hand and the lines of his arm. She had tasted delicacies from every province, and she understood the importance of this moment. As they ate, the two of them, neither looked away from the other. And as they set down their chopsticks after the last mouthful, Chuan said, "I am, of course, far from being a perfect magician."

This disappointed her. "And why is that?" She knew the coquette's art of gazing down and to the side, of the hesitant touch, and disdained to use it. Such gestures belonged to younger women first of all and to women with shallower purposes most of all. A forthright gaze suited her better.

"The near-perfect magician," he said, "desires a single thing only, when desire he must. He desires it so perfectly that nothing else exists, and this is the root that nourishes his magic-making. At other times, in other places, he may live as ordinary men. But magic with nothing to distract it from its purpose—that is what he shapes."

"So a perfect magician desires nothing," said Horanga, who believed in stating things plainly. "And everything becomes possible as a solution to the desire he does not have."

"That is it," said Chuan, and his sober tone pleased her. She had spoken with many a magician in her travels, and not all of them had taken her seriously. "You must have a philosophical turn of mind, to grasp it so quickly. Was it to learn magic that you came here?"

"No," said Horanga with perfect honesty, and her gaze moved to the plates whence they had sated themselves. It was her turn to smile, and she averted her gaze to avoid alarming the man with what was in her eyes. "I am not interested in magic so much as I am interested in magicians."

She spoke of a category rather than a particular, but he understood her well enough.

Once, a tiger watched outside a window, yearning after human skin and human manners, but knew no means of obtaining them except by eating human hearts.

During the night, when half the moon hung low in the sky and its other half shone in fragments from the city's great river, Horanga said to the man beneath her, "For the desire that consumes your heart, O magician, what would you do?"

Other men had answered this question amid silks, or satins, or furs. She was offended by furs, though she should not be. In any case, they had said the expected thing to a woman above them. Chuan pleased her by saying, albeit in a teasing, dream-laden voice, "Other than this? I might walk blindfolded during the darkest hours, with no star overhead, no path underfoot."

It always came back to darkness above all other forms of deprivation. "Would you go into a cave, a place where no light has ever lived, and no wind has ever blown, and even the water has forgotten its wellspring?"

Chuan reached up to stroke a lock of her hair that would otherwise have fallen upon his face. "A perfect magician would see no need, having mastered all distraction. He would also see no reason why not. But a near perfect magician—why, yes."

"Into a cave while you have only the scantest of provisions to sustain you, and only a trickle of water?" Her voice grew lower, deeper, descending.

"Yes," he breathed, letting go of her hair.

"Into a cave with no space to lie down, and scarcely enough room to turn around and around?"

"Yes," he said again.

"Into a cave where the seasons blur into one long languid chill, and nothing varies but the speed of your pulse?"

"Yes."

Even a tiger can only eat so many hearts before they start to taste bitter, then sour, then like nothing at all. By that point, even a tiger's own heart, that rarest of delicacies, loses all savor.

Our tiger, who once watched outside windows, is not incapable of learning this.

Toward morning, when languor had fallen upon them and words returned, Chuan asked his own question. "You only ask about reasons to go into the cave and to stay there. Why not reasons to leave it?"

"You are here, and not in a cave. I should think that the question answers itself."

"And so it does," said the far-from-perfect magician. "How many hearts have you eaten, my dear?"

"Too many," she said, indifferent to numbers, but honest in essence.

"Were they all magicians' hearts?"

"Only later," Horanga said, unsurprised by his astuteness. He was a magician, after all.

"If you are waiting for a perfect magician," Chuan said, "you are looking for the wrong thing. You have a mantle of hair wholly black and you walk upon two legs. You did the better thing by refusing to let the cave consume you, long ago. You wanted to be something other than virtuous, which is to say, you wanted freedom. And you have it, which is one thing more than the mother of that long-ago king ever had."

"It is kind of you to say so," Horanga murmured. "But only humans become perfect magicians through their desire, because they need not become human first. I have discovered no way to eat hearts, of magicians or otherwise, while leaving them intact. I am willing to be enlightened if it does not require sitting still in meditation to find out."

"Nonsense," said Chuan, and took her hand, which had strong, slender fingers and fingernails that were merely fingernails. "About eating hearts, I mean."

Horanga gazed at him in astonishment.

"I have spent this last night demonstrating how to consume a heart while leaving it intact, as have you," said Chuan. "And it seemed to me that you were quite awake for it. Or do you, in the perfection of your desire, have no heart left for me to consume?"

They tell many stories in that land surrounded on three sides by ocean, sometimes of foxes with small sharp smiles, sometimes of rats wearing men's clothing. They tell stories of the magician whose tomb was found empty after his death and of bones that beg for proper burial. Sometimes they speak of their first human king, a son of heaven, and his mother, a bear who had become human by meditating in the deepest and most dreadful of caves.

If they mention the bear's companion, it is to describe her pacing in the darkness, unable to sit still, then running out of the cave in shame, unable to become human.

But the children of tigers, who are sometimes also the children of men, tell a different story.

*Jay Lake lives in Portland, Oregon with his books and two inept cats, where he works on numerous writing and editing projects, including the World Fantasy Award-nominated Polyphony anthology series from Wheatland Press. His current project is **Trial of Flowers** from Night Shade Books, followed by **Mainspring**, coming summer, 2007 from Tor. Jay is the winner of the 2004 John W. Campbell Award for Best New Writer, and a multiple nominee for the Hugo and World Fantasy Awards.*

Regarding "Dancing in the Light of Giants," Jay's young daughter wandered through the house one day singing, "I dance in the light of giants." He wondered what it meant, and so wrote the story to find out.

Dancing in the Light of Giants
Jay Lake

Red as an old man's eye, sun finally sets. Silver moon-braid glitters within the fog of stars in night's sky as I go forth. My time is come, I am to be a woman, but before I can take up with Kamm or henna my hair or keep chickens of my own, I must do this dance.

I am done with being a girl. I smile and ease my way shadow-soft through the stand of pecans gnarled and old that fence our little village. People watch me from behind tight-woven curtains or in their brass mirrors fogged with breath, but still I am alone for the first time in my life.

Rugged hills to the west are yet warm from the sun's kind regard. My feet tickle among moss and ferns, catch tiny sticks with a prick to remind me who and where I am. I arrive at the ridge and stand before the Man-High Gate. Here our people come when we grow large enough to be women and men, and here is where we finally go again when we are grown too large to be ourselves.

I slip through the standing stones with their glittering eyes, into the meadow beyond. "Look," I say aloud, laughing, "there is Grandfather Stott."

He lies buried, huge and proud, the great hook of his nose a thunderous echo of my own face's sharp curve. I run to Grandfather Stott. His eyes gleam like any star as I curtsey before him, stroking the long bridge of his nose, now taller than I am. I whirl into dance, exploding like a robin in a dust bath, throwing head and hair and arms out as offerings to the world. I will be a woman, see me dance.

After a while, the gleam in Grandfather Stott's eyes brightens to a beacon, casting my shadow on the hill and lighting the ridge so that from the village beyond it will look as if I have set a fire. I kiss his porous, stony cheek where his head swells above the bulging earth, then run on to dance for Auntie Swallowtail. There is a whole night yet, and dozens of the giants are still awake enough to see.

Dawn comes, orange and pure borne on wings of birdsong, as I lie gasping and sweating, coated with chilly dew just outside the Man-High Gate. My clothes are long gone to the dance, but as Kamm approaches me, I just smile. Knowing what he would find, he has brought a blanket and a shovel.

"Your mother sends this," Kamm says, draping the blanket over me. "And your father this." He lays the shovel down next to me. "Shall we dig?"

Now that I am a woman, I must begin to dig my pit, for someday when I am grown too large for the Man-High Gate I will come at dusk to lower myself into the earth and watch through the ages for new children to come dance in my light. But there are years between here and there, and Kamm to kiss and invite beneath my blanket and the birds sing their promise of morning.

In my life, dawn will never end.

Kelly Link is the author of two collections, ***Stranger Things Happen*** *and* ***Magic For Beginners.*** *She and her partner Gavin J. Grant publish books as Small Beer Press and also produce the 'zine* ***Lady Churchill's Rosebud Wristlet****. They live in Northampton and co-edit (the fantasy half of)* ***The Year's Best Fantasy and Horror*** *with Ellen Datlow.*

Monster
Kelly Link

No one in Bungalow 6 wanted to go camping. It was raining, which meant that you had to wear garbage bags over your backpacks and around the sleeping bags, and even that wouldn't help. The sleeping bags would still get wet. Some of the wet sleeping bags would then smell like pee, and the tents already smelled like mildew, and even if they got the tents up, water would collect on the ground cloths. There would be three boys to a tent, and only the boy in the middle would stay dry. The other two would inevitably end up squashed against the sides of the tent, and wherever you touched the nylon, water would come through from the outside.

Besides, someone in Bungalow 4 had seen a monster in the woods. Bungalow 4 had been telling stories ever since they got back. It was a no-win situation for Bungalow 6. If Bungalow 6 didn't see the monster, Bungalow 4 would keep the upper hand that fate had dealt them. If Bungalow 6 did see a monster—but who wanted to see a monster, even if it meant that you got to tell everyone about it? Not anyone in Bungalow 6, except for James Lorbick, who thought that monsters were awesome. But James Lorbick was a geek and from Chicago and he had a condition that made his feet smell terrible. That was another thing about camping. Someone would have to share a tent with James Lorbick and his smelly feet.

And even if Bungalow 6 did see the monster, well, Bungalow 4 had seen it first, so there was nothing special about that, seeing a monster after Bungalow 4 went and saw it first. And maybe Bungalow 4 had pissed off that monster. Maybe that monster was just waiting for more kids to show up at the Honor Lookout where all the pine trees leaned backwards in a circle around the bald hump of the hill in a way that made you feel dizzy when you lay around the fire at night and looked up at them.

"There wasn't any monster," Bryan Jones said, "and anyway if there was a monster, I bet it ran away when it saw Bungalow 4." Everybody nodded. What Bryan Jones said made sense. Everybody knew that the kids in Bungalow 4 were so mean that they had made their counselor cry like a girl. The Bungalow 4 counselor was a twenty-year-old college student named Eric who had terrible acne and wrote poems about the local girls who worked in the kitchen and how their breasts looked lonely but also beautiful, like melted ice cream. The kids in Bungalow 4 had found the poetry and read it out loud at morning assembly in front of everybody, including some of the kitchen girls.

Bungalow 4 had sprayed a bat with insect spray and then set fire to it and almost burned down the whole bungalow.

And there were worse stories about Bungalow 4.

Everyone said that the kids in Bungalow 4 were so mean that their parents sent them off to camp just so they wouldn't have to see them for a few weeks.

"I heard that the monster had big black wings," Colin Simpson said. "Like a vampire. It flapped around and it had these long fingernails."

"I heard it had lots of teeth."

"I heard it bit Barnhard."

"I heard he tasted so bad that the monster puked after it bit him."

"I saw Barnhard last night at dinner," Colin Simpson's twin brother said. Or maybe it was Colin Simpson who said that and the kid who was talking about flapping and fingernails was the other twin. Everybody had a hard time telling them apart. "He had a Band-Aid on the inside of his arm. He looked kind of weird. Kind of pale."

"Guys," their counselor said. "Hey guys. Enough talk. Let's pack up and get going." The Bungalow 6 counselor was named Terence, but he was pretty cool. All of the kitchen girls hung around Bungalow 6 to talk to Terence, even though he was already going out with a girl from Ohio who was six-feet-two and played basketball. Sometimes before he turned out the lights, Terence would read them letters that the girl from Ohio had written. There was a picture over Terence's camp bed of this girl sitting on an elephant in Thailand. The girl's name was Darlene. Nobody knew the elephant's name.

"We can't just sit here all day," Terence said. "Chop chop."

Everyone started complaining.

"I know it's raining," Terence said. "But there are only three more days of camp left and if we want our overnight badges, this is our last chance. Besides it could stop raining. And not that you should care, but everyone in Bungalow 4 will say that you got scared and that's why you didn't want to go. And I don't want to everyone to think that Bungalow 6 is afraid of some stupid Bungalow 4 story about some stupid monster."

It didn't stop raining. Bungalow 6 didn't exactly hike; they waded. They splashed. They slid down hills. The rain came down in clammy, cold, sticky sheets. One of the Simpson twins put his foot down at the bottom of a trail and the mud went up all the way to his knee and pulled his tennis shoe right off with a loud sucking noise. So they had to stop while Terence lay down in the mud and stuck his arm down, fishing for the Simpson twin's shoe.

Bryan Jones stood next to Terence and held out his shirt so the rain wouldn't fall in Terence's ear. Bryan Jones was from North Carolina. He was a big tall kid with a friendly face, who liked paint guns and BB guns and laser guns and pulling down his pants and mooning people and putting hot sauce on toothbrushes.

Sometimes he'd sit on top of James Lorbick's head and fart, but everybody knew it was just Bryan being funny, except for James Lorbick. James Lorbick was from Chicago. James Lorbick hated Bryan even more than he hated the kids in Bungalow 4. Sometimes James pretended that Bryan Jones's parents died in some weird accident while camp was still going on and that no one knew what to say to Bryan and so they avoided him until James came up to Bryan and said exactly the right thing and made Bryan feel better, although of course he wouldn't really feel better, he'd just appreciate what James had said to him, whatever it was that James had said. And of course then Bryan would feel bad about sitting on James's head all those times. And then they'd be friends. Everybody wanted to be friends with Bryan Jones, even James Lorbick.

The first thing that Terence pulled up out of the mud wasn't the Simpson twin's shoe. It was long and round and knobby. When Terence knocked it against the ground, some of the mud slid off.

"Hey. Wow," James Lorbick said. "That looks like a bone."

Everybody stood in the rain and looked at the bone.

"What is that?"

"Is it human?"

"Maybe it's a dinosaur," James Lorbick said. "Like a fossil."

"Probably a cow bone," Terence said. He poked the bone back in the mud and fished around until it got stuck in something that turned out to be the lost shoe. The Simpson twin took the shoe as if he didn't really want it back. He turned it upside down and mud oozed out like lonely, melting soft-squeeze ice cream.

Half of Terence was now covered in mud, although at least, thanks to Bryan Jones, he didn't have water in his ear. He held the dubious bone as if he was going to toss it off in the bushes, but then he stopped and looked at it again. He put it in the pocket of his rain jacket instead. Half of it stuck out. It didn't look like a cow bone.

By the time they got to Honor Lookout, the rain had stopped. "See?" Terence said. "I told you." He said it as if now they were fine. Now everything would be fine. Water plopped off the needles of the pitiful pine trees that leaned eternally away from the campground on Honor Lookout.

Bungalow 6 gathered wood that would be too wet to use for a fire. They unpacked their tents and tent poles, and tent pegs, which descended into the sucking mud and disappeared forever. They laid out their tents on top of ground cloths on top of the sucking, quivering, nearly-animate mud. It was like putting a tent up over chocolate pudding. The floor of the tents sank below the level of the mud when they crawled inside. It was hard to imagine sleeping in the tents. You might just keep on sinking.

"Hey," Bryan Jones said, "look out! Snowball fight!" He lobbed a brown mudball which hit James Lorbick just under the chin and splashed up on James's glasses. Then everyone was throwing mudballs, even Terence. James Lorbick even threw one. There was nothing else to do.

When they got hungry, they ate cold hot dogs for lunch while the mud dried and cracked and fell off their arms and legs and faces. They ate graham crackers with marshmallows and chocolate squares and Terence even toasted the marshmallows with a cigarette lighter for anyone who wanted. Since they couldn't make a fire, they made mud sculptures instead. Terence sculpted an elephant and a girl on top. The elephant even looked like an elephant. But then one of the Simpson twins sculpted an atom bomb and dropped it on Terence's elephant and Terence's girlfriend.

"That's okay," Terence said. "That's cool." But it wasn't cool. He went and sat on a muddy rock and looked at his bone.

The twins had made a whole stockpile of atom bombs out of mud. They decided to make a whole city with walls and buildings and everything. Some of the other kids from Bungalow 6 helped with the city so that the twins could bomb the city before it got too dark.

Bryan Jones had put mud in his hair and twisted it up in muddy spikes. There was mud in his eyebrows. He looked like an idiot, but that didn't matter, because he was Bryan Jones and anything that Bryan Jones did wasn't stupid. It was cool. "Hey man," he said to James. "Come and see what I stole off the clothes line at camp."

James Lorbick was muddy and tired and maybe his feet did smell bad, but he was smarter than most of the kids in Bungalow 6. "Why?" he said.

"Just come on," Bryan said. "I don't want anyone else to see this yet."

"Okay," James said.

It was a dress. It had big blue flowers on it and James Lorbick got a bad feeling.

"Why did you steal a dress?" he said.

Bryan shrugged. He was smiling as if the whole idea of a dress made him happy. It was big, happy, contagious smile, but James Lorbick didn't smile back. "Because it will be funny," Bryan said. "Put it on and we'll go show everybody."

"No way," James said. He folded his muddy arms over his muddy chest to show he was serious.

"I dare you," Bryan said. "Come on, James, before everybody comes over here and sees it. Everybody will laugh."

"I know they will," James said. "No."

"Look, I'd put it on, I swear, but it wouldn't fit me. No way would it fit. So you've got to do it. Just do it, James."

"No," James said.

James Lorbick wasn't sure why his parents had sent him off to a camp in North Carolina. He hadn't wanted to go. It wasn't as if there weren't trees in Chicago. It wasn't as if James didn't have friends in Chicago. Camp just seemed to be one of those things parents could make you do, like violin lessons, or karate, except that camp lasted a whole month. Plus, he was supposed to be thankful about it, like his parents had done him a big favor. Camp cost money.

So he made leather wallets in arts and crafts, and went swimming every other day, even though the lake smelled funny and the swim instructor was kind of weird and liked to make the campers stand on the high diving board with their eyes closed. Then he'd creep up and push them into the water. Not that you didn't know he was creeping up. You could feel the board wobbling.

He didn't make friends. But that wasn't true, exactly. He was friendly, but nobody in Bungalow 6 was friendly back. Sometimes right after Terence turned out the lights, someone would say, "James, oh, James, your hair looked really excellent today" or "James, James Lorbick, I wish I were as good at archery as you" or "James, will you let me borrow your water canteen tomorrow?" and then everyone would laugh while James pretended to be asleep, until Terence would flick on the lights and say, "Leave James alone—go to sleep or I'll give everyone five demerits."

James Lorbick knew it could have been worse. He could have been in Bungalow 4 instead of Bungalow 6.

At least the dress wasn't muddy. Bryan let him keep his jeans and T-shirt on. "Let me do your hair," Bryan said. He picked up a handful of mud pushed it around on James's head until James had sticky mud hair just like Bryan's.

"Come on," Bryan said.

"Why do I have to do this?" James said. He held his hands out to the side so that he wouldn't have to touch the dress. He looked ridiculous. He felt worse than ridiculous. He felt terrible. He felt so terrible that he didn't even care anymore that he was wearing a dress.

"You didn't have to do this," Bryan said. He sounded like he thought it was a big joke, which it was. "I didn't make you do it, James."

One of the Simpson twins was running around, dropping atom bombs on the sagging, wrinkled tents. He skidded to a stop in front of Bryan and James. "Why are you wearing a dress?" the Simpson twin said. "Hey, James is wearing a dress!"

Bryan gave James a shove. Not hard, but he left a muddy handprint on the dress. "Come on," he said. "Pretend that you're a zombie. Like you're a kitchen girl zombie who's come back to eat the brains of everybody from Bungalow 6, because you're still angry about that time we had the rice pudding fight with Bungalow 4 out on the porch of the dining room. Like you just crawled out of the mud. I'll be a zombie too. Let's go chase people."

"Okay," James Lorbick said. The terrible feeling went away at the thought of being a zombie and suddenly the flowered dress seemed magical to him. It gave him the strength of a zombie, only faster. He staggered with Bryan along toward the rest of Bungalow 6, holding out his arms. Kids said things like, "Hey, look at James! James is wearing a DRESS!" as if they were making fun of him, but then they got the idea. They realized that James and Bryan were zombies and they ran away. Even Terence.

After a while, everybody had become a zombie. So they went for a swim. Everybody except for James Lorbick, because when he started to take off the dress, Bryan Jones stopped him. Bryan said, "No, wait. Keep it on. I dare you to wear that dress until we get back to camp tomorrow. I dare you. We'll show up at breakfast and say that we saw a monster and it's chasing us, and then you come in the dining room and it will be awesome. You look completely spooky with that dress and all the mud."

"I'll get my sleeping bag all muddy," James said. "I don't want to sleep in a dress. It's dumb."

Everybody in the lake began to yell things.

"Come on, James, wear the dress, okay?"

"Keep the dress on! Do it, James!"

"I dare you," said Bryan.

"I dare you," James said.

"What?" Bryan said. "What do you dare me to do?"

James thought for a moment. Nothing came to him. "I don't know."

Terence was floating on his back. He lifted his head. "You tell him, James. Don't let Bryan talk you into anything you don't want to do."

"Come on," Bryan said. "It will be so cool. Come on."

So everybody in Bungalow 6 went swimming except for James Lorbick. They splashed around and washed off all the mud and came out of the pond and James Lorbick was the only kid in Bungalow 6 who was still covered in crusty mud. James Lorbick was the only one who still had mud spikes in his hair. James Lorbick was the only one wearing a dress.

The sun was going down. They sat on the ground around the campfire that wouldn't catch. They ate the rest of the hotdogs and the peanut butter sandwiches that the kitchen girls always made up when bungalows went on overnight hikes. They talked about how cool it would be in the morning, when James Lorbick came running into the dining room back at camp, pretending to be a monster.

It got darker. They talked about the monster.

"Maybe it's a werewolf."

"Or a were-skunk."

"Maybe it's from outer space."

"Maybe it's just really lonely," James Lorbick said. He was sitting between Bryan Jones and one of the Simpson twins, and he felt really good, like he was really part of Bungalow 6 at last, and also kind of itchy, because of the mud.

"So how come nobody's ever seen it before?"

"Maybe some people have, but they died and so they couldn't tell anybody."

"No way. They wouldn't let us camp here if somebody died."

"Maybe the camp doesn't want anybody to know about the monster, so they don't say anything."

"You're so paranoid. The monster didn't do anything to Bungalow 4. Besides, Bungalow 4 is a bunch of liars."

"Wait a minute, do you hear that?"

They were quiet, listening. Bryan Jones farted. It was a sinister, brassy fart.

"Oh, man. That's disgusting, Bryan."

"What? It wasn't me."

"If the monster comes, we'll just aim Bryan at it."

"Wait, what's that?"

Something was ringing. "No way," Terence said. "That's my cell phone. No way does it get reception out here. Hello? Hey, Darlene. What's up?" He turned on his flashlight and shone it at Bungalow 6. "Guys. I've gotta go down the hill for a sec. She sounds upset. Something about her car and a chihuahua."

"That's cool."

"Be careful. Don't let the monster sneak up on you."

"Tell Darlene she's too good for you."

They watched Terence pick his way down the muddy path in a little circle of light. The light got smaller and smaller, farther and farther away, until they couldn't see it any more.

"What if it isn't really Darlene?" a kid named Timothy Ferber said.

"What?"

"Like what if it's the monster?"

"No way. That's stupid. How would the monster know Terence's cell phone number?"

"Are there any marshmallows left?"

"No. Just graham crackers."

They ate the graham crackers. Terence didn't come back. They couldn't even hear his voice. They told ghost stories.

"And she puts her hand down and her dog licks it and she thinks everything is okay. Except that then, in the morning, when she looks in the bathtub, her dog is in there and he's dead and there's lots of blood and somebody has written **HA HA I REALLY FOOLED YOU** with the blood."

"One time my sister was babysitting and this weird guy called and wanted to know if Satan was there and she got really freaked out."

"One time my grandfather was riding on a train and he saw a naked woman standing out in a field."

"Was she a ghost?"

"I don't know. He used to like to tell that story a lot."

"Were there cows in the field?"

"I don't know, how should I know if there were cows?"

"Do you think Terence is going to come back soon?"

"Why? Are you scared?"

"What time is it?"

"It's not even 10:30. Maybe we could try lighting the fire again."

"It's still too wet. It's not going to catch. Besides, if there was a monster and if the monster was out there and we got the fire lit, then the monster could see us."

"We don't have any marshmallows anyway."

"Wait, I think I know how to get it started. Like Bungalow 6 did with the bat. If I spray it with insecticide, and then—"

Bungalow 4 fell reverently silent.

"Wow. That's awesome, Bryan. They should have a special merit badge for that."

"Yeah, to go with the badge for toxic farts."

"It smells funny," James Lorbick said. But it was nice to have a fire going. It made the darkness seem less dark. Which is what fires are supposed to do, of course.

"You look really weird in the firelight, James. That dress and all the mud. It's kind of funny and kind of creepy."

"Thanks."

"Yeah, James Lorbick should always wear dresses. He's so hot."

"James Lorbick, I think you are so hot. Not."

"Leave James alone," Bryan Jones said.

"I had this weird dream last year," Danny Anderson said. Danny Anderson was from Terre Haute, Indiana. He was taller than anyone else in Bungalow 6 except for Terence. "I dreamed that I came home from school one day and nobody was there except this man. He was sitting in the living room watching TV and so I said, 'Who are you? What are you doing here?' And he looked up and smiled this creepy smile at me and he said, 'Hey, Danny, I'm Angelina Jolie. I'm your new dad.'—

"No way. You dreamed your dad was Angelina Jolie?"

"No," Danny Anderson said. "Shut up. My parents aren't divorced or anything. My dad's got the same name as me. This guy said he was my new dad. He said he was Angelina Jolie. But he was just some guy."

"That's a dumb dream."

"I know it is," Danny Anderson said. "But I kept having it, like, every night. This guy is always hanging out in the kitchen and talking to me about what we're going to do now that I'm his kid. He's really creepy. And the thing is, I just got a phone call from my mom, and she says that she and my dad are getting divorced and I think maybe she's got a new boyfriend."

"Hey, man. That's tough."

Danny Anderson looked as if he might be about to cry. He said, "So what if this boyfriend turns out to be my new dad? Like in the dream?"

"My stepdad's pretty cool. Sometimes I get along with him better than I get along with my mom."

"One time I had a dream James Lorbick was wearing a dress."

"What's that noise?"

"I didn't hear anything."

"Terence has been gone a long time."

"Maybe he went back to camp. Maybe he left us out here."

"The fire smells really bad."

"It reeks."

"Isn't insect stuff poisonous?"

"Of course not. Otherwise they wouldn't be able to sell it. Because you put it on your skin. They wouldn't let you put poison on your skin."

"Hey, look up. I think I saw a shooting star."

"Maybe it was a space ship."

They all looked up at the sky. The sky was black and clear and full of bright stars. It was like that for a moment and then they noticed how clouds were racing across the blackness, spilling across the sky. The stars disappeared. Maybe if they hadn't looked, the sky would have stayed clear. But they did look. Then snow started to fall, lightly at first, just dusting the muddy ground and the campfire and Bungalow 6 and then there was more snow falling. It fell quietly and thickly. It was going to be the thirteenth of June tomorrow, the next-to-last day of camp, the day that James Lorbick wearing a dress and a lot of mud was going to show up and scare everyone in the dining room.

The snow was the weirdest thing that had ever happened to Bungalow 6.

One of the Simpson twins said, "Hey, it's snowing!"

Bryan Jones started laughing. "This is awesome," he said. "Awesome!"

James Lorbick looked up at the sky, which had been so clear a minute ago. Fat snowflakes fell on his upturned face. He wrapped his crumbly mud-covered arms around himself. "*Awesome*," he repeated.

"Terence! Hey Terence! It's snowing!"

"Nobody is going to believe us."

"Maybe we should go get in our sleeping bags."

"We could build a snow fort."

"No, seriously. What if it gets really cold and we freeze to death? All I brought is my windbreaker."

"No way. It's going to melt right away. It's summer. This is just some kind of weather event. We should take a picture so we can show everybody."

So far they had taken pictures of mud, of people pretending to be mud-covered zombies, of James Lorbick pretending to be a mud-haired, dress-wearing monster. Terence had taken a picture of the bone that wasn't a cow bone. One of the Simpson twins had put a dozen marshmallows in his mouth and someone took a picture of that. Someone had a digital photo of Bryan Jones's big naked butt.

"So why didn't anyone from Bungalow 4 take a picture of the monster?"

"They did. But you couldn't see anything."

"Snow is cooler anyway."

"No way. A monster is way better."

"I think it's weird that Terence hasn't come back up yet."

"Hey, Terence! Terence!"

They all yelled for Terence for a few minutes. The snow kept falling. They did little dances in the snow to keep warm. The fire got thinner and thinner and started to go out. But before it went out, the monster came up the muddy, snowy path. It smiled at them and it came up the path and Danny Anderson shone his flashlight at it and they could all see it was a monster and not Terence pretending to be a monster. No one in Bungalow 4 had ever seen a monster before, but they all knew that a monster was what it was. It had a white face and its hands were red and dripping. It moved very fast.

You can learn a lot of stuff at camp. You learn how to wiggle an arrow so that it comes out of a straw target without the metal tip coming off. You learn how to make something out of yarn and twigs called a skycatcher, because there's a lot of extra yarn and twigs in the world, and someone had to come up with something to do with it. You learn how to jam your feet up into the mattress of the bunk above you, while someone is leaning out of it, so that they fall out of bed. You learn that if you are riding a horse and the horse sees a snake on the trail, the horse will stand on its hind legs. Horses don't like snakes. You find out that tennis rackets are good for chasing bats. You find out what happens if you leave your wet clothes in your trunk for a few days. You learn how to make rockets and you learn how to pretend not to care when someone takes your rocket and stomps on it. You learn to pretend to be asleep when people make fun of you. You learn how to be lonely.

The snow came down and people ran around Honor Lookout. They screamed and waved their arms around and fell down. The monster chased them. It moved so quickly that sometimes it seemed to fly. It was laughing like this was an excellent fun game. The snow was still coming down and it was dark which made it hard to see what the monster did when it caught people. James Lorbick sat still. He pretended that he was asleep or not there. He pretended that he was writing a letter to his best friend in Chicago who was spending the summer playing video games and hanging out at the library and writing and illustrating his own comic book. *Dear Alec, how are you? Camp is almost over, and I am so glad. This has been the worst summer ever. We went on a hike and it rained and my counselor found a bone. This kid made me put on a dress. There was a monster which ate everybody. How is your comic book coming? Did you put in the part I wrote about the superhero who can only fly when he's asleep?*

The monster had one Simpson twin under each arm. The twins were screaming. The monster threw them down the path. Then it bent over Bryan Jones, who was lying half inside one of the tents, half in the snow. There were slurping noises. After a minute it stood up again. It looked back and saw James Lorbick. It waved.

James Lorbick shut his eyes. When he opened them again, the monster was standing over him. It had red eyes. It smelled like rotting fish and kerosene. It wasn't actually all that tall, the way you'd expect a monster to be tall. Except for that, it was even worse than Bungalow 4 had said.

The monster stood and looked down and grinned. "You," it said. It had a voice like a dead tree full of bees: sweet and dripping and buzzing. It poked James on the shoulder with a long black nail. "What are you?"

"I'm James Lorbick," James said. "From Chicago."

The monster laughed. Its teeth were pointed and terrible. There was a smear of red on the dress where it had touched James. "You're the craziest thing I've ever seen. Look at that dress. Look at your hair. It's standing straight up. Is that mud? Why are you covered in mud?"

"I was going to be a monster," James said. He swallowed. "No offense."

"None taken," the monster said. "Wow, maybe I should go visit Chicago. I've never seen anything as funny as you. I could look at you for hours and hours. Whenever I needed a laugh. You've really made my day, James Lorbick."

The snow was still falling. James shivered and shivered. His teeth were clicking together so loudly he thought they might break. "What are you doing here?" he said. "Where's Terence? Did you do something to him?"

"Was he the guy who was down at the bottom of the hill? Talking on a cell phone?"

"Yeah," James said. "Is he okay?"

"He was talking to some girl named Darlene," the monster said. "I tried to talk to her, but she started screaming and it hurt my ears so I hung up. Do you happen to know where she lives?"

"Somewhere in Ohio," James said.

"Thanks," the monster said. He took out a little black notebook and wrote something down.

"What are you?" James said. "Who are you?"

"I'm Angelina Jolie," the monster said. It blinked.

James's heart almost stopped beating. "Really?" he said. "Like in Danny Anderson's dream?"

"No," the monster said. "Just kidding."

"Oh," James said. They sat in silence. The monster used one long fingernail to dig something out between its teeth. It belched a foul, greasy belch. James thought of Bryan. Bryan probably would have belched right back, if he still had a head.

"Are you the monster that Bungalow 4 saw?" James said.

"Were those the kids who were here a few days ago?"

"Yeah," James said.

"We hung out for a while," the monster said. "Were they friends of yours?"

"No," James said. "Those kids are real jerks. Nobody likes them."

"That's a shame," the monster said. Even when it wasn't belching, it smelled worse than anything James had ever smelled before. Fish and kerosene and rotting maple syrup poured over him in waves. He tried not to breathe.

The monster said, "I'm sorry about the rest of your bungalow. Your friends. Your friends who made you wear a dress."

"Are you going to eat me?" James said.

"I don't know," the monster said. "Probably not. There were a lot of you. I'm not actually that hungry anymore. Besides, I would feel silly eating a kid in a dress. And you're really filthy."

"Why didn't you eat Bungalow 4?" James said. He felt sick to his stomach. If he looked at the monster he felt sick, and if he looked away, there was Danny Anderson, lying facedown under a pine tree with snow on his back and if he looked somewhere else, there were Bryan Jones's legs poking out of the tent. There was Bryan Jones's head. One of Bryan's shoes had come off and that made James think of the hike, the way Terence lay down in the mud to fish for the Simpson twin's shoe. "Why didn't you eat them? They're mean. They do terrible things and nobody likes them."

"Wow," the monster said. "I didn't know that. I would have eaten them if I'd known, maybe. Although most of the time I can't worry about things like that."

"Maybe you should," James said. "I think you should."

The monster scratched its head. "You think so? I saw you guys eating hot dogs earlier. So do you worry about whether those were good dogs or bad dogs when you're eating them? Do you only eat dogs that were mean? Do you only eat bad dogs?"

"Hot dogs aren't really made from dogs," James said. "People don't eat dogs."

"I never knew that," the monster said. "But see if I worried about that kind of thing, whether the person I was eating was a nice guy or a jerk, I'd never eat anyone. And I get hungry a lot. So to be honest, I don't worry. All I really notice is whether the person I'm chasing is big or small or fast or slow. Or if they have a sense of humor. That's important, you know. A sense of humor. You have to laugh about things. When I was hanging out with Bungalow 4, I was just having some fun. I was just playing around. Bungalow 4 mentioned that you guys were going to show up. I was joking about how I was going to eat them and they said I should eat you guys instead. They said it would be really funny. I have a good sense of humor. I like a good joke."

It reached out and touched James Lorbick's head.

"Don't do that!" James said.

"Sorry," said the monster. "I just wanted to see what the mud spikes felt like. Do you think it would be funny if I wore a dress and put a lot of mud on my head?"

James shook his head. He tried to picture the monster wearing a dress, but all he could picture was somebody climbing up to Honor Lookout. Somebody finding pieces of James scattered everywhere like pink and red confetti. That somebody would wonder what had happened and be glad that it hadn't happened to them. Maybe someday people would tell scary stories about what had happened to Bungalow 6 when they went camping. Nobody would believe the stories. Nobody would understand why one kid had been wearing a dress.

"Are you shivering because you're cold or because you're afraid of me?" the monster said.

"I don't know," James said. "Both. Sorry."

"Maybe we should get up and run around," the monster said. "I could chase you. It might warm you up. Weird weather, isn't it? But it's pretty, too. I love how snow makes everything look nice and clean."

"I want to go home," James said.

"That's Chicago, right?" the monster said. "That's what I wrote down."

"You wrote down where I live?" James said.

"All those guys from the other bungalow," the monster said. "Bungalow 4. I made them write down their addresses. I like to travel. I like to visit people. Besides, if you say that they're jerks, then I should go visit them? Right? It would serve them right."

"Yeah," James said. "It would serve them right. That would be really funny. Ha ha ha."

"Excellent," the monster said. It stood up. "It was great meeting you, James. Are you crying? It looks like you're crying."

"I'm not crying. It's just snow. There's snow on my face. Are you leaving?" James said. "You're going to leave me here? You aren't going to eat me?"

"I don't know," the monster said. It did a little twirl, like it was going to go running off in one direction, and then as if it had changed its mind, as if it was going to come rushing back at James. James whimpered. "I just can't decide. Maybe I should flip a coin. Do you have a coin I can flip?"

James shook his head.

"Okay," the monster said. "How about this. I'm thinking of a number between one and ten. You say a number and if it's the same number, I won't eat you."

"No," James said.

"Then how about if I only eat you if you say the number that I'm thinking of? I promise I won't cheat. I probably won't cheat."

"No," James said, although he couldn't help thinking of a number. He thought of the number four. It floated there in his head like a big neon sign, blinking on and off and back on. Four, four, four. Bungalow 4. Or six. Bungalow 6. Or was that too obvious? Don't think of a number. He would have bet anything that the monster could read minds. Maybe the monster had put the number four in James's head. Six. James changed the number to six hundred so it wouldn't be a number between one and ten. Don't read my mind, he thought. Don't eat me.

"I'll count to six hundred," the monster said. "And then I'll chase you. That would be funny. If you get back to camp before I catch you, you're safe. Okay? If you get back to camp first, I'll go eat Bungalow 4. Okay? I tell you what. I'll go eat them even if you don't make it back. Okay?"

"But it's dark," James said. "It's snowing. I'm wearing a dress."

The monster looked down at its fingernails. It smiled like James had just told an excellent joke. "One," it said. "Two, three, four. Run, James! Pretend I'm chasing you. Pretend that I'm going to eat you if I catch you. Five, six. Come on, James, run!"

James ran.

Nick Mamatas is the author of the novel of neighborhood nuclear superiority ***Under My Roof*** *(Soft Skull, 2006) and the Lovecraftian Beat road novel* ***Move Under Ground*** *(Prime, 2006). His short fiction has appeared in the men's magazine* ***Razor,*** *the German pop culture mag* ***Spex,*** *and a variety of fantasy and horror magazines including* ***Polyphony, Chizine, Strange Horizons,*** *and the anthologies* ***Shivers V, Corpse Blossoms,*** *and* ***Poe's Lighthouse.*** *He lives in Massachusetts.*

At the End of the Hall
Nick Mamatas

My earliest fear, the one I remember anyways, was of great pulp magazine robots with hot water heater bodies and vacuum tube eyes. My brother loved the pulps and forbade me to even touch his precious magazines, so I wouldn't. I'd stare and stare at the covers though; hourglassed damsels in diaphanous gowns draped over thick slab altars, knives inches from the cleavage of their breasts; the glowing eyes of PIs; pinheaded little green men in flying saucers with convertible bubble roofs; and the robots, always the robots with their cylindrical torsos and pincer claws for hands. I'd want to tear off the cover, or at least flop another magazine on top of it to hide the thing, but I *wasn't allowed to touch*. So I studied the picture, memorized every detail.

Later, I was afraid of being raped and killed on some quiet street rounding through the woods. Glowing headlights, unctuous come-ons by a too-slick man with thin lips, then his meaty hand over my mouth — what would it smell like?—the knife held high in the dark with those headlights glinting in the steel . . .

After I got married and had children, I was afraid that I'd come home from some errand or maybe just wake up one morning and my little boys would be dead and blue in their beds. Then it happened and I swallowed every pill in the medicine cabinet, lost my husband in the fog of grief and hospital stays, and spent the rest of my life typing addresses on envelopes for a community college library and baking cakes for office birthday parties. If I liked the co-worker, pineapple upside down cake. If I didn't, devil's food cake from no-frills powdery mix. I was afraid someone would realize what I was doing, but nobody cared.

Forty years later, I'm in a hospital bed again, sans one lung, tubes everywhere, my roommate humming her way through a BM while a fat nurse boredly watches, and I fear nothing anymore, not even death. My son, my surviving son, William was just here visiting, his mouth full of wishes for my recovery, and he stoked my distaste for his visits with every platitude.

It's not William's fault, well, much of it isn't anyway. He's just another foolish man with balding pate and a necktie my granddaughter Madicyn—and what a name that is, whatever happened to Betty?—bought him for his birthday with money I gave her for her own birthday. That's the circle of life, these days. After Harold died, I'm afraid I just never liked William that much. I loved him, I love him still dearly, and my heart leaps whenever he comes to visit, which is daily and more than my roommate gets from her loud clan of rawboned mustachios.

William, unfortunately, picked up the awful habit of wishing from my husband and father. Harold wasn't like that; he never wished for anything. Me neither, and not because I'm one of those sour women who keeps hopes and dreams at arm's length, the type who loudly declares over coffee that she "doesn't hope" so she "won't ever be disappointed." Disappointment is a birthright, there's no avoiding it. But I don't refrain from wishing for fear of my wishes not coming true, but for fear of one of them, and only one of them, coming true.

"I wish I were dead." I nearly said it the day I saw Harold, cold and still in his little room, but I swallowed the wish along with sleeping pills and I'm glad I did, despite it all. There have been moments of joy since. Madicyn's birth, for example, or the time I went to Egypt on vacation and saw the pyramids; I even rode a camel down to Cheops and the kind men who worked for the tour laughed like American men rarely do. Joyfully, not ruefully. I don't wish I were dead, not yet. There is one last thing to do.

William's visits rake me over the coals. What a fool I raised. He expends wishes in the way only someone who knows they won't ever come true could. If only one or two had come true, he might have learned something, but I'd be the worse for it. I remember when he was three, his face oddly serious when he announced at dinner, "I wish I were an ice cream man!" I cringe at the thought of him shuffling in to the room every day during visiting hours in a paper hat and white slacks. With sticky hands. With loose change jingling in his pockets.

I'm glad he works in a bank and keeps banker's hours. It means he visits early and leaves early. If only he had left earlier a month ago, back when I lived at home. Instead he waltzed in, sweaty and in shorts, put his feet up on my coffee table, and after nattering some pleasantries and trivia about my granddaughter, wished for a cheese sandwich. Of course I made him one, and a glass of lemonade, and heard his excuses between bites and slurping sips as to why he couldn't mow my lawn. He wasn't halfway through the sandwich before the phone ran. My doctor had the test results; he'd need to operate. There would be chemotherapy. It was Stage IIIa cancer, but if I didn't check in to the hospital right away it might soon become IIIb and then surgery would be futile. After sickly hugs and consolation, William left with promises to do whatever he could, and to visit me every day. He said he'd pray for me, which is just another form of wish. Too bad for me that he wasted the wish that actually came true on the sandwich. He left the cheese sandwich to dry on its plate. I threw it out the next morning, having interrupted my packing to tidy the house.

"Don't touch me," I tell him. "You're not allowed to touch me. The doctor says." In truth, I just can't stand being touched at all, and William is the only one who would listen, so I tell him to keep his hands at his sides. The medical staff, from my doctor down to the lowliest CNA, all take endless liberties, poking and turning and brushing the hair from my forehead as if I were an infant or already dead and needing to look presentable for the wake. I don't dread their forced clockwork cheerfulness and grasping hands anymore, I am beyond that, numb to it. I'd simply rather have it end sooner rather than later.

Even worse than the poking are the endless measurements, and that I cannot dissuade even William from participating in. "Did you eat today, Mama?" he asks. "Did you eat all your pudding? Did you have a glass of water?" he asks. "Would you like another? I'm sure you can have two glasses of water. How about a nice orange? Maybe just two *slices* of orange?"

"Two slices?" I ask. "William, two slices of *what size*? One can slice an orange in half and have two slices."

"Oh Mama, you know what I mean. Two *quarters*." His emphasis suggests that he's not done treating me like a child.

"Ah, so you mean to offer me one half of an orange. Is that right? Well, in that case, why didn't you just say so in the first place?"

William sighs, so easily defeated. "That's right, half an orange. Can I cut this here orange in two, right down the middle, and offer you one half? I can leave the other half on a napkin on the night table, in easy reach."

"No thank you," I say. "I don't believe that I'm hungry for orange right now, and I certainly wouldn't be hungry for a dried-out, shriveled-up half of an orange later." Later, I give the orange to my roommate, and she smiles appreciatively. I feel warm and she shrugs her shoulders in a little dance, imitating Harold's woebegone gait. I smile.

The staff keeps track of my evacuations as studiously as William does my ingestions. It's demeaning and a worthless endeavor, as foolish as counting the seconds to the ground after falling from an airplane, but I cannot stop them. I find myself tearing up; what is the point of all this empty medical ritual? I am not going to live. I feel sorry for William and the hours he wastes here.

Nobody ever asks me if I'd like a book other than the trashy paperbacks with the creased spines the hospital has to read to while away the days, but every day some intern or other says something like, "You sure do read a lot, Ms. Moss. Can you really finish a whole book in two days?" *Yes dear, between scooter rides and sock hops.* I think, but I speak only the first clause. William promises to bring me some books from my shelves, but he turns up empty-handed. "I'm so sorry, Mama," he says, "I must have forgotten." The edge in his voice hints that he has a screw of his own to turn.

Later, a nurse ups my pain medication, as if to thwart even my reading time. They even measure my television viewing but never ask me what I think of any of the shows. I no longer have opinions, as far as my son or my doctors are concerned, unless it's regarding how high I want my feet at night or whether I'd prefer the blue or gray comforter from my home. Fear, I am bereft. Wishes, I'm waiting. But opinions, I still have.

Madicyn, the poor thing, takes after her father, with her big round head. It won't serve her well in adolescence. With luck, she may grow to be handsome, but never beautiful. And like her father, she is full of specious wishes. "Grandmama," she says when she visits, "I wish you'd feel better, just for one day, so you can see me in my recital." Madicyn takes ballet, and is in that awkward stage between the cutesy stomping of kindergartners dressed in sequined costumes and the beginnings of real dance. She twirls about constantly, but is scarcely better at it than she is at wishing. Better for one day, indeed. Her eyes are hazel, like Harold's were, and she looks up at me happily, like she just told me a secret, truly not seeing all the tubes or my desiccated state. I cannot correct her.

"Dance as well as you would were I in the audience, child." I wonder if Harold would have married, had he lived. What would his children have been like? I'm running out of things to say.

"I will, Grandmama. I wish I was a prima ballerina already!" She twirls again. My roommate turns away from the television to smile indulgently at her and me. It goes on like this, but thankfully Madicyn mostly stays home with her mother when William visits me. I prefer William's company, as at least he will occasionally fall into silence after some struggle over how much of my breakfast I consumed, and I need silence to gather my will.

You see, I have a theory. I have never, and I do mean not even once, made a wish. Not even as a little girl, not for a kitten nor for the happy revelation that I was not an ordinary child, but the lost adopted daughter of foreign princes. Kittens grow to be cats, after all as my mother often reminded me, and as exotic as they sounded, I suspected that lost princes could be cruel. Most wishes are as useless as my son's verbiage, but some do come true. My roommate this morning wished that her own sons would stop by, even though it's a Saturday and they only come after church on Sundays. Twenty minutes later the four of them, and some wives and kids, spilled into the room, violating all the rules of visiting hours. They bellowed well-wishes, messed around with the foot pedals of her adjustable bed, and even sang some ethnic song. One of their children even moved as though to pull out my IV tube. Exhausting. The novel I was reading, about some lusty pirate with a V-shaped latissimus that he often flexed while swaggering against ruby skies, was no escape. Oh, for Faulkner. I nearly wished. William got his cheese sandwich, did he not? Madicyn wished for and received a pink tutu and a purple top for her recital costume last week.

I never made wishes because I was afraid they'd come true. Now, on the edge of my consciousness I feel some hint of apprehension that my one wish won't. I push it away, into the miasma of morphine in which my thoughts have to float. Then I pinch the tube of my morphine drip, to stop the flow of the drug, to bring the pain, and to focus on my memories of him. I wish and wish and wish, like a shivering child.

That night, at the end of the hall, I hear his footfalls. They're quiet at first, but soon there is no mistaking them in the otherwise quiet hours of early Sunday. My roommate awakens with a start and grabs the handrails of her bed to pull herself up and peer at the door. For a moment, he is still and she squints into the darkness. The drywall explodes, and pincer arms flailing, he is here. "Oh my God!" the woman shrieks and I laugh as I drag myself to a ready seated position up as best I can. The robot's eyes blaze with arc light as he steps around my roommate's bed and plucks me from mine. Let the tubes fall to the floor, let my roommate shriek and scream and pray—tomorrow you'll have a tale for your oafish brood, won't you!

The steel of the robot's torso is warm and rumbling from whatever unearthly clockwork motivates its form—I thought it would cool and unyielding, but I'm glad for the heat as I'm wearing nothing but my embarrassing hospital gown. He cradles me close and stomps into the hallway, where the night nurses have already gathered with fire extinguishers and wheelchairs. Beyond them, a chunky intern dives for the nurse's station phone.

"Robot! The death rays!" I shout. My hair stands on end as his vacuum tube eyes blaze. Twin white squiggles of lightning erupt and hit the phone; it explodes in a cascade of sparks and black flame. Then intern wails and skids across the floor, his smoldering hand tucked under his pendulous stomach. The robot steps over him and carries me down the hall as the patients awaken and call pathetically for their nurses.

I wrap my arms as tightly as I can around the base of the robot's head, freeing his right arm to swing and menace with clanking pincers; my legs are cradled at the knee by his thick left arm. We're flanked by that easily-marveled idiot intern from the other day as he stumbles from the men's room.

"No! What is it?" he cries out stupidly, and I declare, as the robot caves in his sternum with a single blow and sends him down to the tiles, "It's a robot, fool. Read a book!" At the end of the hall, the robot swivels his torso 180 degrees, so that I can be safe as he backs into and then through the bearing wall. The dust of brick and wallboard, the whine and burning air of ignited boot rockets, they deaden all my senses save the feeling of our featherfall decent into the parking lot. The robot kindly gives me few moment to compose myself and comb the dust from my hair with my fingers before beginning our march again.

Two blocks later we come across the first cordon of police. Three cars, lights flashing, and six officers, two with shotguns and four with their sidearms drawn, are arrayed behind the open doors of their black and whites. One of them shouts to me, "Stop the robot, or we'll fire!" I don't bother calling back that I don't control the automaton; I'm too short of breath, my heart is a timpani. I can't speak; all my resources are devoted to holding on as tightly as I can. I have no fear. I know that, even in these coarse times, the police would never open fire on an old woman. I bury my head in the nook of steel and rubber between arm and cylinder and smile as I hear his eyes charge and fire. My fillings tingle; he fires again. The heat of his steel skin burns my cheek; he fires again. I turn to the scene and am jostled as the robot kicks his way through the wreckage of the police cruisers, and we stomp on toward—where? Another wish. They're easy to make now, that there isn't much time left.

William! "To William's house," I say, and the robot obeys, turning the corner at Allston Way. Yes, William, the time has come, and Madicyn too, you must know the truth. We're coming for you! Do not fear, children, grandmama won't hurt you, nor will her friend with the lightning-bottle eyes. We're cutting across lawns, trudging through the spray of late-night sprinkler systems and pushing past fences so that you may know the last secret of a long, sour life. Don't waste your time and breath on propriety and nonsense, William. Forget your girlish dreams, little Madicyn . . . no, Betty, I will call you Betty. Your middle name is Elizabeth, after me. I'll call you what I want, when I want to—damn your cuckold father and that tramp of a long-gone mother with her ridiculous affectations.

March on robot; never mind the barking dogs or the distant shrieks from foolish women in curlers and mud packs. Let them gawk! Let William and little Betty gawk too; anything to shake them out of their complacency and ridiculous little wishes for winning touchdowns and snow days. The world can be theirs, if they would just reach out and take it. We're at the edge of the driveway. Go on, crush the rhododendrons, let the mailbox fall to the ground. Let the tiles on the steps crumble to powder under our weight, but yes, oh yes, ring the bell like midnight's own Fuller Brush man. You're a clever dream-thing, aren't you? The lights are coming on. William will likely struggle into a robe before tromping down the steps, but my breath is leaving me, so nudge down the door.

Inside. Betty on the opposite end of the vestibule, her bucket jaw hanging low as she stares. In the distance, William squeaks with fear and outrage, calling on his daughter to run. He's so afraid, and of nothing at all! He has a ball bat, how funny. He drops it and the end lands on his toe when he sees me cradled, half-dead, in the nut-and-bolt crook of the robot's arms, but he doesn't even wince, because a little pain doesn't matter. He's learning already, but he's never been a quick study.

"Grandmama?" Betty says quietly. I look at them both and laugh and laugh. "Never fear!" I cry out, sharper and more joyous than I've ever spoken to her. "It isn't worth it, child, don't be afraid!" and she's not, but my son squats and grabs her roughly about the shoulders, for his own fearful sake, not hers. She shrugs him off and steps forward. I want to see my granddaughter. "Harold!" I say. It's a command, and at that word my Harold's eyes spark and cast the room in the whitest of light and long stark shadows. They are waiting to discharge.

"Make a wish!" I tell my William, and I can only hope he grants me a next full breath.

Holly Phillips lives in Trail, British Columbia, Canada, in an old house with fabulous views of the river and the smelter. Her first novel, ***The Burning Girl****, has just hit the bookstores this year.*

"I wrote "Summer Ice" after a long series of very dark stories full of violence and suffering. I was hungry for some light, and although the character Manon is struggling with loneliness, among other things, I'm still delighted at how bright and open the story is. It's one of my favorites."

Summer Ice

Holly Phillips

Today Manon arrives at a different time, and sits at a different table. Her sketchbook stays in her bag: a student had lingered after class to show her his portfolio of drawings and her mind is full of his images. Thick charcoal lines smudged and blended without much room for light. She has not found solace in her own work since she moved to the city and began to teach. Her life has become a stranger to her, she and it must become reacquainted. She has always been tentative with strangers. Art has become tentative with her.

The table she sits at today is tucked against the wall opposite the glass counter that shields long tubs of ice cream. Summer sunlight is held back from the window by a blue awning, but it glazes the trolley tracks in the street. Heat shimmers above chipped red bricks. Inside, the walls are the colors of sherbet, patched paint rippled over plaster, and the checkerboard floor is sticky. Children come and go, keeping the counterman busy. He is dark in his damp white shirt and apron, his hands drip with flavors as he wields his scoop. An electric fan blows air past his shaved head. Through a doorway behind him Manon sees someone walk toward the back of the store, a man as dark but older, slighter, with tight gray hair and a focused look.

Manon scoops vanilla from her glass bowl and wonders at the fan, the hard cold of the ice cream. This small store must be rich to afford so much electricity in a power hungry town. She imagines the latest in roof solars, she imagines a freezer crowded with dessert and mysterious frozen riches. The dark man in white clothes behind curved glass is an image, a movement, that defies framing. A challenge. Her sketchbook stays in her bag. The last of her ice cream hurts the back of her skull. She does not want to go back to the apartment that has not yet and may never become home.

The stream of customers pauses and the counterman drops his scoop in a glass of water and turns his back on the tables to wash his hands. Through the doorway Manon sees the older man open the freezer door. She catches a glimpse of a dark, half empty space: part of a room through a door through a door behind glass. Depth and cold, layers of distance. The fan draws into the storefront a chill breeze that dies a moment after the freezer door slams shut. Manon rises and takes her bowl to the counter. The young man thanks her, and as she turns to the door he says, "See you."

"See you," she says. She steps into the gritty heat and carries with her the image of dimness, depth, cold. The memory of winter, except they don't have winters like that here.

In the winter Manon and her sister tobogganed down the hill behind their mother's house. Snow would sometimes fall so thickly it bowed the limbs of pine trees to the ground, muffling charcoal-green needles in cozy coats of white. Air blended with cloud, snowy ground with air, until there was nothing but white, shapes and layers and emptinesses of white, and the plummet down the hill was a cold dive on swan wings and nothing. Manon and her sister tumbled off at the bottom, exalted, still flying despite the snowmelt inside cuffs and boots. Perhaps to ground themselves they burrowed down until they found the pebbled ice of the stream that would sing with frogs come spring. Black lumpy glass melted slick and mirroring beneath their breath and tongues. Then they would climb the hill, dragging the rebellious toboggan behind them, and begin the flight again.

The city is still greening itself, a slow and noisy process. Pneumatic drills chatter the cement of Manon's street, tools in the hands of men and women who seem to revel in the work, the noise, the destruction of what others once labored to build. The art school is already surrounded by a knot-work of grassy rides and bicycle paths and trolley ways, buildings are crowned with gardens, the lush summer air is bright with birds and goat bells, but Manon's neighborhood is rough with dust that smells of dead automobiles, the dead past. She skirts piles of broken pavement, walks on oily dirt that will have to be cleaned and layered with compost before being seeded, and eases herself under the plastic sheet the landlord has hung over the front door to keep out the grime. A vain attempt, all the tenants have their windows open, hopeful of a cooling breeze.

Manon opens the bathtub tap and lets a few liters burble into the blue enamel bowl she keeps over the brown-stained drain. The darkness of the clear water returns the image of the frozen stream to her mind. She takes off her dusty clothes and steps into the tub, strokes the wet sponge down her skin. The first touch is a shock, but after that not nearly cool enough. The bathroom is painted Mediterranean blue, the window hidden by a paper screen pressed with flowers. It smells of dampness, soap, old tiles, some previous tenant's perfume. Manon squeezes the sponge to send a trickle down her spine. Black pebbled ice. Layers of distance. The counterman's eyes.

She turns her attention to her dirty feet, giving the structures of imagery peace to build themselves in the back of her mind, in a place that has been empty for too long.

Ira, the landlord of Manon's building, has been inspired by the work racketing in the street below. Even though the parking lot that once serviced the four-story building has already been converted to a garden (raised beds of the same dimensions of the parking spaces, each one assigned to the appropriate apartment) Ira has decided that the roof must be greened as well.

"Native plants," he says at the tenant meeting, "that won't need too much soil or water." That way he can perform the conversion without reinforcing the roof.

Lupe, Manon's right-hand neighbor, says as they climb the stairs, "The old faker. Like we don't know he only wants the tax rebate."

"It will mean a reduction in rent, though, won't it?" Manon says.

Lupe shrugs skeptically, but there are laws about these things. And anyway, Manon likes Ira's enthusiasm, whatever its source. His round pink face reminds her of a ripening melon. She also likes the idea of a meadow of wild grass and junipers growing on the other side of her ceiling. Lupe invites her over for a beer and they talk for a while about work schedules ("We'll have to make sure the men do their share, we always do, they're a bunch of bums in this building," Lupe says) and splitting the cost and care of a rabbit hutch ("'Cause I don't know about you," Lupe says, "but I'd rather eat a bunny than eat like a bunny."). Then Lupe's son comes home from soccer practice and Manon goes back to her place. The evening has gone velvety blue. In the quiet she can hear a trolley sizzle a few blocks away, three different kinds of music, people talking by open windows. She lies naked on her bed and thinks about Ira's plans and Lupe's earthy laughter so she doesn't have to wonder when she'll sleep.

The art school can't afford to pay her much. The people who run the place are her hosts as much as her employers, the work space they give her counts as half her salary. She has no complaints about the room, tall, plaster-walled, oak-floored, with three double-hung windows looking north and east up a crooked street, but her tools look meager in all this space. She feels meager herself, unable to supply the quantity of life the room demands. Create! the bare walls command. Perform! She carries the delicate lattice of yesterday's images like a hollow egg into the studio, hopeful, but cannot decide where to put it down. Paper, canvas, clay, all inert, doors that deny her entry. She paces, she roams the halls. Other people teach to the sound of industry and laughter. She teaches her students as if she were teaching herself how to draw, making every mistake before stumbling on the correct method. Unsure whether she is doing something necessary or cowardly, or even dangerous to her discipline, she leaves the building early and walks on grass and yellow poppies ten blocks to her other job.

During the years of awkward transition from continental wealth to continental poverty, the city's parks were abandoned to flourish or die.

Now, paradoxically, as the citizens sow green across the cityscape these pockets of wilderness are being reclaimed. Lush lawns have been shoved aside by boisterous crowds of wild oats and junipers and laurels and manzanita and poison oak and madrone and odorous eucalyptus trees shedding strips of bark and long ribbon leaves that crumble into fragrant dirt. No one expects the lawns to return. The city does not have the water to spare. But there are paths to carve, playgrounds and skateboard parks and benches to uncover, throughways and resting places for a citizenry traveling by bike and foot. It's useful work, and Manon mostly enjoys it, although in this heat it is a masochistic pleasure. The crew she is assigned to has been working together for more than a year, and though they are friendly people she finds it difficult to enter into their unity. The fact that she only works with them part-time does not make it easier.

Today they are cleaving a route through the wiry tangle of brush that fills the southwest corner of the park. Bare muscular branches weave themselves into a latticework like an unsprung basket, an organic form that contains space yet has no room for storage. Electric saws powered by the portable solar generator buzz like wasps against dead and living wood. Thick yellow sunlight filters through and is caught and stirred by dust. Birds and small creatures flurry away from the falling trees. A jay chooses Manon to harangue as she wrestles with a pair of long-handled shears. Blisters start up on her hands, sweat sheets her skin without washing away debris, and her eye is captured again and again by the woven depths of the thicket, the repeated woven depths hot with sun and busy with life, the antithesis of the cold layered ice of yesterday. She drifts into the working space that eluded her in the studio, and has to be called repeatedly before she stops to join the others on their break.

Edgar says, "Do you ever get the feeling like they're just growing in again behind your back? Like you're going to turn around and there's going to be no trail, no nothing, and you could go on cutting forever without getting out?"

"We have been cutting forever," Anita says.

"Like the prince who has to cut through the rose thorns before he can get to the sleeping princess," Gary says.

"That's our problem," Anita says. "We'll never get through if we have no prince."

"You're right," Gary says. "All the other guys that tried got stuck and left their bones hanging on the thorns."

"Man, that's going to be me, I know it." Edgar tips his canteen, all the way up, empty. "Well, come on, the truck's going to be here in an hour, we might as well make sure it drives away full."

The cut branches the crew has hauled to the curbside lace together like the growing chaos squared, all their leaves still a living green. As the other three drag themselves to their feet, Manon says, "Do you think anyone would mind if I took a few branches home?"

Her crewmates glance at each other and shrug.

"They're just going to city compost," Edgar says.

Manon thanks him. They go back to work in the heavy heat of late afternoon.

She kneels to wash spiders and crumbs of bark out of her hair, the enamel basin precarious on the rim of the tub. Lupe and her son have guests for dinner. Manon can hear talk and laughter and the clatter of pans, and the smell of frying and hot chilies slips redolent under her door. She should be hungry, but she is too tired to cook, and is full with loneliness besides. Her sister's partner introduced the family to spicy food. He cooked Manon a celebratory dinner when she got this job at the art school, and everyone who was crowded around the small table talked a lot and laughed at jokes that no one outside the family would understand. They were pleased for her, excited at the thought of having someone in the southern city, a preliminary explorer who could set up a base camp for the rest. Her sister had promised she would visit this summer before she got too big to travel, but the last Manon had heard they were in the middle of suddenly necessary roof repairs and might not be able to afford the fare. Manon puts on a favorite dress and goes with wet hair into the dusk that still hovers between sunset and blue. It is hard to look at the rubbled street and not think of armies invading.

The ice cream shop is dim behind glass, but the open sign is still in the window so she goes in. Bad to spend her money on treats, bad to eat dessert without dinner, bad to keep coming back to this one place as if she has nowhere else in the whole city to go. There is no one behind the counter, no one at the tables — well, it is dinner time — or perhaps the sign is meant to say closed. But then the older man with tight gray curls comes through the inner doorway and smiles and asks her what he can get for her. Vanilla, she says, but with a glance for permission he adds a scoop of pale orange.

"Lemon-peach sorbet," he says. "It's new, tell me what you think."

She tastes it standing there at the counter. "It's good."

He nods as if he'd been waiting for her confirmation. "We make everything fresh. My cousin has trees outside the city."

"It's really good."

He busies himself with cleaning tasks and she sits at the table by the wall. Despite the unfolding night, he does not turn on any lights. When the counter's glass is spotless he steps outside a moment, then comes in shaking his head. "Still hotter out there than it is in here." He lets the door close.

While Manon eats her ice cream, the vanilla exotic and rich after the sorbet, he scrapes round chocolate scoops from the bottom of a tub and presses them into a bowl. He takes the empty tub to the back, and she sees the shift of white door and darkness as he opens the freezer. The fan snares the cold and casts it across the room, so the hairs on her arms rise. The freezer has its own light and she can see the ice cream man shifting tubs, looking for more chocolate. There is a lot of room, expensive to keep cold, and what looks like a door to the outside insulated by a silver quilt. When he comes back with the fresh tub and drops it into its place behind the counter, she gets up and carries over her empty bowl. "Thanks. The peach was really good."

"Good while it lasts. You can only make it with fresh fruit." He rubs his hands together as he escorts her to the door. "Time for the after-dinner rush," he says, and he flips on the lights as she steps outside.

It is still hotter out than in.

The house at the top of the tobogganing hill grew long icicles outside the kitchen window. Magical things, they were tusks spears wands to

Manon and her sister. The side yard was trampled by the playful feet of white boars that could tell your fortune, and warriors that clad themselves in armor so pure they were invisible against the snow, and witches who could turn your heart to ice and your body to stone, or conjure you a cloak of swan's down and a hat of perfect frost. Two angels, one a little bigger than the other, lay side by side and spread their wings, giggling at the snow that slipped down their collars, and struggled to rise without marring the imprints of their bodies, their pinions heavy with snow. Thirsty with cold and the hard work of building the warriors' fortress, they would snap off the sharp ends of their tusks/spears/wands and with their tongues melt them by layers as they had grown, water slipping over a frozen core, almost but not quite clear, every sheath catching a bit of dirt from the roof, or a fleck of bark, a needle-tip of pine. Half a winter down their throats, too cold, leaving them thirstier than before.

Manon does her share for the roof garden on the evenings of her teaching days. Her other job has made her strong, and the physical work helps drive out the difficulties of the day. Too many of her students are older than she is, she hasn't figured out how to make them believe her judgments and advice. Or perhaps they are right not to believe her, perhaps she is too young, or too inept. Lupe's son shovels dirt from the pile left in the alley by the municipal truck, loading a wheelbarrow that he pushes through the garden beds to the bucket which he fills so Manon can haul it up on the pulley and dump the contents in the corner where Lupe leans with her rake. The layers of drainage sheets, pebbles, sand have already been put down by the tenants on other floors. Dirt is the fourth floor's responsibility.

"I've got the easy job," Lupe says again as Manon dumps the heavy bucket. "Let's switch."

Manon grins. Lupe is in her forties, graying and soft. Manon has muscles that spring along her bones, visible under her tanned skin in the last slant of sun. It feels good to drop the bucket down to Marcos, warm slide of rope through her hand, and then heave it up again, competent, strong. Lupe rakes with elegant precision, a Zen nun with a haywire braid crown and a T-shirt with a beer slogan stretched across her breasts. The third floor tenants have spread the sand too unevenly for her liking and she rakes it, too, in between bucket loads of soil. Marcos and Manon, communicating by the zizz of the dropping bucket and the thump of shoveled dirt, decide to force Lupe to abandon her smooth contours. She catches on and grins fiercely, wielding her rake with a virtuosic flourish. They work until Marcos, four stories down, is only a shadow among the lighter patches of garden green. Then they go to Lupe's apartment for beer and spicy bean tacos.

"Don't worry about the dirt," Lupe says. "Living with a teenage boy is like living in a cave anyway."

Marcos scowls at her and slopes off to his room.

Lupe rolls her eyes. "Have another beer. And try the salsa, it's my mother's recipe. She always makes this one with the first tomatoes from the garden."

Manon had taken the branches from the park to her studio, and this morning she carries a canvas knapsack full of left-over roof pebbles to join them. The strap is heavy on her aching shoulder. She isn't strong enough yet not to feel the pain of work. Spilled on the wood floor the stones, some as small as two knuckles, some as big as her fist, look dull and uninteresting, although she chose them with care. Next to the twisted saw-cut branches of manzanita and red madrone, they look like what they are: garden trash. She kicks them into a roughly square beach and tries binding the branches with wire, an unsturdy contraption that more or less stands on its own, footed in pebbles. She steps back. Weak, clumsy, meager. The word keeps recurring in this room. Meager.

She has to teach a class.

Life drawing is about volume and line. She tells her students to be hasty. "Throw down the lines, capture some space, and move on. Be quick," she says. "Quick!" And then watches them frown earnestly over painstaking pencils while the model sits, naked and patient, and reads her book.

"Look," Manon tells them. She takes her pad and a pencil and sweeps her hand, throwing down the lines. "Here, here, here. Fast! A hint, a boundary, a shape. Fast!" Her hand sweeps and the figure appears. It's so easy! See the line and throw it down.

They don't get it. They look at her sketch with admiration and dismay, and are more discouraged than before.

"Start again," she says.

They start again, painstaking and frowning.

After class she goes back to her studio and takes apart the pathetic bundle of wired twigs. Meager! She doesn't get it either.

Lupe has a meeting, Marcos has soccer. Manon spends some time in her garden bed, weeding herbs and carrots and beans. She uncovers an astonishing earthworm, a ruddy monster as thick as her thumb that lengthens absurdly in its slow escape. Mr. Huang from the second floor comes out and gives her a dignified nod as he kneels to weed his mysterious greens. Manon's mother always planted carrots and beans, but Manon's carrots don't look right, the delicate fronds have been seared by the sun. Mr. Huang's greens, like Lupe's tomatoes, burgeon amongst vivid marigolds. The blossoms are as orange as the eyes of the pigeons Lupe strings netting against, thieves worse than raccoons and wandering goats. Manon's tidy plot is barren in comparison. She has planted the wrong things, planted them too late, something. When she goes in she finds a message from her sister on her telephone.

Sorry I missed you. It looks like I might not be coming after all . . .

One of the other art teachers has a show opening in a gallery across town. Manon finds a note about it in her box in the staff room, a copied invitation, everyone has one. She carries it up to her studio where she is confronted by the mess of branches and stones. The madrone cuttings have begun to lose their leaves, but the red bark splits open in long envelope mouths to reveal pistachio green. She picks up a branch, carries it around the room, pacing, thinking. Nothing comes but the reminder of someone else's show. The teacher is one she likes, an older man with a beard and a natural tonsure. She has thought about asking him for advice on her classes, but has not, yet. He was on her hiring committee. She knows he did not invite her especially, but it would be rude not to go. She puts the branch down and digs into her bag to consult her trolley timetable.

She cuts brush in the park again this afternoon, and is relieved to find that her vision of layered space and interstitial depth repeats itself. Branches crook and bend to accommodate each other, red tawny gray arms linked in a slow maneuver, a jostle for sky. She thinks back to her studio and realizes she has missed something crucial. Something. She works her shears, then wrestles whole shrubs out of the tangle without stopping to cut them smaller, determined on frustration. When, on their break, Edgar asks if she is going to join the rest of the crew for a beer after work, she tells them she has a friend's opening to attend. Then berates herself, partly for the "friend," partly because now she will have to go.

She wears her favorite dress again, the long blue one patterned with yellow stars, the one her sister gave her. The trolley is crowded, the windows all wide open. She stands and has to cling to a strap too high for her, her arms and shoulders hurting, the hot breeze flickering through the armholes of the dress. A young man admires her from a seat by the door, but she would rather be invisible. The trolley car sways past lighted windows, strolling pedestrians, a startled dog that has escaped its leash. She has never been to the gallery before. She only realizes she has missed her stop when one of the bright windows blinks an image at her, a colorful canvas with the hint of bodies beyond. She eases past the admiring boy, steps down, and has to walk back four blocks. She remembers how tired she is, remembers she won't really know anyone there. The sunwarmed bricks breathe up her bare legs in the darkness.

Karl, the artist whose show this is, is surrounded by well-wishers. Manon gives him a small wave, but cannot tell if he sees her. The gallery is a remodeled house with many small rooms, and there are many people in each one. Every corner sports an electric fan so the air rushes around, bearing odors of bodies, perfume, wine the way the waiters bear trays of food and drink. They are casual in T-shirts and jeans, while most of the guests have dressed up, to be polite, to have fun. The people stir around, looking at the canvases on the walls, looking for friends, talking, laughing, heating up the rumpled air, and they impart a notion of animal movement to the paintings. Karl works in pillows of color traced over by intricate lines. Nets, Manon decides, to keep the swelling colors contained. She likes the brightness, the warmth, the detail of brushwork and shading, but recognizes with a tickle of chagrin that she still is more fond of representative than abstract art. Immature, immature. She takes a glass of wine and then wishes she hadn't. She is thirsty for water or green tea, for air that has not been breathed a hundred times. She decides she will pay her respects to Karl and go.

"Hi!" one of the waiters says.

"Hi?" Manon says, and then realizes the young man with the dark face glossy with heat is the counterman from the ice cream store. "Oh, hello."

"I wasn't sure you'd remember me," he says. He rearranges glasses to balance his tray.

"Of course I do," she says, then wonders why of course.

"Big crowd," he says.

"Yes, it's good."

"Good for business. We do the catering, my family I mean."

Someone takes one of the full glasses on his tray and he rebalances the rest.

Manon looks for something to say. "I teach with Karl. At the art school."

"Who's Karl?"

"The artist?"

"Oh." They both laugh. He says, "I'm Luther, by the way."

"Manon."

"It's nice to meet you."

She smiles.

"Well, I'd better get back to work. I'll see you around, huh?"

"Yes."

Luther raises his tray and turns sideways to slip between two groups of talkers, then glances back at her. "Manon?"

"Right."

He grins and eases himself into his round. Manon smiles. A lot of people don't get her name the first time around.

She works her way into Karl's circle and he introduces her around as "the brilliant new artist we managed to snare before some place with real money snapped her up."

Lupe decides to make a pond for the roof garden with left over plastic sheeting and stones. She and Manon dig out a hollow in the dirt, line it with plastic, fill the bottom with pebbles from the left-over pile. Ira the landlord, who is impatient to sow some seeds, points out that it will have to be filled by hand in the dry season. Lupe smiles with implausible sweetness and says she knows. When he bustles off on other business, Lupe goes downstairs to fill the bucket at the garden tap, leaving Manon to haul it up on the pulley. The first time, Lupe fills the bucket too full and gets a muddy shower when Manon starts to pull (her swearing sounds more fiery than her salsa) so after that she only fills it halfway, which means Manon is raising and carrying and pouring and lowering until dark. She doesn't mind. The sky is a deep arch of blue busy with evening birds, and there is something good about working with water, which has voice and character but no form. The wet pebbles glow with color and the water swirls, the pond growing layer by layer, dark mirror and clear window all at the same time. She goes to bed with that image in her mind.

At the end of winter Manon and her sister dug out the stream at the bottom of the tobogganing hill, as if by their excavations they could hasten spring. The packed toboggan run stood above the softer sublimating snow, a ski-jump track grubby with sled-marks. They walked down this steep ramp, stomping it into steps with their boot soles, and at the bottom frayed their wool mittens by terrier digging. The ice revealed was a mottled shield over mud and sand. Suspended brown leaves made stilled layers of time out of the fall's spilling water. Although Manon and her sister would never drink from the summer stream, they broke wafers of ice free from the edges of stones and reeds and melted them on their tongues. There was always a muddy, gritty taste. The flavor of frogs, Manon's sister insisted, which made Manon giggle and squeal, but did not prevent her from drinking more ice. She always looked, too, for the frogs buried under ice and mud, waiting, but never saw them. The first she ever knew of them was their tentative peeping after dark in the start of spring.

Luther is behind the counter when she returns to the ice cream store a day or two after Karl's opening. He has a cheerful smile for the succession of customers (the store is busy today) but lights up especially when he sees Manon standing in line.

"Hi!" he says. "Vanilla, right? It'll be just a second."

"I'm in no hurry," she says. He has lovely eyes, dark and thickly lashed.

"So, Manon," he says when he hands her the dish, "can you stick around for a little while? My dad's out on a delivery, but he wanted to talk to you, and he should be back soon."

"Talk to me?"

Luther grins. "We have a proposition to make." Then, as if worried he has been too familiar, "I mean, about work, about maybe doing some work for us. As an artist."

There is a boisterous family behind her deciding on flavors. She smiles and shrugs. "I'll be around."

"Great," he says. "Great!" And then the family is giving him their requests.

Engaged by curiosity, she doesn't mind sitting at the narrow counter shelf at the back of the room. She feels as if last night's work, last night's idea, has turned a switch, shunted a trolley from a siding to the street, set her running back on the tracks of her life. A happy feeling, but precarious: it is, after all, only an idea. Even good ideas sometimes die. But this idea inside her head has met its reflection (perhaps) in the ideas of the ice cream family, and this, she feels, is a hopeful thing. Hope, like inspiration, is fragile, and she tries to think of other things while she eats her ice cream and waits for Luther's dad.

He arrives not long after she has finished her bowl. The store has emptied a little, and after a brief word with his son he comes around the counter and suggests she join him at a table. He says his name is Edward Grant. "Call me Ed."

"Manon."

"That's French, isn't it?"

She nods.

"I've got a cousin in New Orleans." He shrugs that aside. "Anyway, about this proposition. We've been working to expand our catering business, but we haven't had much to spare for advertising. Word of mouth is pretty good for the kind of business we do, but lately I've thought even just pamphlets we could hand around would be good. I know Luther said you're a real artist, so I hope I'm not insulting you by asking. I just thought how everyone can use whatever work they can get these days."

"I could use the work. I mean, I'd be happy to, only I don't know much about graphic design," Manon says regretfully. "That's computer stuff, and I'm pretty ignorant."

Ed shrugs that off too. "We've got a computer program. What I was thinking was maybe you could come up with a picture for us, not a logo exactly, but an image that would catch peoples' imaginations, and then," he takes in a breath, as if this is the part that makes him uncertain, and he is suddenly very much like his son, "maybe you could paint it for us, too, here in the store. So what do you think?"

Manon eyes the melting-sherbet walls. Luther takes advantage of a lull and comes out from behind the counter to wipe down the tables. He leans over his father's shoulder and says, "So what do you think?"

"We can pay a flat fee of five hundred dollars," Ed says. "And materials, of course."

"Well actually," Manon says, "I was thinking maybe we could barter a trade?"

Ed looks doubtful. "What kind of trade?"

Manon smiles. "How about some space in your freezer?"

After that, everything becomes folded into one.

The savor of Ed's cinnamon rolls mingled with the watery smell of acrylic paint and the electric tang of the first trolley of the cool and limpid morning.

The busy hum of her classes, that she feels she has stolen from Karl's, except he gave his advice freely, as a gift.

The gritty sweat of work in the park, sunshine rich with sawdust, and after, the cool of conversation and bitter beer.

The green sprout of tough roof seeds, careless of season, and the plash of birds bathing in the pool that has to be filled by hand, and the recipe for Lupe's mother's salsa that calls for cilantro fresh from Manon's garden bed.

The cold enfolding fog of the freezer and the chirp and crackle of ice as another layer of water gets poured into the wood and plastic form.

Vanilla, dusk, and Luther's smile.

And somehow even time. The southwest corner of the park has been cleared to reveal a terrace floored in rumpled bricks and roses. The tree of winged fruits and ripening birds burgeons on Ed's and Luther's wall. The form in the freezer is full. And there is a message on Manon's telephone. *I can come, I can come after all! The train arrives at dawn, call and tell me how to find you . . .*

Manon's sister arrives on the first trolley from the station. The early sky is a blue too sweet to become the furnace glare of noon, a promise that delights though it does not deceive. The demolition crews have taken their jackhammers to another street, leaving quiet and a strange soft carpet of turquoise where the pavement used to be, the detoxifiers that will leach spent oil from the earth. Manon walks to the trolley stop, happy to be early, and then stands amazed when her sister climbs down, balancing a belly and a bulging yellow pack.

"Elise!" cries Manon. "You're so big!"

Elise laughs and maneuvers into an embrace. "You're so slender! Look how beautiful you are, so fit and tanned!"

"Look how beautiful you are!" Manon says, laughing back. The sister's known face is new, round and gently shining, warm with the summer within. Manon takes the pack and says, "You must be so tired. Are you hungry? Or do you just want to sleep? It's only a couple of blocks."

"What I really need," Elise says, "is a pee. But we can wait if it's only a couple of blocks."

"Two and a half," Manon says. And then, "We!"

They link arms and laugh.

While Elise sleeps, Manon walks to the ice cream shop where Ed and Luther are waiting. Margot, Luther's mother and Ed's wife, is also there. She and Ed have collaborated on a feast of a breakfast, eggs scrambled with tomatoes and peppers, fresh bread and rolls, peaches like soft globes of sunrise, cherries like garnet jewels. There is so much food they can feed Edgar when he comes with the park crew's truck, and Lupe and Marcos when they finally show up, almost an hour late. Edgar can't get over Manon's tree on the sherbet-colored wall, he keeps getting up to stand with his back to the counter and stare at it all over again. "There's something new every time I look," he says. When Lupe arrives she stands next to him to admire Manon's work, while Marcos slumps sleepy-eyed over the last of the eggs.

It takes all of them to lift the form full of frozen water. They crowd into the freezer, breath smoking extravagantly, and fit poles through the pallet that makes up the bottom of the form. Edgar opens the freezer's alley door and the back of the truck, and in a confusion of warmth and cold the seven of them jockey the heavy thing outside and up onto the truck bed. Margot and Lupe massage their wrists. Edgar, in the back of the truck, leans against the crate-like form and says, "Wow!" Manon grins in secret relief: she had wondered if they'd be able to shift it at all. But now everyone except Margot and Ed pile into the truck that farts and grumbles its anachronistic way through the green streets to the park.

Elise declares herself to be amazed at the city. "I thought it would be all falling down and ugly. But look!" She points out the trolley window. A grape vine weaves its way up a trellis bonded to tempered glass and steel, drinking in the reflected heat of noon. "It's like that game we used to play when we were little, do you remember? Where we'd pretend that everyone had vanished from the earth except for us and everything was growing back wild. Remember? In the summer we used to say the old barn was the town all grown over in blackberry canes."

Manon remembers. "Like a fairy story. Sleeping Beauty, or something."

"Right! And I'd make you crawl inside and wait for me to rescue you." Elise laughs. "And we'd get in so much trouble for ruining our clothes! Good thing no one ever knew where we were playing, we'd never have been allowed."

The trolley drops them at the northeast corner of the park. Manon leads her sister through the half-wild tangle of chaparral and jungle gyms.

"I can't believe you made this whole park!" Elise says.

"There's still a lot of poison oak," Manon says absently.

Elise breathes in dry spicy air. "It smells so good. Ooh, what is that, it's like cough drops only delicious?"

Manon laughs. "Eucalyptus trees."

Elise's belly slows her down and her nap is still mellow in her, or maybe that's pregnancy too. She is happy to stroll, to stop and sniff the air, to peer after the jay she hears chattering in the bush. Manon keeps starting ahead, she can hear people talking and laughing on the rose terrace, but then she has to wait, to pause, to stroll, until she is ready to burst like a seed pod with anticipation. But finally the path takes one final curve and it is Elise who looks ahead and says, "Oh look, I wonder what's happening."

Manon takes her sister's hand to urge her on.

Amongst the determined roses a crowd of people mills. There are people from the park crews, people from the art school, people from the ice cream store, people from the city who have come to see the new/old park, people who were passing by. At the heart of the crowd, on the center space of the rose garden where a fountain once had played, surrounded by a lively ring of children, stands Manon's sculpture. Free from its wood and plastic form, it gleams in the late morning sun, an arc of ice, a winter stream's limb, an unbound book written on sheets of time. The sunlight fingers through the pages, illuminating the suspended branches of red and green madrone, the butterfly bouquets of poppies, the stirred-up stream-pebble floor: layers and depths all captured by the water poured and frozen one day after another and already melting.

"Did you make this?" Elise says, her eyes unaccountably bright with tears.

"Yes," says Manon, suddenly shy.

"Oh," says Elise. "Oh." And carrying her belly she pushes gently among the children to drink.

ACKNOWLEDGEMENTS

"Pip and the Fairies," copyright © 2005 by Theodora Goss, first appeared in *Strange Horizons*, 3 October 2005.

"My Father's Mask," copyright © 2005 by Joe Hill, first appeared in *20th Century Ghosts*, PS Publishing, 2005.

"Heads Down, Thumbs Up," copyright © 2005 by Gavin J. Grant, first appeared in *SCIFICTION*, 27 April 2005.

"Returning My Sister's Face," copyright © 2005 by Eugie Foster, first appeared in *Realms of Fantasy*, February 2005.

"The Farmer's Cat," copyright © 2005 by Jeff VanderMeer, first appeared in *Polyphony 5*, Wheatland Press, 2005.

"A Very Little Madness Goes a Long Way," copyright © 2005 by M. Rickert, first appeared in *F&SF*, August 2005.

"The Language of Moths," copyright © 2005 by Christopher Barzak, first appeared in *Realms of Fantasy*, April 2005.

"The Dybbuk in Love," copyright © 2005 by Sonya Taaffe, first appeared in *The Dybbuk in Love*, Prime, 2005.

"Gulls," copyright © 2005 by Tim Pratt, first appeared in *Polyphony* 5, Wheatland Press, 2005.

"The Maiden Tree," copyright © 2005 by Catherynne M. Valente, first appeared in *Cabinet des Fees*, website, 2005.

"Proboscis," copyright © 2005 by Laird Barron, first appeared in *F&SF*, February 2005.

"Eating Hearts," copyright © 2005 by Yoon Ha Lee, first appeared in *F&SF*, June 2005.

"Dancing in the Light of Giants," copyright © 2005 by Jay Lake, first appeared in *Realms of Fantasy*, April 2005.

"Monster," copyright © 2005 by Kelly Link, first appeared in *Noisy Outlaws*, McSweeney's, 2005.

"At the End of the Hall," copyright © 2005 by Nick Mamatas, first appeared in *Fantasy Magazine* 1, 2005.

"Summer Ice," copyright © 2005 by Holly Phillips, first appeared in *In the Palace of Repose*, Prime Books, 2005.